SOFT
And
OTHERS

Tor Books by F. Paul Wilson

BLACK WIND
SOFT AND OTHERS

SOFT
And
OTHERS

16 Stories of Wonder and Dread
by
F. PAUL WILSON

A TOM DOHERTY ASSOCIATES BOOK
NEW YORK

SOFT AND OTHERS

A TOR BOOK
Published by Tom Doherty Associates, Inc.
49 West 24 Street
New York, NY 10010

First edition: May 1989
0 9 8 7 6 5 4 3 2 1

ACKNOWLEDGMENTS

"The Cleaning Machine" first appeared in *Startling Mystery Stories* 18, March 1971, © 1970 by Health Knowledge, Inc. Reprinted by permission.

"Ratman" first appeared in *Analog*, August 1971, © 1971 by Condé Nast Publications, Inc. Reprinted by permission.

"Lipidleggin'" first appeared in *Isaac Asimov's Science Fiction Magazine*, May-June 1978, © 1978 by Davis Publications, Inc. Reprinted by permission.

"To Fill the Sea and Air" first appeared in *Isaac Asimov's Science Fiction Magazine*, February 1979, © 1979 by Davis Publications, Inc. Reprinted by permission.

"Green Winter" first appeared in *Analog*, January 6, 1981, © 1981 by Davis Publications, Inc. Reprinted by permission.

"Be Fruitful and Multiply" first appeared in *Perpetual Light* (Warner Books), edited by Alan Ryan, © 1982 by F. Paul Wilson.

"Soft" first appeared in *Masques* (Maclay), edited by J. N. Williamson, © 1984 by F. Paul Wilson.

"The Last 'One Mo' Once Golden Oldies Revival'" first appeared in *Whispers* V (Doubleday), © 1985 by Stuart David Schiff. Reprinted by permission.

"The Years the Music Died" first appeared in *Whispers* VI (Doubleday), © 1987 by Stuart David Schiff. Reprinted by permission.

To the editors who variously inspired, encouraged, niggled, nit-picked, nursed, and guided these stories into print:

John W. Campbell, Jr.
Robert A. W. Lowndes
George Scithers
Stanley Schmidt
Alan Ryan
J. N. Williamson
Stuart David Schiff
Alan Rogers
Charles L. Grant
Edward Ferman
John Betancourt and Darrell Schweitzer
David J. Schow

CONTENTS

AUTHOR'S NOTE

Sixteen stories written between 1969 and 1987. Not an all-inclusive collection. Some early stuff is missing. Rereading your old fiction can be enlightening and, at times, embarrassing. Some stories hold up well and you find nice little bits of prose here and there that you don't remember writing. Then there are other stories—in some you wince at the wandering point of view, and a few you wonder how you ever sold. So equal parts vanity and empathy figured into the decision against inflicting some of my abecedarian efforts twice upon the reading public. They have been left to moulder in the pages of old back-date magazines.

Other stories, such as "Pard," "He Shall Be John," and the novelette "Wheels Within Wheels," have been expanded or extended into novels; "Demonsong" and "Dydeetown Girl" eventually will be put to similar use, so they too are excluded here. And the comic book pieces wouldn't fit.

The stories appear in the order in which they were written.

F. Paul Wilson
The Jersey Shore
July 1987

Introduction

I couldn't *give* this story away. It was rejected by practically every short-fiction magazine in existence at the time. Only John Campbell bothered to tell me why. (He always told me why, and I revere his memory for that.) He said: "It's not a story, because it doesn't go anywhere. (The tenants did, but the story doesn't!) It's a vignette."

He was right, as usual. I'd been reading too many horror stories, and it showed. There was no market for sf-horror at the time. The story didn't work as pure science fiction, but as a quiet little horror story, it wasn't too bad.

Finally I found a home for it.

Although not my first sale, "The Cleaning Machine" turned out to be my first published story. It appeared in April 1971, in *Startling Mystery Stories* #18. The magazine folded with that issue. (Pure synchronicity, of course—no cause-effect relationship, I'm sure. I hope.) *SMS* was one of a series of reprint digests edited by Bob Lowndes for Health Knowledge, Inc., during the late sixties and early seventies. Occasionally he accepted new material by unknowns. Greg Bear, Stephen King, and other names that may sound familiar first got into print courtesy of Bob Lowndes.

I never got paid for "The Cleaning Machine"—*twice*. Health Knowledge stiffed me when they folded the magazine. But worse than that, the story was immediately pirated by a *Creepy* clone called *Galaxy Mission*. I found out about this sixteen years later. The irony is too much: The story I couldn't give away was stolen and reprinted within months of publication!

THE CLEANING MACHINE

Dr. Edward Parker reached across his desk and flipped the power switch on his tape recorder to the "on" position.

"Listen if you like, Burke," he said. "But remember: She has classic paranoic symptoms; I wouldn't put much faith in anything she says."

Detective Ronald Burke, an old acquaintance on the city police force, sat across from the doctor. "She's all we've got," he replied with ill-concealed exasperation. "Over a hundred people disappear from an apartment house and the only person who might be able to tell us anything is a nut!"

Parker glanced at the recorder and noticed the glowing warm-up light. He pressed the button that started the tape.

"Listen."

". . . and I guess I'm the one who's responsible for it but it was really the people who lived there in my apartment who drove me to it—they were jealous of me.

"The children were the worst. Every day as I'd walk to the store they'd spit at me behind my back and call me names. They even got other little brats from all over town and would wait for me on corners and doorsteps. They called me terrible names and said that I carried awful diseases. Their parents put them up to it, I know it! All those people in my apartment building laughed at me. They thought they could hide it but I heard it. They hated me because they were jealous of my poetry. They knew I was famous and they couldn't stand it.

"Why, just the other night I caught three of them rummaging through my desk. They thought I was asleep and so they sneaked in and tried to steal some of my latest works, figuring they could palm them off as their own. But I was awake. I could hear them laughing at me as they searched. I grabbed the butcher knife that I always keep under my pillow and ran out into the study. I must have made some noise when I got out of bed because they ran out into the hall and closed the door just before I got there. I heard one of them on the other side say, 'Boy, you sure can't fool that old lady!'

"They were fiends, all of them! But the very worst was that John Hendricks fellow next door who was trying to kill me with an ultra-frequency sonicator. He used to turn it on me and try to boil my brains while I was writing. But I was too smart for him! I kept an ice pack on my head at all hours of the day. But even that didn't keep me from getting those awful headaches that plague me constantly. He was to blame.

"But the thing I want to tell you about is the machine in the cellar. I found it when I went down to the boiler room to see who was calling me filthy names through the ventilator system. I met the janitor on my way downstairs and told him about it. He just laughed and said that there hadn't been anyone down in the boiler room for two years, not since we started getting our heat piped in from the building next door. But I *knew* someone was down there—hadn't I heard those voices through the vent? I simply turned and went my way.

"Everything in the cellar was covered with at least half an inch of dust—everything, that is, except the machine. I didn't know it was a machine at that time because it hadn't done anything yet. It didn't have any lights or dials and it didn't make any noise. It just sat there being clean. I also noticed that the floor around it was immaculately clean for about five foot in all directions. Everywhere else was filth. It looked so strange, being clean. I ran and got George, the janitor.

"He was angry at having to go downstairs but I kept pestering him until he did. He was mighty surprised.

" 'What *is* that thing?' he said, walking toward the machine. Then he was gone! One moment he had been there, and then he was gone. There was no blinding flash or puff of smoke . . . just gone! And it happened just as he crossed into that circle of clean floor around the machine.

"I immediately knew who was responsible: John Hendricks! So I went right upstairs and brought him down. I didn't bother to tell him what the machine had done to George since I was sure he knew all about it. But he surprised me by walking right into the circle and disappearing, just like George.

"Well, at least I wouldn't be bothered by that ultra-frequency sonicator of his anymore. It was a good thing I had been too careful to go anywhere near that thing.

"I began to get an idea about that machine—it was a *cleaning* machine! That's why the floor around it was so clean. Any dust or *anything* that came within the circle was either stored away somewhere or destroyed!

"A thought struck me: Why not 'clean out' all of my jealous neighbors this way? It was a wonderful idea!

"I started with the children.

"I went outside and, as usual, they started in with their name-calling. (They always made sure to do it very softly but I could read their lips.) There were about twenty of them playing in the street. I called them together and told them I was forming a club in the cellar and they all followed me down in a group. I pointed to the machine and told them that there was a gallon of chocolate ice cream behind it and that the first one to reach it could have it all. Their greedy little faces lighted up and they scrambled away in a mob.

"Three seconds later I was alone in the cellar.

"I then went around to all the other apartments in the building and told all those hateful people that their sweet little darlings were playing in the old boiler room and that I thought it was dangerous. I waited for one to go downstairs before I went to the next door. Then I met the husbands as they came home from work and told them the same thing. And if anyone came looking for someone, I sent him down to the cellar. It was all so simple: In searching the cellar they had to cross into the circle sooner or later.

"That night I was alone in the building. It was wonderful— no laughing, no name-calling, and no one sneaking into my study. Wonderful!

"A policeman came the next day. He knocked on my door and looked very surprised when I opened it. He said he was investigating a number of missing-persons reports. I told him that everyone was down in the cellar. He gave me a strange look but went to check. I followed him.

"The machine was gone! Nothing was left but the circle of clean floor. I told the officer all about it, about what horrible people they were and how they deserved to disappear. He just smiled and brought me down to the station where I had to tell my story again and they sent me here to see you.

"They're still looking for my neighbors, aren't they? Won't listen when I tell them that they'll never find them. They don't believe there ever *was* a machine! But they can't find my neighbors, can they? Well, it serves them right! I told them I'm the one responsible for 'cleaning out' my apartment building but they don't believe me. Serves them *all* right!"

* * *

"See what I mean?" said Dr. Parker with the slightest trace of a smile as he turned the recorder off. "She's no help at all."

"Yeah, I know," Burke sighed. "As looney as they come. But how can you explain that circle of clean floor in the boiler room with all those footprints around it?"

"Well, I can't be sure, but the 'infernal machine' is not uncommon in the paranoid's delusional system. You found no trace of this 'ultra-frequency sonicator' in the Hendricks apartment, I trust?"

Burke shook his head. "No. From what we can gather, Hendricks knew nothing about electronics. He was a short-order cook in a greasy spoon downtown."

"I figured as much. She probably found everybody gone and went looking for them. She went down to the boiler room as a last resort and, finding *it* deserted, concluded that everybody had been 'cleaned out' of the building. She was glad but wanted to give herself the credit. She saw the circle of clean floor—probably left there by a round table top that had been recently moved—and started fabricating. By now she believes every word of her fantastic story. We'll never really know what happened until we find those missing tenants."

"I guess not," Burke said as he rose to go, "but I'd still like to know why we can find over a hundred sets of footprints approaching the circle but none leaving it."

Dr. Parker didn't have an answer for that one.

Introduction

"Ratman" was my first sale. After years of detailed rejection slips from John W. Campbell, editor of *Analog*, I finally broke the barrier: A check from Condé Nast for $375 arrived in the mail. A nickel a word and no comment from Campbell. Just a check. Typical. He was the kind of guy who liked to argue. If he disagreed with you, he could go on for pages. If he agreed, he had nothing to say. The check said it all.

I was a first-year medical student at the time, with a wife, no job, no money, and a baby on the way. You can't imagine how $375 looked to us.

"Ratman" grew out of the psychopharmacological research I did at CIBA between pre-med and med school. Day in, day out, we dosed white rats with new drugs and placed them in Skinner boxes. Lots of times I felt sorry for the rats. But there were times when I thought they might be doing a number on us fellows in the white coats. After all, intraperitoneal injections of amphetamine were part of the protocol.

(Please forgive the size of the computers mentioned here. "Ratman" was written in 1970, years before Steve Jobs began playing with microchips.)

RATMAN

S ince its purpose was neither to load nor unload cargo, his converted tramp freighter was directed to a landing pad at the far end of the field where it wouldn't get in the way. Orz, red-haired and of average height and build though somewhat stoop-shouldered, didn't mind. As long as he was in the general area his efficiency would be unimpaired.

When the viewscreen picked up an approaching ground car, Orz snapped his fingers and a half-kilo space rat leaped from the control console to his shoulder.

"Let's go, 62," he said to his favorite employee.

The space rat grasped the fabric of his master's shirt tightly in his tiny paws and lashed his tail about nervously. He didn't like meeting strangers, but it was part of his job; his master had found that there was a definite psychological advantage in appearing with a space rat on his shoulder.

. Orz and 62 reached the hatch just as the ground car pulled up alongside. They scrutinized the two occupants as the freighter's loading ramp descended.

The first to debark was a portly little man wearing a stylish orange tunic that should have been two sizes larger. His companion probably weighed as much but was taller and better proportioned.

Orz's long legs carried him swiftly down the ramp after it had settled and the portly one came forward to meet him.

"Mr. Samuel Orzechowski?" he asked, mangling the pronunciation.

Orz smiled. "That's right, but you can call me Sam, or Orz, or, as some people prefer, Ratman." *And being a client,* he thought, *you'll no doubt choose the last one.*

"Well," the little man replied, "I guess 'Ratman' will do. I'm Aaron Lesno, president of the Traders League, and this is Evan Rabb, our treasurer," he said, indicating the man beside him.

"Welcome to Neeka," said Lesno.

"Could I ask you something, Ratman?" Rabb hastily interjected. He couldn't take his eyes off 62. "Is that a space rat?"

"A small one," Orz nodded. "A baby, really."

"Aren't you afraid of . . ."

"Of losing my ear?" he grinned. "Not at all. I imagine you two and the rest of the League are somewhat in the dark as to my methods, and you've probably got a lot of questions. I've found it best in the past to get everyone together and explain things to everybody at once. It saves me time and you money."

"An excellent idea!" Lesno agreed. "We've all been anxiously awaiting your arrival . . . Well," he corrected himself with a glance at Rabb, "almost all . . . but I'm sure there would be no problem in getting everyone together."

"What did you mean by 'almost all'?" Orz asked.

Rabb spoke up. "One of our more influential members was vehemently opposed to the idea of retaining you."

"Oh, really? Why?"

"Have no fear, Ratman," Lesno assured him with a smile, "he'll let you know why at the meeting tonight."

"Fair enough," Orz said. "Can someone come back and pick me up in a few hours for the meeting?"

"Why not come with us now and let us show you around a bit?" Lesno offered.

Orz shook his head and gestured over his shoulder to the ship. "Sorry . . . feeding time."

Rabb and Lesno stiffened and glanced nervously from 62 to the open hatch. "Yes, quite," Lesno muttered. "Very well, then, we'll have someone call for you in, say, three hours."

"That'll be fine." This settled, the two-man welcoming committee lost little time in putting some distance between themselves and the squat little freighter.

"Seem like pretty decent fellows," Orz told 62 as he made his way up the ramp and down the central corridor. As they approached the rat room, 62 began to prance excitedly on his master's shoulder and was literally doing a dance by the time Orz hit the door release.

His several hundred fellow employees inside took up the same excited dance at the sound of the door sliding open. The cages were arranged five high along the walls of the long, narrow room. They were simple, steel-sided boxes with front doors of quarter-inch steel mesh; each was self-cleaning, had its own water supply, and was equipped with an automatic feeder.

But Orz had never trusted automatic feeders, so now he went from cage to cage and shoved food pellets through the tiny feeding hole in the front of each. He had to be nimble, for the rats were greedy and anxious and a fingertip could easily be mistaken for a pellet. His practiced eye decided how much each rat should get. This was important: A rat became fat and lazy if overfed and would gnaw his way out of the cage if underfed. A rat in either condition was of little use to Ratman.

Fifty cages stood open and empty and Orz placed a few pellets in each. 62 was frantic by now so he decided to give the little fellow something before he jumped off his shoulder and into one of the empty cages. The rat rose up on his hind legs, snatched the pellet from Orz's proffering fingers with his tiny, handlike paws, and began to gnaw noisily and voraciously.

Three hours later, Orz flipped a particular switch on the console, checked to make sure the door to the rat room was open, then headed for the hatch. There, after casting an eye through the dusk at the approaching ground car, he secured the hatch, but opened a small panel at its bottom. With 62 perched watchfully upon his shoulder, he was waiting at the bottom of the ramp when the car arrived.

Lesno was alone inside. "Well, Ratman," he said with a smile, "everybody's waiting, so—" then he spotted 62 and his face fell. "Does he have to come along? I mean, he won't get too excited, will he?"

"Don't worry," Orz replied, sliding into his seat, "he won't bite you." To lessen the man's anxiety he made a point of keeping 62 on his far shoulder.

"Your advertising literature was quite timely," Lesno remarked as they got under way, hoping conversation would take his mind off those two beady eyes peering at him around the back of his passenger's head. "The rat problem was reaching its peak when we received it. I trust that wasn't just coincidence."

"No coincidence at all. I keep my ear to the ground and word got around that there was a space rat plague on Neeka. I figured you could use my services."

Lesno nodded. "We had heard a few stories about you but didn't know whether to believe them or not. Your advertising claims were quite impressive. I just hope you can live up to them."

About twenty exporters and importers were waiting in the conference room on the second floor of the Traders League office complex. It was a motley group of discordant colors, shapes, sizes, and ages. Lesno entered ahead of Orz and lost no time in bringing the meeting to order.

"We all know why we're here," he said, tapping the gavel twice, "so there's really no use in wasting time with introductions." He pointed to Orz. "The creature on this man's shoulder is introduction enough: Ratman has arrived and he's going to tell us something about himself and about space rats." So saying, he relinquished the podium.

Nothing like a businesslike business, Orz thought as he stood up and received a slight spattering of applause. They knew of his claim to be able to control space rats with space rats and were frankly dubious. But this was nothing new to Orz.

Without even a glance at the audience, he nonchalantly snapped his fingers and tapped the top of the podium. 62 immediately leaped from his shoulder to the podium and began to sniff the wood curiously.

"This," he began, "although a specimen of *Rattus interstellus*, is not a true 'space rat' in the full sense of the word; but his parents were. Lab-raised space rats—such as 62, here—can turn out to be quite friendly, but they are no less cunning, no less intelligent, and certainly no less vicious when cornered. These are the rats I 'employ,' so to speak.

"But first let's puncture a few of the myths that have grown up around the space rat. First of all, no matter what the spacers tell you, space rats have no psi powers; they don't know what you're going to do next . . . it's just that their reflexes are developed to such a high degree that it almost seems that way when you take pot shots at one with a blaster. They will respond to ultra-frequency tones but by no means do they have a language . . . they're intelligent, all right, but they're a long way from a language."

His eyes flicked over the audience. These were traders, barterers; they recognized a man who knew what he was talking about, and they were all listening intently.

He continued. "But just what is it that distinguishes the space rat from other rats?" To dramatize his point, he allowed 62 to crawl onto the back of his hand and then held the fidgety creature aloft.

"This is the product of centuries in the pressurized but

unshielded holds of interstellar cargo ships. Wild genetic mutation and the law of survival of the fittest combined to produce a most adaptable, ferocious, and intelligent creature.

"Everyone knew of the space rat's existence, but no one paid much attention to him until an ensign aboard the freighter *Clinton* was kept awake one night by the continuous opening and closing of the compartment door outside his cabin. The ship was in port, and, under normal circumstances, he would have spent the night in town, but for one reason or another he had returned to his quarters.

"Now, these doors which divide the corridors into compartments open automatically when you touch the release panel and remain open as long as a simple electric eye beam is broken; when the beam makes contact again, the door closes. The doors naturally make some noise when they operate, and this is what was disturbing the ensign. But, every time he checked to see who was wandering up and down the corridor, he found no one. Checking with the guard detail he found that he was the only person authorized to be in that area of the ship.

"So he set up watch. Opening his door a crack, he peeked through to the corridor and waited. But no one came and he was about to give up when he spotted this large space rat come running down the corridor. As it approached the door it leaped over a meter into the air and threw itself against the release panel. The door slid open as the creature landed on the floor and it scurried through before the door closed again."

The traders were smiling and shaking their heads in wonder as Orz paused and placed 62 back on the podium. "Since it is doubtful that the rat could have accidentally leaped against the release panel, it must be assumed that he learned by watching. That would make him a highly unusual rat . . . they thought. Then they discovered that the whole colony aboard the *Clinton* knew how to operate the doors! Then other spacers on other ships began watching for space rats while their ships were in port—that's when their movements are the greatest; they stick pretty much to the cargo holds in transit—and it was discovered that the *Clinton* rats were not so extraordinary. These reports fired the interest of researchers who figured they would go out and catch themselves a few space rats and put them through some tests."

The audience broke into laughter at this point. They were all well familiar with the elusiveness of the space rat.

"Another characteristic of the space rat was soon discovered: viciousness. It took quite a while, but after much effort and many scars a number of space rats were caught. And, as expected, they proved virtually untrainable. We hoped to do better with their offspring.

"I was working with the offspring when I heard about a rat problem in the nearby spaceport. Traps, poison, even variable frequency sonic repellers had failed to control them. I went to investigate and found that a good many space rats were jumping ship and setting up residence in the warehouses which ring every spaceport. Another factor was added: In the warehouses they meet other strains of space rat from other ships and the resultant cross-breeding produces a strain more intelligent and more ferocious than even the cargo-ship rat. I managed to catch half a dozen in as many months, mated them and began to go to work on the offspring. Through a mixture of imprinting and operant conditioning, second-generation space rats proved quite tractable.

"But I needed more wild rats and tried the wild idea of training my lab rats to help catch other rats. It worked out so well that I decided to go into the business of space-rat control."

He paused and glanced around the room. "Any questions?"

An elderly trader in the front row raised a bony hand. "Just how does one rat go about catching another?" he asked in a raspy voice.

"I'll demonstrate that tomorrow," Orz replied. "It'll be easier to understand once you see the equipment."

A huge, balding man with a grizzled beard stood up without waiting to be recognized. "I've got a question, Ratman," he said belligerently. "If all you've got are a few trained rats, why do you charge so much?"

This elicited a few concurring mutters from other members of the audience. Here, no doubt, was the man Lesno had referred to earlier that day.

"You have me at a disadvantage, sir," Orz replied with a smile.

"I'm Malcomb Houghton and I guess I rank third, or fourth, around here in cubic feet of warehouse space."

Orz nodded. "Very glad to meet you, sir. But let me answer your question with another question: Do you have any idea what it costs to operate a privately owned freighter, even a small one such as mine? My overhead is staggering."

Being a businessman, this argument seemed to make sense to Houghton, but he remained standing. "I just wonder," he began slowly. "If you can train rats to catch other rats, how do we know you didn't land some special trouble-making rats here on Neeka a few months ago to aggravate the situation to the point where we had to call you in?"

The audience went silent and waited for Ratman's reply. Orz cursed as he felt his face flushing. This man was dangerously close to the truth. He hesitated, then cracked a grin.

"How'd you like to go into partnership with me?" he quipped.

The tension suddenly vanished as the audience laughed and applauded. Orz gathered up 62 and left the podium before Houghton could zero in on him again. He couldn't tell whether the man was stabbing in the dark, or whether he really knew something.

Lesno escorted him out the door. "Wonderful!" he beamed. "I think you're the man to solve our problems. But time is of the essence! The port residents have been on our necks for months; their pets are being killed, they're afraid for their children and they're afraid for themselves. And since the rats are based in the warehouse district, we might be held liable if we don't do something soon. And"—he put his hand on Orz's shoulder and lowered his voice—"we've been keeping it quiet, but a man went after a few of the rats with a blaster the other night. They turned on him and chewed him up pretty badly."

"I'll start as early as possible," Orz assured him. "You just send somebody around tomorrow with a good-sized truck and I'll be waiting."

Rabb must have overheard them as he approached. "That won't be necessary," he said. "We're placing a truck at your disposal immediately. I'll drive it over to your ship and Lesno will bring me back after dropping you off."

Orz said that would be fine and he arranged a time and place of meeting with Lesno for early the next morning on the way back to the ship. A few minutes later he and 62 were standing next to the borrowed truck watching the two League officers drive away.

"*Ratman!*" whispered a voice from the deep shadows under the ramp.

Orz spun around. "Who's there?" he asked guardedly.

"I'm your contact."

"You'd better come out and identify yourself," he said.

Muttering and brushing off the knees of her coveralls, a tall, statuesque brunette stepped out of the shadows. "Where have you been for the past hour? We were supposed to meet as soon as it was dark!"

"Just who are you, miss?" Orz asked.

She straightened up and stared at him. "You don't take any chances, do you?" she said as a wry smile played about her lips. "O.K. I'm Jessica Maffey, Federation agent NE97. I'm the one who received a smuggled shipment of fifty of your best harassing rats, drove them into town, and let them go in the warehouse district. Satisfied, Ratman?"

Orz grinned at her annoyance. "You're Maffey, all right . . . I've got a picture of you inside, but you can't be too careful." He glanced around. "Let's get inside where we can talk."

"Speaking of going inside," she said, "there's been a steady stream of rats going through that little opening in the hatch."

He nodded. "Good. I activated a high-frequency call before I left. All the harassers you loosed should be snug in their cages by now."

He unlocked the hatch and led her to the rat room. As he busied himself with transferring 62 to a cage and checking on the harassing rats, Jessica looked around. From the darkened recess of each cage shone two gleaming points of light, and all those several hundred points of light seemed to be fixed upon her. She shuddered.

"Three missing," Orz was saying. "That's not too bad . . . accidents do happen." He pressed a button on the wall and the open doors on the cages of the harassing rats swung shut with a loud and simultaneous clang.

"How about a drink?" he offered his guest.

"As a matter of fact, I'd love one!" she replied, sighing with relief as they stepped back into the corridor. Orz looked at her curiously. "It gets a little dry and dusty sitting under a loading ramp," she explained with a tight smile.

With Jessica seated in his spartan, fastidiously neat living quarters with her hand around a cold gin and tonic, Orz began to talk business. "Federation Intelligence only gave me a sketchy idea of what's going on here. You were to fill me in on the rest, so why don't I tell you what I know and you take it from there."

"Go ahead," she told him.

Drink in hand, Orz paced the room as he spoke. "Let's start

with this planet. Neeka is a fiercely independent, sparsely populated world which exports a lot of food and imports a lot of hardware. Formerly a splinter world, it agreed to trade with the Federation but refused to join it. They were asked to join the Restructurists in their revolt against the Federation but turned them down. They want absolutely no part of the war . . . and I can't say as I blame them.

"*However:* The Haas Warp Gate is right outside this star system and the convoys stack up in this area before being shot through to the battle zones. Fed agents discovered a turncoat feeding information on the size and destinations of the convoys to someone on this planet. That someone, in turn, was transmitting the info to the Restructurists via subspace radio. He's been stopped temporarily, but as soon as he makes another contact, he'll be in business again. I was told to meet you here and stop him. That's all I know."

Jessica nodded and drained her drink. "Right. But subspace transmissions can't be traced so we had to depend on deductive reasoning. First of all, you're allowed to be pro-Federation, or pro-Restructurist on Neeka, and you're allowed to talk all you want about either cause. Nobody minds. But try to do something to aid either cause and you wind up in prison. Strict neutrality is enforced to the letter on Neeka. Therefore, partisan natives, such as myself and the man we're after, have to go underground.

"Now, it would be as easy to smuggle in a subspace transmitter as it was to smuggle in your rats, but hiding it would be an entirely different matter. It's a huge piece of hardware and it needs a large power supply."

"So the man we're after," Orz broke in, "is someone with easy access to an off-planet source of information, and a place big enough to hide a subspace transmitter without arousing suspicion."

"And a warehouse right here in port has the size and access to the necessary power," Jessica concluded. "Since the members of the Traders League own all the warehouses, they are the obvious target for investigation."

"But which one?"

She shrugged. "Their security is too tight for me to do much snooping. The only way to get into those warehouses is to be invited in. That's where Ratman comes in."

Orz was thoughtful. "It really shouldn't be too difficult. I was informed by the Traders League when they retained me that their warehouses are fully automated and computer-operated."

"With a population density as low as Neeka's," Jessica added, "labor is anything but cheap."

"Right," he continued. "And, if I wanted to hide a subspace radio in one of those warehouses, I'd disguise it as part of the automation works and no one would ever be the wiser. All I've got to do tomorrow when I go into the warehouses is keep my eyes open for an unusually large computer-automation rig. When I find it I'll just 'accidentally' expose it as a subspace transmitter. The Neekan authorities will take care of our spy after that."

He suddenly halted his pacing and snapped his fingers. "Forgot to turn off the call signal for the rats . . . I'll be right back."

"Mind if I come along?" Jessica asked.

"Not at all."

She watched Orz's back as he led her down the narrow corridor to the bridge. "Can I call you something other than 'Ratman'?"

He grinned over his shoulder. "Sam will do fine."

"O.K., Sam: How did you get started in all this?"

"Well, I got the idea a few years ago and thought I was a genius until I started looking for backers. Everyone I approached thought I was either a swindler or a nut. As a last desperate hope I went to IBA."

"What's IBA?"

"Interstellar Business Advisors. It's a private company with some pretty canny people working for them. They dug up somebody who promised to back me halfway, then they approached the Federation with this undercover idea. Since I'd be able to get on otherwise unfriendly planets, the Federation put up the rest of the money. So now I'm a full-time Ratman and a part-time Fed man. And when my reputation spreads, IBA has got some ideas for starting a corporation and selling franchises."

They entered the bridge as he was speaking and Jessica noticed that it was as meticulously ordered as his quarters. Two additions to the standard console caught her eye immediately.

"Improvements?" she asked, pointing to a brace of toggle switches.

Orz flipped one of the toggles to "off" and turned to her. "Those are the high-frequency signals for my rats. They've got an effective range of about two kilometers and when a rat hears the proper tone, he makes a beeline for this ship."

"And what's that?" She indicated a bright red lever with three safety catches and "Danger" written in white letters along its length.

The lightness left his voice. "For the direst of emergencies only," he replied.

Feminine curiosity aroused, Jessica went to touch it. "What does it do?"

"That's my secret," Orz replied with a tight smile and snatched her wrist away from the lever. "I've yet to use it and I hope the day never comes when I do." To draw her attention elsewhere he pointed to the far wall. "See that inconspicuous little switch over there by the intercom speaker? When that's in the down position—like now—the controls are locked."

"You're just full of tricks, aren't you?" she said, trying to hide a smile. He was like a little boy showing off a new toy.

"Can't be too careful."

*   *   *

Lesno, Rabb, Houghton, and a few others were ready and waiting when Orz pulled up in front of the Traders League offices with the truck.

"Straight ahead," said Lesno as he hopped in beside Orz. "We'll start with Rabb's places first since they're the closest." Two left turns brought them up before a huge structure with a "Rabb & Co." sign above the sliding doors. Orz waited until the others had arrived, then addressed the group.

"First of all," he told them, "you must keep all humans away from any warehouse where my rats are at work, so give whatever employees you have the day off. Next, let me explain that space rats set up a close-knit community within a warehouse—one community per warehouse—and that each community has a leader who achieved his position by being the most cunning and the most ferocious in the community."

He reached into the back of the truck and brought out a simple cage. Inside was a very large and very vicious-looking space rat. "This is one of my Judas rats. I've selectively bred them for ferocity and any one of these is a match for any three ordinary space rats. Within hours after his release, my Judas rat will have established himself at the top of the community's pecking order."

Once again Orz reached into the back of the truck and brought out a cage, but this one was larger and empty. "Normally a space rat wouldn't go near a trap like this, but he'll follow the Judas if the Judas is the community leader. And once the community has followed him inside and is busy at the bait, the Judas hops outside, releases this catch and a spring closes and locks the door. He then returns to the ship. The cage is made of a lightweight titanium alloy that not even a space rat's teeth can dent." He held up the cage. "Tomorrow morning this should be filled with a community of very angry space rats."

"Is that all there is to it?" Houghton blurted incredulously. Orz could imagine the man's mind tallying and totaling, and deciding that no matter what his overhead, Ratman charged too much. "This is outrageous! I'll have nothing to do with such nonsense! We're being hoodwinked!"

Somebody doesn't want me in his warehouse, Orz thought and was about to say something when Rabb beat him to it.

"The League has already retained Ratman, Malcomb, and we voted to use the treasury to do so . . . remember? So you have, in effect, already paid for his services, and it would be foolish of you not to take advantage of them."

Houghton paused, considering Rabb's words, then he glanced at the cage and shrugged. "I guess I don't have much choice," he said sullenly and turned toward his car. "Let me know when you get around to my places."

It was late in the day when they finally did get around to Houghton's warehouses, but Orz had preferred it that way. He had his suspicions and wanted to see as many of the other warehouses as possible before confronting Houghton. There had been nothing suspect in the others, although Lesno's computer setups had been somewhat larger than most, but nowhere near big enough to house a subspace radio.

Houghton met them outside.

"I've only got a few cages left," Orz told him, "so we'll do as many as we can and I'll get the rest tomorrow after I collect the cages I've set out today."

"Might as well start with the main house," Houghton replied and led them toward the largest building of his complex. The doors slid open to reveal a huge expanse of concrete floor with crates and boxes stacked almost to the ceiling. Huge cranes—controlled by a computer that knew the exact location of every item in storage—swung from above. Looming against the far wall was a large, metal-paneled structure.

Orz pointed to it. "Is that your computer?"

"Yes," the bearded man replied absently, "now let's get on with this . . . I haven't got all day."

"Mind if I take a look at it?" Orz asked and started walking toward it. This was what he had been looking for; it was big enough to house two subspace transmitters. "Rats love to nest in those things, you know."

"I assure you there are no rats in there so stay away from it!" Houghton almost shouted. He began to follow Orz, and Lesno and Rabb trailed along.

Orz went to the nearest inspection plate and began loosening the screws which held it in place.

"Get away from there!" Houghton yelled as he came up. "You don't know what you're doing! You could mess up my whole operation!"

"Look, if I'm going to do my job right, I've got to check this out!" The inspection plate came off in his hands then and he stuck his head inside. Nothing unusual. He replaced it and went to the next plate with the same result. Four more inspection plates later he was sure there was no subspace transmitter hidden within.

Houghton was standing behind him and tugging angrily on his beard as Orz replaced the last screw. "Are you quite through, Ratman?"

Orz stood and faced him. "Awful big computer you've got there, Mr. Houghton," he said matter-of-factly. He was chagrined, but refused to show it.

"That's the computer for my whole operation. I found it easier to centralize the system: Instead of installing new units all the time, I just add to the central unit and feed it into the new buildings as they are built. It's much more convenient."

"More economical, too, I'll bet," Orz added laconically.

"Why, yes," Houghton replied. "How did you know?"

"Lucky guess."

Jessica was waiting for him back at the ship. "Don't bother telling me you didn't find anything," she said as he collapsed in a chair. "That look on your face tells me the whole story."

"I was so sure it was Houghton! The way he objected to the League retaining me, the way he tried to rake me over the coals at the meeting last night, the way he blew up this morning, I was sure he had something to hide. Turns out he's only a cheapskate with a centralized computer."

"What makes you so sure he hasn't got it stashed somewhere else?" Jessica asked, coming over and handing him a drink.

He accepted it gratefully and took a long slow swallow before answering. "I'm not sure of anything right now. But, if that transmitter's here—and we know it is—it's got to be in one of those warehouses. Which reminds me . . ." He got to his feet slowly and trudged to the rat room.

Jessica didn't follow, but glanced out into the corridor when she heard the clang of cage doors. Furry gray and brown shapes were scurrying toward the hatch.

"What are you up to?" she asked as Orz reappeared.

"I had a brainstorm on my way back to the ship. We'll find out if it worked tomorrow."

Orz noticed Jessica in the crowd outside Rabb's main warehouse. She smiled and winked mischievously, knowing he couldn't acknowledge her. The crowd was waiting to see if Ratman could live up to his claims and watched intently as he and Rabb disappeared inside. An uncertain cheer began and died as he reappeared dragging—with little help from Rabb—a cageful of clawing, squealing, snarling, snapping space rats. Having retreated to what it considered a safer distance, the crowd applauded.

Lesno strode forward, beaming. "Well, Ratman, I knew you could do it! But what are you going to do with the little monsters now that you've caught them?"

"Most of them will have to be gassed and killed, but I'll save a few of the best for breeding purposes . . . I like to keep my working stock as strong as possible."

They completed the rounds of Rabb's buildings, then

moved on to Lesno's. The novelty had worn off and the crowd was beginning to thin by the time they got around to Lesno's third warehouse, but interest was renewed at the sound of Orz's voice calling from within.

"Mr. Lesno! There's something you ought to see in here!"

Lesno went in. Rabb, Houghton, and some of the braver members of the crowd—Jessica among them—followed him.

It looked as if a bomb had gone off inside. Every crate, every package had been torn open. Even some of the computer paneling had been torn away.

"What happened?" Lesno cried, staggered by the destruction.

Orz shrugged and pointed to the full cage. "I don't know. There's your community, caged and ready to go. But I've never seen anything like this before."

Houghton was looking over the ravaged computer. "Never seen a computer that looked like this," he muttered. "Is this some new model, Aaron?" he asked Lesno.

Rabb came up. "Looks like part of a subspace radio!"

"Ridiculous!" Lesno sputtered. "What would I be doing with—"

"You're a spy!" Houghton declared. "A Federation spy!"

A blaster suddenly appeared in Lesno's hand. "Don't insult me by linking me to the Federation!"

Houghton shrugged. "So you're a Restructurist spy, then. Just as bad. You get twenty years either way."

"I'm not going to argue with you, Malcomb. Just stay where you are."

"You can't escape, Aaron!" Rabb warned.

Lesno smiled. "Of course I can," he said and pointed the blaster at Orz. "Ratman is going to volunteer the use of his ship. He's even going to come along for the ride to make sure no one gets trigger-happy."

Orz caught Jessica's eye. She was readying to make a move, but he shook his head. They had succeeded in destroying

Lesno's effectiveness as a spy. It didn't matter if he escaped. And so, with a blaster at the back of his head, Orz preceded the little man to the truck.

"You work for the Federation, don't you?" Lesno said as Orz drove them toward the spaceport.

"I'm afraid I don't have time to work for anyone other than Sam Orzechowski."

"Come now, Ratman. I was suspicious yesterday when I saw the way you gave Houghton's computer a going over and this morning's revelation confirmed it. Why deny it?"

Orz shrugged. "O.K., I occasionally do some snooping for the Federation."

"How did you get on to me?" Lesno asked earnestly. "I thought I had a foolproof arrangement."

"Well, I wasn't sure, but Houghton's centralized setup started me on a new approach. I figured that if one man could centralize his computers, another could *de*centralize a subspace transmitter. Then it struck me that you'd have to take the transmitter apart in order to sneak it into town. And since it was already in pieces, why not leave it that way? At least that's what I would have done. So the next thing to do was to look for the man with the *slightly* larger computers. You fit the bill."

"But how did you manage to tear the place apart?"

"That was easy. If you could go back to that warehouse now, you'd find a tiny, high-frequency *labeler* attached to the door. I have a number of vandal rats trained to be specialists in making a mess out of a building. The *labeler* told them where to go to work."

Shaking his head in admiration, Lesno remarked, "You should be working for us."

"But I don't want a restructured Federation," Orz replied. "I sort of like it the way it is."

"But there are such inequalities in the galaxy! Some planets are drowning in their surpluses while other planets are starving, and the Federation does nothing!"

"The Federation doesn't think such matters are within its scope."

"They will be when we win!" he replied righteously.

Orz knew argument was futile and allowed a shrug to be his only reply.

Once on the ship, it was evident to Orz that Lesno knew his way around freighters. He retracted the ramp, secured the hatch, and then followed Orz to the bridge.

He gestured to the extra seat. "You just sit there and keep out of the way, Mr. Ratman, and you won't get hurt. I'm not a murderer. If all goes well, I'll drop you off at the first neutral port we reach. But I won't hesitate to shoot you if you try anything."

"Don't worry," Orz told him. "My mission was to stop you, not capture you. I really don't care if you get away."

Lesno's eyes narrowed. This lack of chauvinism did not fit his conception of a Fed man. Something was up. His suspicions were reinforced when he found the console inoperable.

"Where's the lock?" he demanded.

Orz pointed across the room. "By the speaker." But Lesno made no move. Instead his eyes roved the room until they came to rest on the red lever. His face creased into a smile.

"You didn't think anyone would be fooled by that, did you?"

Orz nearly leaped from his seat as the Restructurist reached for the lever. "Don't touch that!"

"Sit down!" Lesno warned, pointing the gun at Orz's chest. "I told you before, I'm not a killer but—"

"I know you're not!" Orz said frantically. "Neither am I. That's why you've got to leave that lever alone!"

Lesno merely smiled and kept him covered while he released the first two safety catches. "Listen to me, Lesno! That lever sets off a special tone stimulus and releases every one of my rats! They've all been trained to attack anyone and everyone but me when they hear that tone . . . I installed it for use in a situation when it was either kill or be killed! This is not one of those situations!"

Lesno was having some trouble with the third catch, but it finally yielded. "A good try, Ratman," he said and, ignoring Orz's cry of protest, pulled the lever.

Faintly, from far down the corridor, came a metallic clang. A loud, wailing tone filled the ship. Lesno paled and turned anxiously toward his captive.

"Why didn't you listen to me, you fool!" Orz yelled.

Lesno suddenly believed. Horror-stricken, he began to push and pull the lever back and forth but with no effect. He was still working at it when the squealing, gray-brown carpet swept through the door.

Orz turned away and tried unsuccessfully to block out the screams and sickening sounds of carnage that filled the bridge. He had trained the rats too well . . . there would be no stopping them.

And when all was quiet again, Orz congratulated himself on having kept his stomach in place. But then 62 leaped up to his accustomed spot on his shoulder and began with great contentment to clean his reddened claws and jowls.

Only Jessica came to see him off. Orz had cleaned up the rat problem and the people were appreciative, but they had either seen the corpse that had been removed from his ship, or they had heard about it. It hadn't been easy to identify it as Aaron Lesno.

"I see the red lever's been removed," Jessica remarked. She hadn't been near the ship since the incident.

Orz avoided her gaze. "Yeah. I took it out . . . can't quite look at it." He changed the subject abruptly. "Well, now that this thing's been cleared up, what'll you be doing with yourself?"

"I've no intention of settling down and becoming a good Neekan citizen, you can be sure of that!" she replied. "I'm putting in for an assignment as soon as possible. There's too much going on out there for me to get tucked away on this rock!"

Orz smiled for the first time in several days. "That's funny. I was thinking of taking on an assistant. This business is getting a little too complicated for me to handle alone."

He paused as Jessica waited eagerly.

"You like rats?" he asked.

Introduction

I had been playing with libertarian themes in my *Analog* stories, mostly as subtexts. I decided to go all out with "Lipidleggin'."

It was the mid-seventies and Senator Ted Kennedy was agitating for national health insurance, the kind that brought Britain to the brink of ruin. Luckily, wiser heads prevailed and another fascist Kennedy scheme was aborted. But the idea of NHI got me thinking (it also spurred me to write a guest editorial for *Analog* on the subject in the April 1975 issue) and I wondered about the long-term consequences of such a program. Wouldn't it be logical to assume that if the federal government was going to be paying for the treatment of disease, it would also want to get actively involved through legislation in the prevention of those same diseases?

I tried a first draft in the third person but wasn't happy with it. For the hell of it, I switched to first person present tense, a voice I usually dislike. But it worked here. George Scithers made a few well-considered suggestions and bought it for *Asimov's*.

The story still makes sense. I mean, if the government is going to foot all the bills when you get sick, pal, it's your duty as a good citizen to do what's necessary to keep yourself healthy, right?

Right?

LIPIDLEGGIN'

Butter.

I can name a man's poison at fifty paces. I take one look at this guy as he walks in and say to myself, "Butter."

He steps carefully, like there's something sticky on the soles of his shoes. Maybe there is, but I figure he moves like that because he's on unfamiliar ground. Never seen his face before and I know just about everybody around.

It's early yet. I just opened the store and Gabe's the only other guy on the buying side of the counter, only he ain't buying. He's waiting in the corner by the checkerboard and I'm just about to go join him when the new guy comes in. It's wet out—not raining, really, just wet like it only gets up here near the Water Gap—and he's wearing a slicker. Underneath that he seems to have a stocky build and is average height. He's got no beard and his eyes are blue with a watery look. Could be from anywhere until he takes off the hat and I see his hair: It's dark brown and he's got it cut in one of those soup-bowl styles that're big in the city.

Gabe gives me an annoyed look as I step back behind the counter, but I ignore him. His last name is Varadi—sounds Italian but it's Hungarian—and he's got plenty of time on his hands. Used to be a Ph.D. in a philosophy department at some university in Upstate New York 'til they cut the department in half and gave him his walking papers, tenure and all. Now he does part-time labor at one of the mills when they need a little extra help, which ain't near as often as he'd like.

About as poor as you can get, that Gabe. The government giraffes take a big chunk of what little he earns and leave him near nothing to live on. So he goes down to the welfare office where the local giraffes give him food stamps and rent vouchers so he can get by on what the first group of giraffes left him. If you can figure that one out . . .

Anyway, Gabe's got a lot of time on his hands, like I said, and he hangs out here and plays checkers with me when things are slow. He'd rather play chess, I know, but I can't stand the game. Nothing happens for too long and I get impatient and try to break the game open with some wild gamble. And I always lose. So we play checkers or we don't play.

The new guy puts his hat on the counter and glances around. He looks uneasy. I know what's coming but I'm not going to help him out. There's a little dance we've got to do first.

"I need to buy a few things," he says. His voice has a little tremor in it and close up like this I figure he's in his mid-twenties.

"Well, this *is* a general store," I reply, getting real busy wiping down the counter, "and we've got all sorts of things. What're you interested in? Antiques? Hardware? Food?"

"I'm not looking for the usual stock."

(The music begins to play)

I look at him with my best puzzled expression. "Just what is it you're after, friend?"

"Butter and eggs."

"Nothing unusual about that. Got a whole cabinet full of both behind you there."

(We're on our way to the dance floor)

"I'm not looking for that. I didn't come all the way out here to buy the same shit I can get in the city. I want the real thing."

"You want the real thing, eh?" I say, meeting his eyes square for the first time. "You know damn well real butter and real eggs are illegal. I could go to jail for carrying that kind of stuff!"

(We dance)

Next to taking his money, this is the part I like best about dealing with a new customer. Usually I can dance the two of us around the subject of what he really wants for upwards of twenty or thirty minutes if I've a mind to. But this guy was a lot more direct than most and didn't waste any time getting down to the nitty-gritty. Still, he wasn't going to rob me of a little dance. I've got a dozen years of dealing under my belt and no green kid's gonna rob me of that.

A dozen years . . . doesn't seem that long. It was back then that the giraffes who were running the National Health Insurance program found out that they were spending way too much money taking care of people with diseases nobody was likely to cure for some time. The stroke and heart patients were the worst. With the presses at the Treasury working overtime and inflation getting wild, it got to the point where they either had to admit they'd made a mistake or do something drastic.

Naturally, they got drastic.

The president declared a health emergency and Congress passed something called the National Health Maintenance Act which said that since certain citizens were behaving irresponsibly by abusing their bodies and thereby giving rise to chronic diseases which resulted in consumption of more than their fair share of medical care at public expense, it was resolved that, in the public interest and for the public good, certain commodities would henceforth and hereafter be either proscribed or strictly rationed. Or something like that.

Foods high in cholesterol and saturated fats headed the list. Next came tobacco and any alcoholic beverage over 30 proof.

Ah, the howls that went up from the public! But those were nothing compared to the screams of fear and anguish that arose from the dairy and egg industry which was facing immediate economic ruin. The Washington giraffes stood firm, however —it wasn't an election year—and used phrases like "bite the bullet" and "national interest" and "public good" until we were all ready to barf.

Nothing moved them.

Things quieted down after a while, as they always do. It helped, of course, that somebody in one of the drug companies had been working on an additive to chicken feed that would take just about all the cholesterol out of the yolk. It worked, and the poultry industry was saved.

The new eggs cost more—of course!—and the removal of most of the cholesterol from the yolk also removed most of the taste, but at least the egg farmers had something to sell.

Butter was out. Definitely. No compromise. Too much of an "adverse effect on serum lipid levels," whatever that means. You use polyunsaturated margarine or you use nothing. Case closed.

Well, almost closed. Most good citizen-type Americans hunkered down and learned to live with the Lipid Laws, as they came to be known. Why, I bet there's scads of fifteen-year-olds about who've never tasted real butter or a true, cholesterol-packed egg yolk. But we're not all good citizens. Especially me. Far as I'm concerned, there's nothing like two fried eggs—fried in *butter*—over easy, with bacon on the side, to start the day off. *Every* day. And I wasn't about to give that up.

I was strictly in the antiques trade then, and I knew just about every farmer in Jersey and eastern Pennsylvania. So I found one who was making butter for himself and had him make a little extra for me. Then I found another who was keeping some hens aside and not giving them any of that special feed and had him hold a few eggs out for me.

One day I had a couple of friends over for breakfast and served them real eggs and toast with real butter. They almost strangled me trying to find out where I got the stuff. That's when I decided to add a sideline to my antiques business.

I figured New York City to be the best place to start so I let word get around the antique dealers there that I could supply their customers with more than furniture. The response was wild and soon I was making more money running butter and eggs than I was running Victorian golden oak.

I was a lipidlegger.

Didn't last, though. I was informed by two very pushy fellows of Mediterranean stock that if I wanted to do any lipid business in Manhattan, I'd either have to buy all my merchandise from their wholesale concern, or give them a very healthy chunk of my profits.

I decided it would be safer to stick close to home. Less volume, but less risky. I turned my antique shop up here by the Water Gap—that's the part of North Jersey you can get to without driving by all those refineries and reactors—into a general store.

A dozen years now.

"I heard you had the real thing for sale," the guy says.

I shake my head. "Now where would you hear a thing like that?"

"New York."

"New York? The only connection I have with New York is furnishing some antique dealers with a few pieces now and then. How'd you hear about me in New York?"

"Sam Gelbstein."

I nod. Sam's a good customer. Good friend, too. He helped spread the word for me when I was leggin' lipids into the city.

"How you know Sam?"

"My uncle furnished most of his house with furniture he bought there."

I still act suspicious—it's part of the dance—but I know if Sam sent him, he's all right. One little thing bothers me, though.

"How come you don't look for your butter and eggs in the city? I hear they're real easy to get there."

"Yeah," he says and twists up his mouth. "They're also spoiled now and again and there's no arguing with the types that supply it. No money-back guarantees with those guys."

I see his point. "And you figure this is closer to the source."

He nods.

"One more question," I say. "I don't deal in the stuff, of course"—still dancing—"but I'm just curious how a young guy like you got a taste for contraband like eggs and butter."

"Europe," he says. "I went to school in Brussels and it's all still legal over there. Just can't get used to these damned substitutes."

It all fit, so I go into the back and lift up the floor door. I keep a cooler down there and from it I pull a dozen eggs and a half-kilo slab of butter. His eyes widen as I put them on the counter in front of him.

"This is the real thing?" he asks. "No games?"

I pull out an english muffin, split it with my thumbs, and drop the halves into the toaster I keep under the counter. I know that once he tastes this butter I'll have another steady customer. People will eat ersatz eggs and polyunsaturated margarine if they think it's good for them, but they want to know the real thing's available. Take that away from them and suddenly you've got them going to great lengths to get what they used to pass up without a second thought.

"The real thing," I tell him. "There's even a little salt added to the butter for flavor."

"Great!" He smiles, then puts both hands into his pockets

and pulls out a gun with his right and a shield with his left. "James Callahan, Public Health Service, Enforcement Division," he says. "You're under arrest, Mr. Gurney." He's not smiling anymore.

I don't change my expression or say anything. I just stand there and look bored. But inside I feel like someone's wrapped a length of heavy chain around my guts and hooked it up to a high-speed winch.

Looking at the gun—a little snub-nosed .32—I start to grin.

"What's so funny?" he asks, nervous and I'm not sure why. Maybe it's his first bust.

"A public health guy with a gun!" I'm laughing now. "Don't that seem funny to you?"

His face remains stern. "Not in the least. Now step around the counter. After you're cuffed we're going to take a ride to the Federal Building."

I don't budge. I glance over to the corner and see a deserted checkerboard. Gabe's gone—skittered out as soon as he saw the gun. Mr. Public Health follows my eyes.

"Where's the red-headed guy?"

"Gone for help," I tell him.

He glances quickly over his shoulder out the door, then back at me. "Let's not do anything foolish here. I wasn't crazy enough to come out here alone."

But I can tell by the way his eyes bounce all over the room and by the way he licks his lips that, yes, he was crazy enough to come out here alone.

I don't say anything, so he fills in the empty space. "You've got nothing to worry about, Mr. Gurney," he says. "You'll get off with a first offender's suspended sentence and a short probation."

I don't tell him that's exactly what worries me. I'm waiting for a sound: the click of the toaster as it spits out the english muffin. It comes and I grab the two halves and put them on the counter.

"What are you doing?" he asks, watching me like I'm going to pull a gun on him any minute.

"You gotta taste it," I tell him. "I mean, how're you gonna be sure it ain't oleo unless you taste it?"

"Never mind that." He wiggles the .32 at me. "You're just stalling. Get around here."

But I ignore him. I open a corner of the slab of butter and dig out a hunk with my knife. Then I smear it on one half of the muffin and press the two halves together. All the time I'm talking.

"How come you're out here messin' with me? I'm small-time. The biggies are in the city."

"Yeah." He nods slowly. He can't believe I'm buttering a muffin while he holds a gun on me. "And they've also bought everyone who's for sale. Can't get a conviction there if you bring the 'leggers in smeared with butter and eggs in their mouths."

"So you pick on me."

He nods again. "Somebody who buys from Gelbstein let slip that he used to connect with a guy from out here who used to do lipidlegging into the city. Wasn't hard to track you down." He shrugs, almost apologizing. "I need some arrests to my credit and I have to take 'em where I can find 'em."

I don't reply just yet. At least I know why he came alone: He didn't want anyone a little higher up to steal credit for the bust. And I also know that Sam Gelbstein didn't put the yell on me, which is a relief. But I've got more important concerns at the moment. I press my palm down on top of the muffin until the melted butter oozes out the sides and onto the counter, then I peel the halves apart and push them toward him.

"Here. Eat."

He looks at the muffin all yellow and drippy, then at me, then back to the muffin. The aroma hangs over the counter in an invisible cloud and I'd be getting hungry myself if I didn't have so much riding on this little move.

I'm not worried about going to jail for this. Never was. I know all about suspended sentences and that. What I *am* worried about is being marked as a 'legger. Because that means the giraffes will be watching me and snooping into my affairs all the time. And I'm not the kind who takes well to being watched. I've devoted a lot of effort to keeping a low profile and living between the lines—"living in the interstices," Gabe calls it. A bust could ruin my whole way of life.

So I've got to be right about this guy's poison.

He can't take his eyes off the muffins. I can tell by the way he stares that he's a good-citizen type whose mother obeyed all the Lipid Laws as soon as they were passed, and who never thought to break them once he became a big boy. I nudge him.

"Go ahead."

He puts the shield on the counter and his left hand reaches out real careful, like he's afraid the muffins will bite him. Finally, he grabs the nearest one, holds it under his nose, sniffs it, then takes a bite. A little butter drips from the right corner of his mouth, but it's his eyes I'm watching. They're not seeing me or anything else in the store . . . they're sixteen years away and he's ten years old again and his mother just fixed him breakfast. His eyes are sort of shiny and wet around the rims as he swallows. Then he shakes himself and looks at me. But he doesn't say a word.

I put the butter and eggs in a bag and push it toward him.

"Here. On the house. Gabe will be back any minute with the troops so if you leave now we can avoid any problems." He lowers the gun but still hesitates. "Catch those bad guys in the city," I tell him. "But when you need the real thing for yourself, and you need it fresh, ride out here and I'll see you're taken care of."

He shoves the rest of the muffin half into his mouth and chews furiously as he pockets his shield and gun and slaps his hat back on his head.

"You gotta deal," he says around the mouthful, then lifts the bag with his left hand, grabs the other half muffin with his right, and hurries out into the wet.

I follow him to the door where I see Gabe and a couple of the boys from the mill coming up the road with shotguns cradled in their arms. I wave them off and tell them thanks anyway. Then I watch the guy drive off.

I guess I can't tell a Fed when I see one, but I can name anybody's poison. Anybody's.

I glance down at the pile of newspapers I leave on the outside bench. Around the rock that holds it down I can see where some committee of giraffes has announced that it will recommend the banning of Bugs Bunny cartoons from theatres and the airwaves. The creature, they say, shows a complete disregard for authority and is not fit viewing for children.

Well, I've been expecting that and fixed up a few mini-cassettes of some of Bugs' finest moments. Don't want the kids around here to grow up without the Wabbit.

I also hear talk about a coming federal campaign against being overweight. Bad health risk, they say. Rumor has it they're going to outlaw clothes over a certain size. That's just rumor, of course . . . still, I'll bet there's an angle in there for me.

Ah, the giraffes. For every one of me there's a hundred of them.

But I'm worth a thousand giraffes.

Introduction

This was another sale to George Scithers when he was editing *Asimov's*. His acceptance note was, "I'll take the fish," and he gave it the cover with a Jack Gaughan painting.

"To Fill" has its origins in my childhood. In his younger days, my father was an indefatigable fisherman. He would surf-cast at dawn or at sunset, sit on the bulkheads of the Manasquan Inlet as the tides changed, or go out on a party boat or a private yacht whenever anyone needed an extra hand. Often he'd bring me along. I never saw the attraction of fishing, or any kind of killing sport, for that matter. But it certainly seems more sporting than hunting. I mean, you aren't trapping a harmless, graceful, defenseless herbivore in the cross hairs of a telescopic sight mounted on a superb killing weapon and snuffing out its life with a twitch of your index finger. A fish has to choose your bait and you have to reel him in before he spits the hook. It's fairer, but the odds still don't seem even.

And sometimes as we trolled through the chum out there on the Atlantic, I'd watch the way the fish would hit or avoid the lines and wonder who was playing with whom. This story is the result of those childhood wonderings.

The title comes from "The Rime of the Ancient Mariner."

I don't go fishing anymore.

TO FILL THE SEA AND AIR

During the period in question there were two items on the interstellar market for which supply could never equal demand. The intricate, gossamer carvings of the Vanek were one, valued because they were so subtly alien and yet so appreciable on human terms. The other was filet of chispen, a seafood delicacy with gourmet appeal all across Occupied Space. The flavor . . . how does one describe a unique gustatorial experience, or the mild euphoria that attends consumption of sixty grams or more of the filet?

Enough to say that it was in high demand in those days. And the supply rested completely on the efforts of the individual chispen fishers on Gelk. Many a large interstellar corporation pressed to bring modern methods to the tiny planet for a more efficient harvesting of the fish, but the ruling council of Gelk forbade the intrusion of outside interests. There was a huge profit to be made and the council members intended to see that the bulk of it went into their own pockets.

from *Stars for Sale:*
An Economic History of Occupied Space,
by Emmerz Fent

I magine the sea, smooth slate gray in predawn under a low drifting carapace of cloud. Imagine two high, impenetrable walls parallel on that sea, separated by ten times the height of a tall man, each stretching away to the horizon. Imagine a force-seven gale trapped between those walls and careening toward you, beating the sea below it to a furious lather as it comes.

Now . . . remove the walls and remove the wind. Leave the onrushing corridor of turbulent water. That was what Albie saw as he stood in the first boat.

The chispies were running. The game was on.

Albie gauged it to be a small school, probably a spur off a bigger run to the east. Good. He didn't want to hit a big run just yet. There were new men on the nets who needed blooding, and a small school like the one approaching was perfect.

He signaled to his men at their posts around the net, warning them to brace for the hit. Out toward the sun stood a long dark hull, bristling amidships with monitoring equipment. Albie knew he was being watched but couldn't guess why. He didn't recognize the design and closed his right eye to get a better look with his left. The doctors had told him not to do that. If he had to favor one of his eyes, let it be the artificial one. But he couldn't get used to it—everything always looked grainy, despite the fact that it was the best money could buy. At least he could see. And if he ever decided on a plastic repair of the ragged scar running across his right eyebrow and orbit, only old friends would know that a chispie wing had ruined that eye. And, of course, Albie would know.

He bore the chispies no animosity, though. No Ahab syndrome for Albie. He was glad to be alive, glad to lose an eye instead of his head. There were no prosthetic heads around.

Most of the experienced men on the nets wore scars or were missing bits of ears or fingers. It was part of the game.

If they didn't want to play, they could stand on shore and let the chispies swim by unmolested. That way they'd never get hurt. Nor would they get those exorbitant prices people all over Occupied Space were willing to pay for filet of chispen.

Turning away from the dark skulking hull, Albie trained both eyes on the chispies. He leaned on the wheel and felt the old tingling in his nerve ends as the school approached. The middle of his sixth decade was passing, the last four of them spent on this sea as a chispen fisher . . . and still the same old thrill when he saw them coming.

He was shorter than most of the men he employed; stronger, too. His compact, muscular body was a bit flabbier now than usual, but he'd be back to fighting trim before the season was much older. Standing straight out from his cheeks, chin, and scalp was a knotty mane of white and silver shot through with streaks of black. He had a broad, flat nose, and the skin of his face, what little could be seen, showed the ravages of his profession. Years of long exposure to light from a star not meant to shine on human skin, light refracted down through the atmosphere and reflected up from the water, had left his dark brown skin with a texture similar to the soles of a barefoot reefclimber, and lined it to an extent that he appeared to have fallen asleep under the needle of a crazed tattooist with a penchant for black ink and a compulsion for cross-hatching. Eyes of a startling gray shone out from his face like beacons in the night.

The stripe of frothing, raging water was closer now. Albie judged it to be about twenty meters across, so he let his scow drift westward to open the mouth of the net a little wider. Thirty meters seaward to his right lay the anchor boat manned by Lars Zaro, the only man in the crew older than Albie. The floats on the net trailed in a giant semi-circle between and behind them, a cul-de-sac ringed with ten scows of Albie's own design—flat-bottomed with a centerboard for greater stability—each carrying one gaff man and one freezer man. The two new hands were on freezer duty, of course. They had a long way to go before they could be trusted with a gaff.

Albie checked the men's positions—all twenty-six, counting himself, were set. Then he glanced again at the big ship standing out toward the horizon. He could vaguely make out *GelkCo I* emblazoned across the stern. He wondered why it was there.

"Incredible! That school's heading right for him!"

"Told you."

Two men huddled before an illuminated screen in a dark room, one seated, the other leaning over his shoulder, both watching the progress of the season's first chispen run. The main body of the run was a fat, jumbled streak of light to the right of center on the screen, marking its position to seaward in the deeper part of the trench. They ignored that. It was the slim arc that had broken from the run a few kilometers northward and was now heading directly for a dot representing Albie and his crew that gripped their attention.

"How does he do it?" the seated man asked. "How does he know where they're going to be?"

"You've just asked the question we'd all like answered. Albie uses outdated methods, decrepit equipment, and catches more than anyone else on the water. The average chispen fisher brings home enough to support himself and his family; Albie is rich and the two dozen or so who work for him are living high."

"Well, we'll be putting an end to that soon enough, I guess."

"I suppose we will."

"It's almost a shame." The seated man pointed to the screen. "Just look at that! The school's almost in his net! Damn! It's

amazing! There's got to be a method to it!"

"There is. And after seeing this, I'm pretty sure I know what it is." But the standing man would say no more.

Albie returned his attention to the onrushing school, mentally submerging and imagining himself at one with the chispies. He saw glistening blue-white fusiform shapes darting through the water around him in tightly packed formation just below the surface. Their appearance at this point differed markedly from the slow, graceful, ray-like creatures that glide so peacefully along the seabottoms of their winter spawning grounds to the south or the summer feeding grounds to the north. With their triangular wings spread wide and gently undulating, the chispies are the picture of tranquillity at the extremes of their habitat.

But between those extremes . . .

When fall comes after a summer of gorging at the northern shoals, the chispen wraps its barbed wings around its fattened body and becomes a living, twisting missile hurtling down the twelve-hundred-kilometer trench that runs along the coast of Gelk's major landmass.

The wings stay folded around the body during the entire trip. But should something bar the chispies' path—a net, for instance—the wings unfurl as they swerve and turn and loop in sudden trapped confusion. The ones who can build sufficient momentum break the surface and take to the air in a short glide to the open sea. The chispen fisher earns his hazard pay then—the sharp barbed edges of those unfurled wings cut through flesh almost as easily as air.

With the school almost upon him, Albie turned his attention to the net floats and waited. Soon it came: a sudden erratic bobbing along the far edge of the semi-circle. There were always a few chispies traveling well ahead of their fellows and these were now in the net. Time to move.

"Everybody hold!" he yelled and started moving his throttle forward. He had to establish some momentum before the main body of the school hit, or else he'd never get the net closed in time.

As the white water speared into the pocket of net and boats, Albie threw the impeller control onto full forward and gripped the wheel with an intensity that bulged the muscles of his forearms.

The hit came, tugging his head back and causing the impeller to howl in protest against the sudden reverse pull. As Albie turned his boat hard to starboard and headed for Zaro's anchorboat to complete the circle, the water within began to foam like green tea in a blender. He was tying up to Zaro's craft when the first chispies began breaking water and zooming overhead. But the circumscribed area was too small to allow many of them to get away like that. Only those who managed to dart unimpeded from the deep to the surface could take to the air. The rest thrashed and flailed their wings with furious intensity, caroming off the fibrous mesh of the net and colliding with each other as the gaffers bent to their work.

The game was on.

The boats rocked in the growing turbulence and this was when the men appreciated the added stability of centerboards on the flat-bottomed scows. Their helmets would protect their heads, the safety wires gave them reasonable protection against being pulled into the water, but if a boat capsized . . . any man going into that bath of sharp swirling seawings would be ribbon-meat before he could draw a second breath.

Albie finished securing his boat to Zaro's, then grabbed his gaff and stood erect. He didn't bother with a helmet, depending rather on forty years of experience to keep his head out of the way of airborne chispies, but made sure his safety wire was tightly clipped to the back of his belt before leaning over the water to put his gaff to work.

There was an art to the gaffing, a dynamic synthesis of speed, skill, strength, courage, agility, and hand-eye coordination that took years to master. The hook at the end of the long pole had to be driven under the scales with a cephalad thrust at a point forward of the chispen's center of gravity. Then the creature's momentum had to be adjusted—*never* countered—into a rising arc that would allow the gaff-handler to lever it out of the water and onto the deck of his scow. The freezer man—Zaro in Albie's case—would take it from there, using hand hooks to slide the flopping fish onto the belt that would run it through the liquid nitrogen bath and into the insulated hold below.

Albie worked steadily, rhythmically, his eyes methodically picking out the shooting shapes, gauging speed and size. The latter was especially important: Too large a fish and the pole would either break or be torn from his hands; too small and it wasn't worth the time and effort. The best size was in the neighborhood of fifty kilos—about the weight of a pubescent human. The meat then had body and tenderness and brought the highest price.

Wings slashed, water splashed, droplets flashed through the air and caught in Albie's beard. Time was short. They had to pull in as many as they could before the inevitable happened. Insert the hook, feel the pull, lever the pole, taste the spray as the winged beastie angrily flapped the air on its way to the deck, free the hook and go back for the next. It was the first time all year Albie had truly felt alive.

Then it happened as it always happened: The furious battering opened a weak spot in the net and the school leaked free into the sea. That, too, was part of the game. After a moment of breath-catching, the men hauled in the remains of the net to pick up the leftovers, the chispies too battered and bloodied by their confused and frantic companions to swim after them.

"*Look at that, will you?*" the seated man said. "*They broke out and now they're heading back to the main body of the run! How do you explain that?*" The standing man said nothing and the seated one looked up at him. "*You used to work for Albie, didn't you?*"

A nod in the dimness. "*Once. Years ago. That was before I connected with GelkCo.*"

"*Why don't you pay him a visit? Never know . . . he might come in handy.*"

"*I might do that—if he'll speak to me.*"

"*Oh? He get mad when you quit?*"

"*Didn't quit. The old boy fired me.*"

"Hello, Albie."

Albie looked up from where he sat on the sand in a circle of his men, each with a pile of tattered net on his lap. The sun was lowering toward the land and the newcomer was silhouetted against it, his features in shadow. But Albie recognized him.

"Vic? That you, Vic?"

"Yeah, Albie, it's me. Mind if I sit down?"

"Go ahead. Sand's free." Albie gave the younger man a careful inspection as he made himself comfortable. Vic had been raised a beach rat but that was hard to tell now. A tall man in his mid-thirties, he was sleek, slim, and dark with blue eyes and even features. The one-piece suit he wore didn't belong on the beach. His black hair was slicked back, exposing a right ear bereft of its upper third, a physical trait acquired during his last year on the chispen nets. Restoration would have been no problem had he desired it, but apparently he preferred to flaunt the disfigurement as a badge of sorts. It seemed to Albie that he had broken Vic in on the nets only a few days ago, and had sacked him only yesterday. But it had been years . . . eleven of them.

He tossed Vic a length of twine. "Here. Make yourself useful. Can I trust you to do it right?"

"You never let a man forget, do you?" Vic said through an uncertain smile.

"That's because *I* don't forget!" Albie knew there was a sharp edge on his voice; he refused to blunt it with a smile of his own.

The other men glanced at each other, frowning. Albie's mellow temperament was legend among the fishermen up and down the coast, yet here he was, glowering and suffusing the air with palpable tension. Only Zaro knew what lay behind the animosity.

"Time for a break, boys," Zaro said. "We'll down a couple of ales and finish up later."

Albie never allowed dull-witted men out on the nets with him: They took the hint and walked off.

"What brings you back?" he asked when they were alone.

"That." Vic pointed toward the ship on the horizon.

Albie kept his eyes down, concentrating on repairing the net. "Saw it this morning. What's *GelkCo I* mean?"

"She's owned by the GelkCo Corporation."

"So they call it *GelkCo I?* How imaginative."

Vic shrugged and began patching a small hole in the net before him, his expression registering surprise and pleasure with the realization that his hands still knew what to do.

"The Council of Advisors put GelkCo together so the planet could deal on the interstellar market as a corporation."

"Since when do you work for the C. of A.?"

"Since my fishing career came to an abrupt halt eleven years ago." His eyes sought Albie's but couldn't find them. "I went into civil service then. Been on a research and development panel for the Council."

"Civil service, eh?" Albie squinted against the reddening light. "So now you get taxes put *into* your pay instead of taken out."

Vic was visibly stung by the remark. "Not fair, Albie. I earn my pay."

"And what's this corporation supposed to sell?" Albie said, ignoring the protest.

"Filet of chispen."

Albie smiled for the first time. "Oh, really? You mean they've still got chispies on their minds?"

"That's *all* they've got on their minds! And since I spent a good number of years with the best chispen fisher there is, it seemed natural that I be put in charge of developing the chispen as a major export."

"And that ship's going to do it?"

"It has to!" Vic said emphatically. "It must. Everything else was tried before they came to me—"

"Came to me first."

"I know." Vic could not suppress a smile. "And your suggestions were recorded as not only obscene, but physically impossible as well!"

"That's because they really aren't interested in anything about those fish beyond the price per kilo."

"Perhaps you're right, Albie. But that boat out there is unique and it's going to make you obsolete. You won't get hurt financially, I know. You could've retired years ago . . . and should have. Your methods have seen their day. That ship's going to bring this industry up to date."

"Obsolete!" The word escaped behind a grunt of disgust. Albie seriously doubted the C. of A.'s ability to render anything obsolete . . . except maybe efficiency and clear thinking. For the past few years he had been keeping a careful eye on the Council's abortive probes into the chispen industry, had watched with amusement as it tried every means imaginable to

obtain a large supply of chispen filet short of actually going out
and catching the fish.

The chrispies, of course, refused to cooperate, persisting in
migratory habits that strictly limited their availability. They
spawned in the southern gulf during the winter and fattened
themselves on the northern feeding shoals during the summer,
and were too widely dispersed at those two locales to be caught
in any significant numbers. Every spring they grouped and ran
north but were too lean and fibrous from a winter of mating,
fertilizing and hatching their eggs.

Only in the fall, after a full summer of feasting on the
abundant bait fish and bottom weed indigenous to their feeding
grounds, were they right for eating, and grouped enough to
make it commercially feasible to go after them. But Gelk's
Council of Advisors was convinced there existed an easier way
to obtain the filet than casting nets on the water. It decided to
raise chispen just like any other feed animal. But chispies are
stubborn. They won't breed in captivity, nor will they feed in
captivity. This held true not only for adult fish captured in the
wild, but for eggs hatched and raised in captivity, and even for
chispen clones as well.

The Council moved on to tissue cultures of the filet but the
resultant meat was said to be nauseating.

It eventually became evident to even the most dunder-
headed member of the Council that there weren't going to be
any shortcuts here. The appeal of chispen filet was the
culmination of myriad environmental factors: The semi-annual
runs along the coast gave the meat body and texture; the
temperature, water quality, and bottom weed found only on
their traditional feeding shoals gave it the unique euphorogenic
flavor that made it such a delicacy.

No, there was only one way to supply the discriminating
palates of Occupied Space with filet of chispen and that was to
go out on the sea and catch them during the fall runs. They
had to be pulled out of the sea and flash-frozen alive before an

intestinal enzyme washed a foul odor into the bloodstream and ruined the meat. No shortcuts. No easy way out.

"I didn't come to gloat, Albie. And I mean you no ill will. In fact, I may be able to offer you a job."

"And how could a lowly old gaffer possibly help out on a monstrosity like that?" He turned back to his net repair.

"By bringing fish into it."

Albie glanced up briefly, then down again. He said nothing.

"You can't fool me, Albie. Maybe all the rest, but not me. I used to watch you . . . used to see you talking to those fish, bringing them right into the net."

"You think I'm a psi or something?" The voice had laughter all around the edges.

"I *know* it! And what I saw on the tracking screen this morning proves it!"

"Crazy."

"No. You're a psi! Maybe you don't even know it, but you've got some sort of influence over those fish. You call them somehow and they come running. That's why you're the best."

"You'll never understand, will you? It's—"

"But I do understand! You're a psi who talks to fish!"

Albie's dark lids eclipsed his eyes until only slim crescents of light gray remained.

"Then why," he said in a low voice, "did I have such a rotten season eleven years ago? Why did I have to fire the best first mate I ever had? If I'm a psi, why couldn't I call the chispies into the net that season? Why?"

Vic was silent, keeping his eyes focused on the dark ship off shore. As he waited for an answer, Albie was pulled pastward to the last time the two of them had spoken.

It had been Albie's worst season since he began playing the game. After an excellent start, the numbers of chispen flowing into the freezers had declined steadily through the fall until that one day at season's end when they sat in their boats and watched the final schools race by, free and out of reach.

That was the day Albie hauled in the net out there on the water and personally gave it a close inspection, actually cutting off samples of net twine and unraveling them. What he found within sent him into a rage.

The first mate, a young man named Vic who was wearing a bandage on his right ear, admitted to replacing the usual twine with fiber-wrapped wire. As Albie approached him in a menacing half-crouch, he explained quickly that he thought too many fish had been getting away. He figured the daily yield could be doubled if they reinforced the net with something stronger than plain twine. He knew Albie had only one hard-and-fast rule among his crew and that was to repair the net exclusively with the materials Albie provided—no exceptions. So Vic opted for stealth, intending to reveal his ploy at season's end when they were all richer from the extra fish they had caught.

Albie threw Vic into the sea that day and made him swim home. Then he cut the floats off the net and let it sink to the bottom. Since that day he had made a practice of being present whenever the net was repaired.

A long time passed before Albie started feeling like himself again. Vic had been in his crew for six years. Albie had taken him on as a nineteen-year-old boy and had watched him mature to a man on the nets. He was a natural. Raised along the coast and as much at home on the sea as he was on land, he was soon a consummate gaffer and quickly rose to be the youngest first mate Albie had ever had. He watched over Vic, worried about him, bled with him when a chispie wing took a piece of his ear, and seriously considered taking him in as a partner after a few more years. Childless after a lifelong marriage to the sea, Albie felt he had found a son in Vic.

And so it was with the anger of a parent betrayed by one of his own that Albie banished Vic from his boats. He had lived with the anguish of that day ever since.

"There's lots of things I can't explain about that season," Vic said. "But I still think you're a psi, and maybe you could help turn a big catch into an even bigger one. If you want to play coy, that's your business. But at least come out and see the boat. I had a lot to do with the design."

"What's in this for you, Vic? Money?"

He nodded. "Lots of it. And a place on the Council of Advisors."

"That's if everything goes according to plan. What if it fails?"

"Then I'm through. But that's not a realistic concern. It's not going to be a question of failure or success, just a question of *how* successful." He turned to Albie. "Coming out tomorrow?"

Albie's curiosity was piqued. He was debating whether or not to let Zaro take charge of the catch tomorrow . . . he'd do an adequate job . . . and it was early in the season . . .

"When?"

"Midmorning will be all right. The scanners have picked up a good-sized run up at the shoals. It's on its way down and should be here by midday."

"Expect me."

A hundred meters wide and at least three times as long: Those were Albie's estimates. The ship was like nothing he had ever seen or imagined . . . a single huge empty container, forty-five or fifty meters deep, tapered at the forward end, and covered over with a heavy wire mesh. Albie and Vic stood in a tiny pod on the port rim that housed the control room and crew quarters.

"And this is supposed to make me obsolete?"

"Afraid so." Vic's nod was slow and deliberate. "She's been ready since spring. We've tested and retested—but without chispies. This'll be her christening, her first blooding." He pointed to the yellow streak creeping down the center of the scanning screen. "And that's going to do it."

Albie noticed a spur off the central streak that appeared to be moving toward a dot at the left edge of the screen.

"My, my!" he said with a dry smile. "Look at those chispies heading for my boats—even without me there to invite them in."

A puzzled expression flitted briefly across Vic's features, then he turned and opened the hatch to the outside.

"Let's go up front. They should be in sight now."

Under a high white sun in a cloudless sky, the two men trod the narrow catwalk forward along the port rim. They stopped at a small observation deck where the hull began to taper to a point. Ahead on the cobalt sea, a swath of angry white water, eighty meters wide, charged unswervingly toward the hollow ship. A good-sized run—Albie had seen bigger, but this was certainly a huge load of fish.

"How many of those you figure on catching?"

"Most of them."

Albie's tone was dubious. "I'll believe that when I see it. But let's suppose you do catch most of them—you realize what'll happen to the price of filet when you dump that much on the market at once?"

"It will drop, of course," Vic replied. "But only temporarily, and never below a profitable level. Don't worry: The Council has it all programmed. The lower price will act to expand the market by inducing more people to take advantage of the bargain and try it. And once you've tried filet of chispen . . ." He didn't bother to complete the thought.

"Got it all figured out, eh?"

"Down to the last minute detail. When this ship proves itself, we'll start construction on more. By next season there'll be a whole fleet lying in wait for the chispies."

"And what will that kind of harvesting do to them? You'll be thinning them out . . . maybe too much. That's not how the game's played, Vic. We could end up with no chispies at all someday."

"We'll only be taking the bigger ones."

"The little guys need those bigger ones for protection."

Vic held up a hand. "Wait and see. It's almost time." He signaled to the control pod. "Watch."

Water began to rush into the hold as the prow split along its seam and fanned open into a giant scoop-like funnel; the aft panel split vertically down the middle and each half swung out to the rear. The ship, reduced now to a huge open tube with neither prow nor stern, began to sink.

Albie experienced an instant of alarm but refused to show it. All this was obviously part of the process. When the hull was immersed to two-thirds of its depth in the water, the descent stopped.

Vic pointed aft. "There's a heavy metal grid back there to let the immature chispies through. But there'll be no escape for the big ones. In effect, what we're doing here is putting a huge, tear-proof net across the path of a major run, something no one's dared to do before. With the old methods, a run like this would make chowder out of anything that tried to stop it."

"How do you know they won't just go around you?"

"You know as well as I do, Albie, these big runs don't change course for anything. We'll sit here, half-sunk in the water, and they'll run right into the hold there; they'll get caught up against the aft grid, and before they can turn around, the prow will close up tight and they're ours. The mesh on top keeps them from flying out."

Albie noticed Vic visibly puffing with pride as he spoke, and couldn't resist one small puncture: "Looks to me like all you've got here is an oversized, motorized seining scoop."

Vic blinked, swallowed, then went on talking after a brief hesitation. "When they're locked in, we start to circulate water through the hold to keep them alive while we head for a plant up the coast where they'll be flash-frozen and processed."

"All you need is some cooperation from the fish."

Vic pointed ahead. "I don't think that'll be a problem. The run's coming right for us."

Albie looked from the bright anticipation in Vic's face to the ship sitting silent and open-mawed, to the onrushing horde of finned fury. He knew what was going to happen next but didn't have the heart to say it. Vic would have to learn for himself.

The stars were beginning to poke through the sky's growing blackness. Only a faint, fading glow on the western horizon remained to mark the sun's passing. None of the moons was rising yet.

With the waves washing over his feet, Albie stood and watched the autumn aurora begin to shimmer over the sea. The cool prevailing breeze carried smoke from his after-dinner pipe away toward the land. Darkness expanded slowly and was almost complete when he heard the voice.

"Why'd you do it, Albie?"

It wasn't necessary to turn around. He knew the voice, but had not anticipated the fury he sensed caged behind it.

"Didn't do a thing, Vic." He kept his eyes on the faint, wavering flashes of the aurora, his own voice calm.

"You diverted those fish!"

"That's what you'd like to believe, I'm sure, but that's not the way it is."

The run had been almost on top of them. The few strays that always travel in the lead had entered the hold and slammed into the grate at the other end. Then the run disappeared. The white water evaporated and the sea became quiet. In a panic, Vic had run back to the control pod where he learned from the scanner that the run had sounded to the bottom of the trench and was only now rising toward the surface . . . half a kilometer aft of the ship. Vic had said nothing, glaring only momentarily at Albie and then secluding himself in his quarters below for the rest of the day.

"It's true!" Vic's voice was edging toward a scream. "I watched your lips! You were talking to those fish . . . telling them to dive!"

Albie swung around, alarmed by the slurred tones and growing hysteria in the younger man's voice. He could not make out Vic's features in the darkness, but could see the swaying outline of his body. He could also see what appeared to be a length of driftwood dangling from his right hand.

"How much've you had to drink, Vic?"

"Enough." The word was deformed by its extrusion through Vic's clenched teeth. "Enough to know I'm ruined and you're to blame."

"And what's the club for? Gonna break my head?"

"Maybe. If you don't agree to straighten out all the trouble you caused me today, I just might."

"And how do you expect me to do that?"

"By guiding the fish *into* the boat instead of under it."

"Can't do that, Vic." Albie readied himself for a dodge to one side or the other. The Vic he had known on the nets would never swing that club. But eleven years had passed . . . and this Vic was drunk. "Can't do it as I am now, and I sure as hell won't be able to do it any better with a broken head. Sorry."

There followed a long, tense, silent moment. Then two sounds came out of the darkness: one, a human cry—half sob, half scream of rage; followed by the grating thud of wood hurled against wet sand. Albie saw Vic's vague outline slump into a sitting position.

"Dammit, Albie! I trusted you! I brought you out there in good faith and you scuttled me!"

Albie stepped closer to Vic and squatted down beside him. He put the bit of his pipe between his teeth. The bowl was cold but he didn't bother relighting it.

"It wasn't me, Vic. It was the game. That ship of yours breaks all the rules of the game."

" 'The game'!" Vic said, head down, bitterness compressing

his voice. "You've been talking about games since the day I met you. This is no game, Albie! This is my life . . . my future!"

"But it's a game to the chispies. That's what most people don't understand about them. That's why only a few of us are any good at catching them: Those fish are playing a game with us."

Vic lifted his head. "What do you take me for—?"

"It's true. Only a few of us have figured it out, and we don't talk it around. Had you stayed with me a few years longer, I might have told you if you hadn't figured it out for yourself by then. Truth is, I'm no psi and I don't direct those fish into my net; they find their way in on their own. If they get caught in my net, it's because they *want* to."

"You've been out on the nets too long, Albie. Chispies can't think."

"I'm not saying they can think like you and me, but they're not just dumb hunks of filet traveling on blind instinct, either. Maybe it only happens when they're packed tight and running, maybe they form some sort of hive-mind then that they don't have when they're spread out. I don't know. I don't have the words or knowledge to get across what I mean. It's a gut feeling . . . I think they look on the net as a game, a challenge they'll accept only if we play by the rules and give them a decent chance of winning."

He paused, waiting for another wisecrack from Vic, but none came. He continued. "They can gauge a net's strength. Don't know how, but they do it. Maybe it's those few fish always traveling in the lead . . . if they find the net too strong, if there's no chance of them breaking out, they must send out some kind of warning and the rest of the run avoids it. Sounds crazy, I know, but there's one inescapable fact I've learned to accept and apply, and it's made me the best: The weaker the net, the bigger the catch."

"So that's why you fired me when you found out I was repairing the nets with wire!"

"Exactly. You were hunting for a shortcut with the chispies and there aren't any. You made the net too strong, so they decided to play the game somewhere else. I wound up with the worse season I ever had."

"And I wound up in the water and out of a job!" Vic began to laugh, a humorless sound, unpleasant to hear. "But why didn't you explain this then?"

"Why didn't you come to me when you wanted to experiment with my nets? Why didn't you go buy your own tear-proof net and try it out on your own time? I may have overreacted, but you went behind my back and betrayed my trust. The entire crew went through pretty lean times until the next season because you broke the rules of the game!"

Vic laughed again. "A game! I must be drunker than I thought—it almost makes sense!"

"After forty years of hauling those winged devils out of the water, it's the only way I can make sense out of it."

"But they get caught and die, Albie! How can that be a game for them?"

"Only a tiny portion of the run challenges me at a time, and only a small percentage of those go into the freezer. The rest break free. What seems like a suicide risk to us may be only a diversion to them. Who knows what motivates them? This is their planet, their sea, and the rules of the game are entirely up to them. I'm just a player—one who figured out the game and became a winner."

"Then I'm a loser, I guess—the biggest damn loser to play." He rose to his feet and faced out toward the running lights of the *GelkCo I* as it lay at anchor a league off shore.

"That you are," Albie said, rising beside him and trying to keep his tone as light as possible. "You built the biggest, toughest damn net they've ever seen, one they'd never break out of . . . so they decided not to play."

Vic continued to stare out to sea, saying nothing.

"That's where you belong," Albie told him. "You were born

for the sea, like me. You tried your hand with those stiff-legged landroamers on the Council of Advisors and came up empty. But you and me, we're not equipped to deal with their kind, Vic. They change the rules as they go along, trying to get what they want by whatever means necessary. They sucked you in, used you up, and now they're gonna toss you out. So now's the time to get back on the water. Get out there and play the game with the chispies. They play hard and fast, but always by the same rules. You can die out there, but not because they cheated."

Vic made no move, no sound.

"Vic?"

No reply.

Albie turned and walked up the dune alone.

"Albieeeeee!"

One of the dock hands came running along the jetty. Albie had just pushed off and was following his crew into the early morning haze. He idled his scow and waited for the man to get closer.

"Guy back at the boathouse wants to know if you need an extra hand today."

Albie held his breath. "What's he look like?"

"I dunno," the dock hand said with a shrug. "Tall, dark hair, a piece missing from his right—"

Albie smiled through his beard as he reversed the scow. "Tell him to hurry . . . I haven't got all day!"

And out along the trench, the chispies moved in packs, running south and looking for sport along the way.

Introduction

Back in 1979, I saw an article in *Medical Tribune* about the successful transplantation of a mammalian nucleus into a plant cell. Naturally, having an sf turn of mind, I foresaw all sorts of possibilities. I put the idea to use immediately, creating photosynthetic cattle for my third novel, *An Enemy of the State*, and making it the central idea for this piece. I promised Stan Schmidt a series of stories in this future scenario, but I haven't got around to writing them yet.

Someday I will. "Green Winter" is the first installment.

This version, by the way, differs from the one Stan bought for *Analog*. I had two endings. This is the other one.

GREEN WINTER

The knife made a crisp, rasping sound as it sliced through Veneem's skin. The area over the left deltoid had been numbed with ice before the procedure and he felt only a sensation of pressure, a mild discomfort.

The dark green of the epidermis parted cleanly to reveal the lighter dermis below. This in turn gave way and exposed the pink of the subcutaneous fat. Blood appeared in a slow, red ooze as the doctor completed the elliptical incision around the growth. It was a tiny hand and forearm this time, mottled green, with minute, articulated fingers. Veneem had put off the excision for as long as he could because the growths so often withered and fell off on their own. But this one had kept on growing, so now he was back at Dr. Baken's adding another scar to his collection.

As the segment of skin supporting the growth was removed, blood filled the cavity and overflowed onto the arm. The doctor quickly wiped it away and began suturing. Three deft ties and the wound was closed. After a compress was applied and a clean cloth wrapped around the area to hold it in place, Veneem rose to his feet.

"See you in five or six days," Dr. Baken said, dropping the excised growth and the excess thread on the garbage pile in the corner. "Those sutures ought to be ready to be pulled by then."

Veneem nodded. He knew the routine.

"Tell me something," he said after a pause. "Don't I get an awful lot of these things?"

"No, not particularly. They're fairly common in regenerated limbs but the incidence varies between individuals. I've got a number of patients who need excisions far more often than you."

Veneem nodded with an overt lack of concern. He didn't want the doctor to think him overly conscious of his health— that would be unseemly for a hunter.

"How's Rana?" Baken asked.

The question surprised Veneem. The doctor had met his daughter, of course—he had been to the house often enough during the early stages of the arm's regeneration, and during Nola's final illness—but he didn't think Rana had made enough of an impression on the man that he'd be asking about her.

"She's well. If I can keep her out of trouble she'll make someone a fine wife someday."

Baken smiled. "If she stayed out of trouble, she wouldn't be Rana."

Veneem had to agree, yet he wondered how the doctor could make such a precise observation. He brushed the matter aside—everyone knew Rana. Now to the matter of settling the fee.

"Get you a rabbit for this—that do?"

"Nicely. Before the half-moon, if you can. My meat supply is getting low."

"You'll have it tomorrow or the next day."

He took his fur jacket from a hook on the wall and gingerly slipped his left arm in first. Veneem was of average height and heavily muscled, more so than most hunters, but moved with a feline grace that was the *sine qua non* of his profession. With the jacket cinched securely around him, he covered his shiny green scalp with a cloth cap, nodded brusquely to Baken, and stepped out into the cold.

His eyes immediately scanned the ground for game tracks. Sheer reflex—he knew he'd find nothing; the ground around Baken's hut was an indecipherable clutter of comings and goings and waitings-around. Pulling his horse out from the shelter, he slid up onto its bare back and trotted eastward along the road. Denuded trees stood stiff and still on either side as an icy gray sky threatened more snow.

Veneem liked snow. He detested the cold that came with it, but winter was inevitable, and so if it must be cold, let it snow. Let it be a wet snow that stuck to the trees and etched them in white against a darkening sky. Let it snow briefly, frequently, no more than a finger's breadth at a time—just enough to erase the stale tracks and highlight the fresh. At such times small-game hunting was as easy as picking wild berries.

He was perhaps halfway home when a movement, a darting shape in the thicket to his right, caused him to pull his mount up sharply and peer into the gloom. His searching eyes found nothing. He could have sworn he'd seen a shadow moving in the tangle. A big shadow. Almost big enough to be a hairy. He cursed the overcast sky. If the sun were out he'd have a better chance for a second look . . . if there was really anything there to see.

His eyes weren't what they used to be; hadn't been for a few years now. This was no casual admission—it was his most carefully guarded secret. He was a hunter and his eyes were his life, his reputation, his means of support, his protection—

Protection! He snorted a disgusted puff of fog into the air. If his vision had been better, perhaps the bolt he'd loosed at that charging boar would have found its eye instead of glancing off its skull. Perhaps then the enraged beast wouldn't have butted Nola, half-crushing her chest, nor gored his left arm so badly that Dr. Baken was forced to remove it at the shoulder. The arm took a full five seasons to regenerate. Nola died of the fever shortly after the accident.

And life had not been quite the same since.

No sound, no further movement came from the thicket. He strained to see but the outlines of objects began to blur beyond two man-lengths. He saw nothing out of the ordinary. Couldn't have been a hairy anyway—they simply weren't seen around here anymore. Just as well . . . his crossbow was at home.

Giving the horse's flanks a jab with his leather-shod heels, he continued on his journey. As he turned off the main road onto the path that led to his home, his gaze roamed the ground in search of wheel tracks. There were none. He began to curse softly and steadily as he rode and was in a foul mood by the time he reached the house.

"Rana!" he called after tethering his horse to the nearest low-hanging branch. The main structure of the house was a low dome of hardened clay with four small windows—boarded now against the cold—and a single entrance. Pushing aside the double hanging of cured hides that covered the doorway, he entered and called again.

"Rana!"

The girl came out of the smaller of the two sleeping rooms at the rear of the house. She had her father's long face and high cheekbones, but her dark eyes were her mother's. The fire in the hearth flickered off her face and bare scalp, darker green than usual now due to the increased time she was spending indoors. It was warm inside and she wore only a simple tunic that hid her thin, wiry frame and reduced her small breasts to an almost imperceptible swell.

"Something wrong?" She was nineteen summers and spoke with a clear, high voice.

"Yes! The delivery was to have been made at sunrise today. Absolutely no later—the Elders promised!"

"We still have some cheese left and there's plenty of meat."

"That's not the point. The supplies were supposed to be here by now and they are not!"

"I'm sure you have a pretty good idea of why they're late," Rana said after a short pause.

"I don't have any such thing!" he lied and pulled his jacket off with angry, jerking motions, oblivious to the discomfort he caused in his left arm.

Of course he knew why the supplies were late: The Elders disapproved of Rana and her overt disrespect for their authority, and this was how they chose to show it. They'd never have dared such a tactic while he was First Hunter, but many things had changed since the accident.

His home, for instance. Rana had moved easily and naturally into the void left in the household by her mother's death— preparing his meals, ministering to his arm while it regenerated, doing her best to keep his spirits up. But nothing she could do would fill the void in his spirit or allay his sense of loss or make him feel *complete* again. Only time would do that.

Time was a friend in that respect, and an enemy in others. Time, along with lots of sun-soaking, food, and rest, had replaced his left arm. But the time needed for convalescence had also preyed on his mind. The other hunters had seen to it that he was kept well stocked with provisions during the regenerative period; this was a tradition, but he'd chafed at being an invalid, dependent on the beneficence of others. He had always been a producer and the role of passive consumer did not sit well. He had been First Hunter before the accident. During his period of forced inactivity other hunters had vied for the vacant position. This was natural and he felt no resentment. However, by the time he was ready to go into the field again, his reputation had faded and there had not been opportunity yet to reassert his prominence. To date, no one in the enclave was generally recognized as First Hunter.

In ways he could see and in ways he could not, Rana had changed, too. She was now prone to long absences from home and to loud, pointed questions whenever she attended a plenum. For every point of the Law she had a "Why?" For every Revealed Truth she had a host of doubts. Rana had become a nettle in the collective breeches of the Elders.

And that could prove dangerous.

"They're goading you," she said. "They want you to bring me into line and this is their way of telling you."

"They'd be falling all over each other trying to supply me with farm goods if I were First Hunter again."

She came over and hugged him. "You *are* First Hunter as far as I'm concerned, and you should be treated as such. You bring more meat into the enclave than any two other hunters combined. It's only because of me that they've held back on restoring your title—they don't want a First Hunter who can't control his daughter."

Veneem ran the fingertips of his left hand lightly over the glossy green smoothness of Rana's scalp. He wanted to tell her that she was the center of his life right now, that although her flagrant disrespect for the Elders distressed him, he admired her fire. But he said nothing of his feelings. It was not his way to show affection, never had been, and he couldn't change now.

"I guess I'm lucky you're not a farmer," she said, "or I'd have been taken off a long time ago."

His voice was a low growl. "Then there'd have been some dead Elders a long time ago. The Elders are the voice of God in the world—I believe that and I revere them as such. But they'll never hurt you, Rana. At least not while I breathe." He pushed her gently to arm's length and, resting both hands on her shoulders, gazed at her face. "But why do you do it? Why do you provoke them so?"

"Because everything they tell us is a lie! Everything!" The utter contempt in her voice made him cringe.

"How can you say that with such certainty? The Elders are older and wiser than either of us. And when they make a pronouncement, it is the Revealed Truth of God."

Rana's white teeth chewed briefly on her lower lip. "Some other time, Father."

"Don't toy with them," he said with an expression that matched the grimness of his tone. "You can push them only so far. If you should ever be deemed a threat to the order, even I won't be able to protect you."

The squeak of wheels and the clop of hooves from down the path halted further discussion as they both went to the door. The supply wagon had arrived.

"See?" Rana said, holding the hangings aside. "They've sent it late enough to irk you, but not late enough to bring you after them."

Orth, who had been driving the supply wagon since Veneem was a child, pulled the pair of horses to a stop in front of the house, set the brake, and slid from the seat—not as smoothly nor as quickly as he had of old, but still with an unmistakable sureness to his movements. He was swathed in furs and blankets to such an extent that he no longer looked quite human. Only his eyes showed through the wraps—quick, dark, darting pupils under heavy green lids ringed with the white lines of age.

"You're late, Orth," Veneem said in a low voice. He knew he couldn't blame the old driver, but neither could he hide the menace in his mood as he went out to meet him.

"I know." Orth's voice was muffled by the layers of cloth covering the lower half of his face. "The Elders wouldn't let me load up until a short while ago. You're the first stop."

Veneem glanced back at Rana and shrugged. Still clad only

in the thin tunic, she came out to help unload the milk, eggs, cheese, and flour.

"Did they give you any reason?" she asked, shivering in the breeze.

"Something about missing supplies. Somebody said it looked like a hairy got into the supply shed last night."

Veneem was reaching for a large wheel of cheese when he heard the word "hairy." His head snapped toward Orth while the rest of his body froze in position.

"A hairy? Last night?"

"Just talk. I wouldn't give it a second—"

Veneem whipped his body around in one abrupt motion and strode toward the house. Rana trotted after him carrying a basket of eggs.

"Where are you going?"

"After that hairy."

"But you heard Orth: just talk. Probably an excuse to make the wagon late."

"Any other time I'd agree with you. But I saw this one just a short while ago." Passing through the doorway, he headed directly for the northwest corner of the room where he kept his crossbow.

Rana's eyes were wide as she followed him. "And you didn't go after it?"

"I didn't know it was a hairy then. I wasn't even sure I'd really seen anything. Now I know."

"But you can't leave now. It's past midday already!"

He made no reply as he pulled his doubly thick hunting cloak from a peg and threw it over his shoulders. His respirations were rapid and his skin tingled with exhilaration. A hairy! There hadn't been a confirmed sighting in years and the last kill had been longer ago than he cared to remember.

He had to bag this one! It meant reaffirmation of his status as First Hunter; no matter how displeased the Elders were with his daughter, they'd have to publicly recognize his primacy if he brought in a hairy. He knew where to start the hunt—that gave him an edge—but he'd have to leave now if he was to have a chance. By morning the beast would be far from the region.

Rana waited for a reply. Receiving none, she hurried to her room and emerged with another crossbow.

"No, Rana," Veneem said in a matter-of-fact tone. "Not this time."

"*Especially* this time, Father. I've never seen a live hairy and may never get another chance—there just aren't any left around here."

"No, Rana." His voice was louder and firmer.

"Yes!" she hissed with sudden, unexplained intensity. "I've handled a bow and followed the trails with you and Mother since I was a child . . . I will *not* be left out of this!"

Veneem knew from her tone and her defiant posture that there was no point in arguing. She was showing her mother's side: When she made up her mind, that was that. He girded his cloak around him with the broad belt that held his supply of hunting bolts, hefted his bow, and brushed past her on his way to the door.

"Get your horse then."

Outside, he helped Orth finish unloading the supplies as Rana hurried around to the lean-to behind the house. The supply wagon had been turned and was on its way down the path toward the road by the time she led her bridled horse around to the front.

Veneem was momentarily awed by her appearance. It had only been two years since her mother's death, yet in that short period she had grown from an awkward adolescent girl into a woman. She stood there, her eyes shining in anticipation, wearing her mother's hunting cloak with her mother's crossbow slung across her shoulder. His eyes were suddenly bleary with excess moisture and his breath did not flow as easily as it should. Shuddering, he pulled himself up on the horse's back. Maybe he didn't deserve to be First Hunter again . . . he seemed to be losing his iron. If he kept on this way, he'd soon be a weepy, wilted old man before his time.

Expression set and teeth clenched, he gathered up the reins, gave the horse a harder than necessary kick on its flanks, and raced off down the path. Rana hopped lightly onto her own mount and took chase.

They rode at full gallop west along the road toward the enclave center until Veneem pulled sharply to a halt and dismounted near a high thicket. Rana overrode the spot and walked her horse back to where her father was now pushing his way into the chaotic tangle of leafless branches. He became a vague shape, thrashing about and cursing as the smaller twigs, stiff with winter, poked at him from all sides. Finally—

"I knew it! Rana, bring the horses around!"

She led the animals back down the road until she found a break in the brush, then guided them through. Veneem awaited her in a clearing behind the thicket, a short distance from the road. He was pointing to the ground.

"Look—cloth-wrapped feet. Tracks everywhere. Cheese rinds, too. He was here. No doubt about it." Veneem followed the tracks a few paces into the trees, then called back over his shoulder. "Tether the horses there. He's headed toward the big rocks."

Rana did as she was bid and hurried after him. The trail was easy to follow.

"Did it ever occur to you," she said, coming abreast and matching his stride with her long thin legs, "that a hairy may be more than just a dumb animal?" She watched him carefully as he replied.

"Never said the hairies were dumb. In fact, they're the craftiest of all animals, as well as the tastiest. That's why they're such a prize."

"But the way they wrap their feet and bodies against the cold . . . doesn't that indicate a high level of intelligence to you?"

"Just imitation. They watch us, they steal our food and materials and copy what we do. They're just game animals. It's Revealed Truth."

"Revealed by whom?"

"Are we going to have to go through that again? You're courting sacrilege—just like at the last plenum when you made everyone so uncomfortable with your impertinence."

"Who revealed the 'truth' that the hairies are animals?" she repeated in a dogged tone.

"Don't ask foolish questions." His voice took on the singsong tone of a recitation: "God made us in his image and speaks through the Elders to guide us back to our place as the lords of creation. Revealed Truths are the word of God."

"God made us, did he?" A taunting smile seeped onto her face. "If that's so, then we're following the tracks of God."

This statement brought Veneem to an abrupt halt. Rana, too, stopped. They faced each other in silence, their breath steaming, streaming from nostrils and parted lips.

"What madness is this?" he said in a hoarse voice. "Why do you torment me with this blasphemy?"

"I don't mean to torment you, believe me. I just want you to know what I know. And now, while you're hunting a hairy . . . it seems to be the best time to tell you."

"Tell me what? That our most highly prized game animal is actually our Creator?" He started walking toward the rocks again. "I'm going to have Dr. Baken take a look at you tomorrow. Maybe he can come up with an elixir or something to—"

"Baken is my source of information!"

Once more Veneem stopped short. The answers to a number of niggling questions were suddenly quite clear. The doctor's inquiries about Rana this morning were also explained.

"Baken, eh? That's where you've been going when you disappear for a whole day." He snorted. "Who'd have thought? So he's the one who's been filling your head with this garbage. I'll have to have a little talk with Dr. Baken."

"He's a good man. We became friends while he was treating you and Mother after the accident."

"He's a fool and worse if he's taught you to blaspheme!"

Veneem resumed his pursuit of the hairy but found it almost impossible to focus his attention on the trail. Dr. Baken had somehow corrupted Rana's thinking. That in itself was bad. But there was more than a few ideas at stake here: The heretical views Rana now held could endanger her life. That was what concerned him most. If she should ever start spouting such madness at a plenum—and she was impulsive enough to do just that given the proper circumstance—the Elders would be duty bound to silence her. Forever.

And that would mean his end, as well. For he'd never allow anything to happen to her while he could raise a hand in her defense. She was all he had left. There was no one he could truly call a close friend—Nola had been that and a wife, too. They had formed a self-sufficient unit, the two of them—a threesome after Rana arrived. There had never been any need for outsiders.

Now they were two; no matter how wrong she was, they would not be divided.

They arrived at the big rocks, a pile of huge stone shards that rose above the forest and stretched away into the haze of the south. Veneem searched along the base of the formation until he found the place where the tracks disappeared.

"He started to climb here." As he began to hoist himself up on the first rock in pursuit, Rana laid a gentle hand on his shoulder.

"Baken has books."

Veneem dropped back to the ground again but remained facing away from his daughter. Utter hopelessness began to settle upon him. Rana was getting in deeper and deeper. Hiding books from the Elders was punishable by death. He ground his teeth in frustration—he couldn't understand her; her constant questioning, her poking into things she should leave alone. It was a good life under the Elders if you just tended to your business. His voice was barely audible as he spoke the law:

"Books are forbidden. They're to be turned over to the Elders as soon as they're found."

"That's so we won't find out what's inside them. Their authority would be destroyed if it became generally known that we're the descendants—worse, yet, the *creations*—of the hairies!"

"Madness!" He still refused to look at her.

"No! Baken's learned to read some of the books and he's teaching me. He's learned things. Incredible things. Things that go against everything we've ever been taught."

"I have no wish to hear them," he said as he found a foothold and began climbing the rocks.

Rana scrambled after him. "You're going to have to listen to me, Father. Baken told me of the time some hunters brought in the carcass of a pregnant bitch hairy. She'd been nearing her time when they got her and he was able to examine the unborn baby. He says it looked just like we do at birth!"

"Be quiet!" Veneem said angrily. He was climbing as quickly as he could, whether in pursuit of the hairy or to escape his daughter's blasphemies, he wasn't quite sure. "The beast will hear us coming!"

But Rana refused to be put off and kept pace.

"Did you know that we're all born with pink skin and hair—hair on our heads and above our eyes? Sometimes fine hair on our arms and legs? And that our skin doesn't turn green until we've been exposed to light? Nobody talks about that . . . the same way nobody admits that if you took a hairy, sheared his fuzz, and stained him green, he'd look as human as we do!

It's obvious to anyone with eyes that we come from the same stock."

Veneem halted his climb and turned to face Rana. Leaning his back against a rock, he studied her a moment before speaking. He hid his anger and adopted the tone of a patient parent speaking to a rather dull-witted child. He raised his forearms diagonally before him, right angles at the elbows, his palms on edge toward Rana. The tips of the right and left middle fingers touched lightly at eye level to form a point.

"This," he said, moving the right arm, "is the animal kingdom. This"—the left arm moved—"is the plant kingdom. At the apex are you and I and our kin: humanity, the highest form of life, the fusion of plant and animal. We have the best attributes of both kingdoms. In lean times we can take a certain amount of nourishment from the sun, and should we lose a limb we can grow a new one. No animal can do that. Yet we can move around and go where we wish, use our hands to build, and eat and drink in the winter months when the sun is weak. No plant can do that."

He sighed. "Don't you see? Not only does what you say go against Revealed Truth, it goes against common sense as well. The hairies belong solely to the animal kingdom. We are superior to them in every way. How could *they* have created *us*?"

"Baken says—"

"'Baken says'!" he mimicked. "'Baken says'! I'm sick of hearing about what Dr. Baken says! I'm after a game animal now—it's my job. If you cannot be silent, go wait by the horses!"

Rana persisted. "Baken says that long ago the hairies took a cell from a—"

"Cell? What's a cell?"

"As Baken explains it, it's one of the uncountable little capsules, invisibly small, that make up the bodies of every living thing."

It was Veneem's turn to taunt. "Look at me! How many 'cells' do you see?"

"When you stand on a hill and look at the beach, how many grains of sand do you see?" She did not wait for an answer. "As I was saying, the hairies took a cell from a plant and removed its nucleus—that's the thing in the center of the cell that controls it—and replaced it with the nucleus from a cell of a hairy. For a while it was just a curiosity, but then they learned how to grow an entire organism from one of these cells. And then we were born. The hairies are the real humans . . . we're their creations."

Veneem made a contemptuous, snorting noise. "And you mock me for blindly accepting the teaching of the Elders! Look what you've just said: You've told me of something called a 'cell' which you admit you've never seen—*can't* see—and then about something else inside this 'cell.' Then you tell me that the beasts who have to steal food from us to survive the winter actually grew us from one of these mythical little capsules. Really, Rana! Who's the fool?"

"We're all fools for believing the Elders for so long! We—"

Veneem's right hand shot out and covered her mouth. A light shower of tiny sand particles had begun to fall, sliding and bouncing down from the rocks above, sprinkling their heads and shoulders.

"He's up there!" he whispered. "And if he has ears he's heard us."

Unslinging his bow, Veneem drew the gut string back to the last notch, set the trigger, and put one of his heaviest bolts in the groove. To his left was a break in the rocks, about a man-length or so wide. He sidled over and peered into it. Empty. A high-walled gully sloped upward for a short distance, then banked off to the right. With weapon at ready, he began his ascent.

The floor of the gully was smooth—it probably served as a water run-off during the spring—and there were patches of ice in scattered recesses. He heard a sudden loud crunch from up around the bend, then nothing. The sound was repeated, followed by a series of lesser noises, and then a large boulder bounded around the curve in the gorge and came rolling at him. Veneem gauged its path and ran upward toward the bend, allowing the stone to bounce off the far wall and pass him on his left.

Reaching the curve, he saw it—a buck hairy. Tall, thin, full mane on head and face; his torso and lower legs were wrapped in tattered cloth and he had just kicked loose a second boulder. With no time to aim properly, Veneem chanced a quick shot from waist level. The hairy howled in pain and clutched its left thigh as Veneem leaped to avoid the oncoming stone juggernaut.

Too late. He misjudged its ungainly wobbling roll and it struck him a glancing blow on the rib cage as it passed. Pain lanced up to his left shoulder and down along his flank as he fell on his back and began to slide down the gully headfirst. For a few heartbeats he could not draw a breath. Then, as his oxygen-starved mind was about to panic, air began to gush in and out of his lungs in ragged gusts. He hauled himself into a sitting position and waited for the pain to subside.

Rana had heard the wail of the wounded hairy and she now peered around the corner of the gully. Seeing her father leaning against the rocks with his hand pressed against his ribs, she dropped her bow and scurried up to his side.

"You all right?" Her expression was frantic.

Still gasping, Veneem nodded and pointed back the way they had come. "Help me up. I wounded him but he still might be dangerous."

Rana took his bow and his arm and led him back to safety. When they reached their previous position, Veneem sank to his knees.

"We'll let him bleed."

"Where'd you get him?"

"Leg."

Her eyes darted back and forth as her mind seemed to race. "Then we can take him alive!"

"*Never!*" Veneem was getting his wind back.

"We must! We may never get another chance like this to learn the truth about the hairies."

"I already *know* the truth!" He spat the words. "And it's part of the law that all hairies must be hunted down and killed like the wild game they are!"

Rana nearly leaped at her father. Her patience was as frayed as his and had been further thinned by seeing him injured. She blamed herself for that—if she hadn't talked so much, they might have been able to take the hairy by surprise instead of the other way around. But it was his unshakable orthodoxy . . .

"How many 'game animals' have set a trap for you, Father? That's not just a wild beast up there!"

Veneem rose slowly, painfully to his feet. "No more of your fever dreams, please. I've more pressing matters to attend to. Silence, now!"

"No! I want you to think about what I've said before you kill it."

"I *am* thinking and I've *been* thinking. *You* must think! If the hairies had the power and the intelligence to create us, what happened to them? Where is their mighty civilization? Answer me that!"

"Baken says"—Veneem growled at the name—"that in their toying with the stuff of life they somehow altered one of the things that make us sick and a great plague swept the world. A famine followed. After that, those who didn't get sick or starve to death went mad, killing each other and destroying their cities. We survived. The plague had no effect on us and we could augment our nourishment by sun-soaking. We multiplied while they died.

"Only a few hairies are left. They hide in the ruined cities.

That's why we're forbidden to go there—because we'd find out that the 'Truths' of the Elders are lies and their hold would be broken!"

"Very clever," Veneem said with a slow, sad shake of his head. "Dr. Baken has managed to twist everything. Everyone knows, and Revealed Truth confirms, that *we* built the cities ages ago. They are now forbidden because they were the cause of our fall from grace. When we built them we separated ourselves from the land and the sun. For that we were punished—the cities were destroyed by God and we were banished from them forever."

He rubbed his injured ribs gingerly, then snatched his bow from Rana.

"No more talk! I'm going to find another way up there, and when I get to him I'll finish him."

Rana watched him briefly as he began to reload the weapon, then wheeled and ran to the edge of the gully where she had dropped her own bow. After checking to see that the bolt was still in place, she called over her shoulder in a low voice:

"I'm going up this way. If I have to hit him in the other leg to bring him down, I will. But I'm going to take him alive."

Veneem's voice was strained as he jolted forward. "Stay out of there—he's still dangerous!"

Rana ignored him and entered the gully. He finished loading as quickly as he could and went after her. He watched as she moved swiftly, cautiously up the center of the gorge. She was almost to the bend when Veneem saw the stone. It was smaller than its predecessors—about the size of a human head—and had been thrown rather than rolled. It bounced once on the granite floor, then flew straight for Rana. She made to dive out of its way but slipped on an icy patch and fell against the far wall.

The bones of her right foot must have made a sickening noise as they were crushed, but it was lost in the loud crack of one rock striking another with shattering force.

Rana writhed on her side, her face contorted in agony. Low guttural sounds, half moan, half grunt, escaped between her clenched teeth as she tried to move the stone off her foot.

After a shocked, frozen instant, Veneem broke into a run and passed Rana without a second look. He had to reach the hairy before the next rock came. Rounding the bend, he saw the beast. It was desperately trying to dislodge a larger stone, one that would surely finish Rana if it started to roll. But it was wounded—its left leg was covered with fresh blood—and its strength wasn't up to the task. When it saw the green fury that was Veneem charging up the gully, it began to retreat.

The hairy clawed and scrambled along the ledge, its wounded leg dragging like an anchor. There was something almost like human fear in its eyes as it glanced over its shoulder at him, something almost human about the gibberish that burst from its mouth, something almost human in the way it rolled on its back and frantically waved its hands as Veneem stood within arm's length and aimed his crossbow at its head.

But it died like any other animal when the bolt split its skull.

"I think you're going to lose it," Veneem said as he gave Rana's foot a final inspection. It was swollen, misshapen, the skin had split in three places and there were numerous spots of brownish discoloration.

A fire was blazing in the hearth, dancing light off the smooth green of Rana's skin as she sat before it. Her wounded foot rested on a folded blanket which in turn rested on a short stool. The bleeding had stopped; so had the pain. Most of it.

"You'll have to get Baken in the morning," she said.

"I'll not have that man near you."

"He's the only doctor in the enclave! If the foot must come off, he'll know where to cut. I won't let anyone else touch me!"

Knowing she was right but refusing to admit it, Veneem said nothing. He turned to the hearth and rotated the spit. He was tired. It had been no easy task to carry Rana to the horses, then fetch the dead hairy, then guide all home. He was feeling his age, especially in his ribs and his left shoulder—there was blood on the dressing over this morning's incision but he hadn't got around to changing it yet.

But at least everything was in its place now. Rana was warming herself by the fire, the carcass of the hairy was dressed and hanging in the cold shed while Veneem roasted a piece of it on the spit. He had cut off the right shank as a celebratory feast of sorts; the rest would go to the central supply shed in the morning. A glance at Rana's wound and he realized there was probably something symbolic in the cut of meat he chose.

He sliced off a small piece and dropped it into a wooden bowl which he then placed in his daughter's lap.

"Come. Eat. You'll need all the nourishment you can get when regeneration starts, especially since there's no sunlight worth mentioning this time of year."

"Not hungry," she said. She was physically and emotionally spent and Veneem did his best to be solicitous.

"Of course you are. You haven't had this much activity in a long, long time. You must be ravenous. And this has always been your favorite."

"No." She swallowed hard—her salivary glands had been activated by the sight and smell of the meat. "You didn't have to kill it."

"Yes, I did. And for more than one reason." He squatted before her and took her hand. "First of all, it hurt you. Nothing can hurt you and be allowed to live. Second, if we had brought it back alive as you wished—and I'm not really sure we could have—you'd have begun publicly spouting the madness that Baken's put into your head. And that would mean the end of you. The Elders would have no choice then but to order your death. Third, because this catch makes me First Hunter beyond any doubt. And last . . ."

He paused, catching and holding her gaze. "And last, I

killed the hairy because it's the law that all hairies are to be killed. They're very scarce now and we might never see one again. But if I should come upon another, I'll kill it. And that settles the matter. I want no more discussion on it. Eat your dinner."

Rana sighed and picked up the piece of meat. It was hot and firm with a thin coating of grease that oozed onto her fingers. She nibbled at it. No sense in letting such a delicacy go to waste.

Introduction

Back in 1981, Alan Ryan was editing *Perpetual Light,* an anthology for Warner Books composed of stories about the religious experience. Over the years, Alan and I had compared our Jesuit educations—I'm a graduate of Xavier in Manhattan (yes . . . I was a Subway Commando) and Georgetown—and he thought I'd be an apt contributor.

The Jesuits taught us to think, to question, never to take anything purely at face value. One result of all that thinking and questioning, at least for me, was an awareness of the negative effects of most religious movements.

I used a variation of the BioCog unit as far back as *Healer* in the mid-seventies, and as recently as "Wires" in *New Destinies IV.* The concept is now a staple of cyberfiction.

"Be Fruitful" was the first story completed on my then brand-new Apple II+ using Applewriter I, a word processor that seems incredibly crude now, but was downright miraculous to me in 1981. The story itself seems to get more timely with each passing year. The Procreationists could be just around the next political corner.

Watch out for them.

BE FRUITFUL AND MULTIPLY

S aw God last week.
    Or maybe it was just St. Bartholomew. Looked more like Bartholomew, but could have been God.

He came to me in the night, a vision dangling from my ceiling, twisting slowly in the air like a corpse hanging from a gibbet. Said the birth rate was down. *Down!* Told me to warn everyone, especially the Church Elders. Told me to warn them right away.

But I've been so busy lately.

Actually, I'm afraid.

(11:40 . . . about twenty minutes to spare)

They'll think I'm crazy. Paranoid, they'll say. But not if I can get everything organized. Not if I can show them in black and white that there's a plot afoot, a plot against the Church, a monstrous conspiracy that threatens everything generations of us have worked for. Been meaning to get organized for so long now, but can't seem to get going.

Maybe that's part of the conspiracy, too. Maybe—

For Birth's sake, don't start blaming your own foot-dragging on someone else! Next thing you know, your stubbed toe is someone else's fault . . . then the pimple on your chin . . . then your backache. Soon you're crazy.

I'm not crazy. My church, the only church, the Church of the Divine Imperative is in danger. God told me so Himself. I may be the only one who knows. But I can prove it. At least I think I can. With God's help and without too much hindrance from Satan and His minions, the Elders will hear and believe. And act.

But got to get organized. Got to sound sane. I have my folks' files and scrapbooks from the old days. That'll help. If I can put the plot in historical perspective, the Elders will be more receptive.

To work! Start with a quote from St. Bartholomew. That'll grab them. They can't turn away from the words of the man who was the inspiration for the Church. And his words are as timely now as they were forty-odd years ago:

> . . . So I say again to you, the Divine Imperative was God's first command to the first man and woman: "Be fruitful and multiply." This was not a casual remark. God created the earth as no more than a staging area. This planet, this life—they are no more than a first evolutionary step toward the ultimate destiny God has planned for His faithful. Nothing more than a staging area. In all the troubles through which you will pass, never forget that.

Words to remember, to be sure. Especially now.

After Bartholomew, how about some of this stuff from the nineties.

. . . these pictures . . . everybody's so plump-ugly. Population was so sparse back then I guess they had to eat more than they needed. Almost obscene to look that well fed. No worry about looking like that nowadays . . .

Here's a magazine article from back then. The non-believers did a lot of empty speculation in the nineties as the movement started to take hold. This looks like a good one:

> . . . *and sociologists are at a loss to explain it. Most of the Church's members were raised in the one- and two-children family units that have been the norm. Yet the whole thrust of the Church of the Divine Imperative runs contrary to the trends of the past few decades. Instead of limiting family size out of concern for the environment and a desire to pursue more personal goals of self-fulfillment, the Procreationists, as they call themselves, have laid aside their cultural, religious, and social backgrounds to band together in a compulsive drive to bring as many new lives as possible into the world.*
>
> *It all started with a pamphlet called "The Next Plateau" by an enigmatic man known only as Bartholomew who is believed to have sprung from the ranks of the now-defunct Moral Majority of the eighties. He is the source of Procreationist theology—a dizzying mixture of right-to-life slogans, Far Eastern mysticism, and rigid fundamentalism. Bartholomew's writings and passionate speeches fired up a significant segment of a generation. Procreationism has caught on. The Church of the Divine Imperative is spreading. Hopefully, for all our sakes, it will be short-lived.*
>
> Time, June 30, 1992

But we showed them—or at least my parents did. Being second-generation Procreationist, I spent most of my life listening to my folks and their friends swap tales about the early days of the Church. Must have been exciting to be in the vanguard, to be shaping history. Wish I could have been there.

The glory of it! They were outsiders in their day, struggling against the Satan-inspired population-control forces that ran the governments of the world. Hard to imagine today, with everybody Procreationist, but back in the old days they were a tiny, persecuted minority. The bureaucratic machinery and its allies in the media did their damnedest—an appropriate word, that—to curb the growth of the Church. Said we threatened to unbalance the environment, accelerate pollution, and trigger famines. Ha!

Goes to show they never understood us. Tried psychoanalytical parlor tricks to explain our growth. They were desperate for any explanation other than the truth: It was God's will!

Listen to this fool:

> *These people are scared. They want a way out—that is all there is to it. They look around and see shortages, unrest, economic and political uncertainty on all sides, and it scares them. But do they pitch in and help? No! They make things worse! They turn to mysticism and embrace practices that exacerbate the very conditions which frighten them. It's mass insanity, that's what it is! And it's got to be stopped!*
>
> Senator Henry Mifflin (D-Neb)
> *Congressional Record*
> November 28, 1997

See? Never understood. The air is thick now, true, because the productive capacity of the entire race must be strained to the utmost to feed, clothe, and house us all. Food is scarce, yes, but there's enough to keep us going until the life force reaches the critical point, the signal to God that we are ready to be transported *en masse* to a higher plane of existence. Even non-believers will be translated to the next plateau. *Then* they'll believe.

Coming soon. I can feel it. We all can.

(11:48 . . . better keep moving)

Getting sidetracked here. Let's see . . . the senator's re-marks make a good lead-in to government attempts to control the Church. Knowing that the Church was doing God's work, the followers of Satan used the governments of the world to suppress it. Communist countries were the most successful—they simply outlawed us and that was that. But wherever there was a spark of democracy, we flourished. And once we were able to organize the faithful into voting blocks, no elected official could stand against us for long. Even after we had gained majority power, anti-Procreationist legislation was still introduced, but was consistently defeated when the final vote came around.

These headlines from some old newsstats ought to be dramatic enough:

BIRTH CONTROL
BILL ABORTED
New York *Daily News*, November 7, 1998

DEFEAT OF POPULATION CONTROL BILL A
CERTAINTY
President Decries Dementia Sweeping Western World
New York *Times*, May 17, 2002

I was born three days after that last headline. Government opposition to the Church folded completely during the first five years of my life. By that time, every head of state and virtually every elected official was a Procreationist. Governments of the free world no longer hindered us because we *became* those governments. Soon, even the inner circles of the communist politburos came under our sway. The world was fast becoming Procreationist.

The media remained a problem for a while longer, probably because they were so full of queers. Queers feared us the most, and with good reason. They knew they were living in defiance of the Divine Imperative: could not be fruitful and multiply, therefore they were an abomination. They offend God and all those who believe in God. But we soon put them in their proper place.

A golden age ensued. The Church continued to expand. It was not enough to have most of humanity as members of the Church—we wanted *everyone*. We inducted new members constantly. Some were reluctant at first, but eventually they saw the Light. Had to. If you weren't with us, you were most certainly against us. The Divine Imperative was frustrated and the goal delayed by anyone who refused to reproduce.

A holy time was upon us. There were pockets of resistance —heretics, die-hard reactionaries who refused to change their ways, queers, feminists—but they didn't last long. All the world was soon one with the Church. Or so I thought.

Something sinister occurred around my ninth birthday. No one recognized it as a threat then, but looking back now I can see the hand of the Devil.

This is the earliest report I could find in the library files:

LEARNING DEVICE TO SEEK MASS MARKET
London (AP)—*Cognition Industries, Ltd., has announced development of a new microcircuit which will make mass distribution of its BioCognitive Learning Unit economically feasible. "It's a major breakthrough," said a spokesman for the Sheffield-based corporation. "Ten years from now there won't be a home without one."*
New York *Times*, March 15, 2011

The company spokesman was wrong: Nearly every home contained a BioCog unit within *five* years, attached to the family vid set with up to a dozen headsets plugged in at once at the educational hours.

After a decade of widespread use, the results were astounding: ten-year-olds doing university-level work, autistic minds reached, brain-damaged kids formerly considered ineducable learning simple math and reading skills. Efforts were made to get BioCog units into as many homes as possible in every corner of the world. A triumphal time for the Church! Not only was the life force growing at an unprecedented rate, but our intellectual powers were increasing beyond our wildest dreams. All for the greater glory of God when He translated us to the next plateau.

Everyone was on guard, of course, for possible misuse of the BioCog device. Mind control was the big bugaboo at first, but that was proved impossible. On a subtler level, however, there was concern over the device's potential for influencing attitudes. Stringent laws were passed to assure the faithful that anti-Procreation ideas would never be put into their heads, nor into the heads of their children while they learned.

All went well until last year . . .

. . . last year . . . Gayle and I produced our fourth life last year, a boy. Still remember how I felt as I cradled him in my arms, knowing I'd helped add another tiny increment to the life force, bringing us all that much closer to our goal . . .

—sidetracked again. Have to concentrate.

Last year, by the time of our fourth, the BioCog unit had become a part of our daily lives. Like all devout Procreationists, we were learning all we could before Translation, to be better prepared for whatever the next plateau might bring. The educational programs were all uniformly effective. And uniformly dull.

Then *The Bobby & Laura Show* made its debut on the late-night vid.

(11:55 . . . still some time left)

Warm in here . . . palms sweaty . . .

The show was controversial from the start. A young couple—Laura a sweet-looking blonde, Bobby darkly virile, both looking mid-twentyish and dressed in light blue kimonos

—had been given an hour to explore methods of enhancing the emotional and physical responses of the procreational act. Discussion would take up the first half of the show; the final half would involve a demonstration via the BioCog unit.

Don't quite recall the details of the discussion that premier night, but the demonstration was unforgettable. Remember the screen dimming as we were instructed to don our headsets. Could see vague shapes of Bobby and Laura disrobing. Then the shapes came together and my body was electrified. Could almost feel Laura's hands on me. Sensations built slowly to a crescendo that was almost unbearable, leaving me weak and limp afterward. I remember turning to Gayle to find her staring at me with an odd expression on her face—she hadn't put her headset on.

Tried to explain it to her. Tried to convey the sensual and emotional warmth that flooded through me, but she just made a face and said it didn't seem right. Took her in my arms right then and showed her how right it was.

Gayle was hardly unique in her doubts about the propriety of the show. Many members of the Church felt there was something scandalous about it. The ensuing investigation revealed that Bobby and Laura were orthodox Procreationists with three lives—a little girl and a set of twin boys—to their credit. Their stated purpose was advancement of Church teachings into new areas. They wanted to explore all the roads of the procreational process in order to better follow the Divine Imperative. They had experimented and had discovered that the BioCog units could influence more than the cognitive areas of the brain, so they were employing the unit's abilities in the emotional and sensual areas as an educational adjunct to their discussions.

Their program was quickly cleared of any wrongdoing. It was, after all, discreetly staged and played only at a late hour. And besides, the reasoning went, weren't they merely doing God's work?

Aided by the notoriety of the investigation, the second *Bobby & Laura* drew the largest audience in the history of this country. Even Gayle put on a headset. She later agreed that it was a remarkably moving experience. It was. Such a feeling of warmth, of being loved, of being needed, of belonging.

With the blessing of the Church, the show quickly moved into all the foreign mass media, vidcast at midnight in every time zone around the world. Dubbing or subtitles were used in the first half; no translation was necessary for the second half. Billions began to look forward to the show each night. Crave it, in fact. Night shifts in factories were interrupted for *Bobby & Laura*. Even stories of hospital patients left unattended during the show.

I remember wondering about Bobby and Laura. Don't care how God-loving and righteous a couple is, they can't generate that level of emotional and physical intensity on a nightly basis. They either had a method of enhancing the signals they transmitted, or had recorded a library of their best procreational sessions and vidcast these to the eager billions wearing their headsets and waiting for the screen to dim.

So what? I'd ask myself. Only showed they were as human as the rest of us. The purpose of their show was not to set some sort of endurance record.

Still went through spasms of uneasiness, though. These would usually hit me after the nightly show was over and Gayle and I were falling asleep in each other's arms, spent without having moved a muscle.

Bobby & Laura had been on for well over a year when it came to me that we hadn't conceived our fifth life as planned. We both knew the reason: Our procreational activity had ebbed to the point where the only thing we did in bed was sleep. That was wrong. Evil. Contrary to everything we believed in. We felt guilty and ashamed.

And confused. Couldn't understand what was happening to me. Loved God and the Church as much as ever. My faith was still strong. Hard for me to admit this, but I'd lost all desire for Gayle as my procreational partner.

I wanted Laura.

Noticed Gayle's righteousness slipping, too. Did Bobby fill her thoughts as Laura did mine?

(11:58 . . . better hurry)

Guilt made me keep all this to myself. Even noticed some hesitation to attend weekly services. Didn't feel as if I was doing my part to follow God's will. But forced myself to go.

Now I know I'm not alone. The vision told me the birth rate is down. Others have been afflicted as I have.

And I know why!

The Devil is sly and ever active. We thought the enemies of the Church had been eliminated. Thought them dispersed and discredited as heretics and blasphemers. Wrong! All wrong! They merely went underground and have been insidiously undermining God's will all along.

And their master plot is *Bobby & Laura!*

Had my suspicions for a long time now, but last week's vision convinced me: We have all become sensually jaded and emotionally dependent on that show. We are exposed to such peaks of pleasure and intimacy via the BioCog unit that the human contact demanded by God seems flat and ordinary.

THE BIOCOG IS AN INSTRUMENT OF THE DEVIL! THROUGH IT WE HAVE BECOME ADDICTED! EMOTIONALLY, PSYCHOLOGICALLY, PHYSIOLOGICALLY, AND NEUROLOGICALLY DEPENDENT ON BOBBY AND LAURA!

But not for long. I'm going to expose this hellish scheme tomorrow. I'll put an end to *The Bobby & Laura Show* for good. I'll reveal them for what they are.

(Only a minute to go)

Exposure of the plot will mean no more Laura for me, but that doesn't matter. God's will is what matters! I can break this addiction and return to the True Path. We all can. I don't need

the show. I can wash it away like sweat and dirt, leaving myself
pure and clean for the coming Translation.

(Midnight)

Bobby & Laura is starting . . . Gayle's by the set . . . I'm
going to join her . . . just for a few minutes . . . then I'll get
back to this . . .

. . . promise . . .

. . . just as soon as the show's over . . .

(I'm coming, Laura!)

Introduction

I think of "Soft" as an AIDS story, possibly one of the very first pieces of fiction influenced by the syndrome.

I began work on an early version of "Soft" in 1982. In early 1983 I received a letter from J. N. Williamson—only a name on some paperback spines to me then—asking for a story for an anthology called *Masques*. He made some heartwarming comments about *The Keep* and generally charmed me into contributing. I met him a few years later at one of the World Fantasy Conventions and found him to be an energetic and endearing gentleman.

I'm a fairly regular reader of the CDC's *Morbidity and Mortality Report Weekly*. I remember seeing the 6/5/81 issue in which patients with the syndrome later to be known as AIDS were first described. The term wasn't coined until more than a year later. Back when I began writing this, AIDS was thought to be a result of the constellation of infections that were part and parcel of the urban male homosexual's promiscuous life-style. There was talk also of a possible single etiologic agent, but that was only theory then.

Although directly triggered by a bodybuilder's remark that the whole country was going soft, the story grew out of these reports. The real-life confusion seen in AIDS's early years is reflected in the confusion and vacillation displayed by the story's authorities regarding the etiology of the softness.

It's not a pleasant piece. *Publishers Weekly* called it "vivid and viscerally wrenching."

That's what I was shooting for.

SOFT

I was lying on the floor watching tv and exercising what was left of my legs when the newscaster's jaw collapsed. He was right in the middle of the usual plea for anybody who thought they were immune to come to 'Rockefeller Center when—*pflumpf!*—the bottom of his face went soft.

I burst out laughing.

"Daddy!" Judy said, shooting me a razorblade look from her wheelchair.

I shut up.

She was right. Nothing funny about a man's tongue wiggling around in the air snake-like while his lower jaw flopped down in front of his throat like a sack of Jell-O and his bottom teeth jutted at the screen crowns-on, rippling like a line of buoys on a bay. A year ago I would have gagged. But I've changed in ways other than physical since this mess began, and couldn't help feeling good about one of those pretty-boy newsreaders going soft right in front of the camera. I almost wished I had a bigger screen so I could watch 21 color inches of the scene. He was barely visible on our 5-inch black-and-white.

The room filled with white noise as the screen went blank. Someone must have taken a look at what was going out on the airwaves and pulled the plug. Not that many people were watching anyway.

I flipped the set off to save the batteries. Batteries were as good as gold now. *Better* than gold. Who wanted gold nowadays?

I looked over at Judy and she was crying softly. Tears slid down her cheeks.

"Hey, hon—"

"I can't help it, Daddy. I'm so *scared!*"

"Don't be, Jude. Don't worry. Everything will work out, you'll see. We've got this thing licked, you and me."

"How can you be so sure?"

"Because it hasn't progressed in weeks! It's over for us— we've got immunity."

She glanced down at her legs, then quickly away. "It's already too late for me."

I reached over and patted my dancer on the hand. "Never too late for you, shweetheart," I said in my best Bogart. That got a tiny smile out of her.

We sat there in the silence, each thinking our own thoughts. The newsreader had said the cause of the softness had been discovered: a virus, a freak mutation that disrupted the calcium matrix of bones.

Yeah. Sure. That's what they said last year when the first cases cropped up in Boston. A virus. But they never isolated the virus, and the softness spread all over the world. So they began searching for "a subtle and elusive environmental toxin." They never pinned that one down either.

Now we were back to a virus again. Who cared? It didn't matter. Judy and I had beat it. Whether we had formed the right antibodies or the right antitoxin was just a stupid academic question. The process had been arrested in us. Sure, it had done some damage, but it wasn't doing any more, and that was the important thing. We'd never be the same, but we were going to live!

"But that man," Judy said, nodding toward the tv. "He said they were looking for people in whom the disease had started and then stopped. That's us, Dad. They said they need to examine people like us so they can find out how to fight it, maybe develop a serum against it. We should—"

"Judy-Judy-Judy!" I said in Cary Grantese to hide my annoyance. How many times did I have to go over this? "We've been through all this before. I told you: It's too late for them. Too late for everybody but us immunes."

I didn't want to discuss it—Judy didn't understand about those kind of people, how you can't deal with them.

"I want you to take me down there," she said in the tone she used when she wanted to be stubborn. "If you don't want to help, okay. But I do."

"No!" I said that louder than I wanted to and she flinched. More softly: "I know those people. I worked all those years in the Health Department. They'd turn us into lab specimens. They'll suck us dry and use our immunity to try and save themselves."

"But I want to help somebody! I don't want us to be the last two people on earth!"

She began to cry again.

Judy was frustrated. I could understand that. She was unable to leave the apartment by herself and probably saw me at times as a dictator who had her at his mercy. And she was frightened, probably more frightened than I could imagine. She was only eighteen and everyone she had ever known in her life— including her mother—was dead.

I hoisted myself into the chair next to her and put my arm around her shoulders. She was the only person in the world who mattered to me. That had been true even before the softness began.

"We're not alone. Take George, for example. And I'm sure there are plenty of other immunes around, hiding like us. When the weather warms up, we'll find each other and start everything over new. But until then, we can't allow the bloodsuckers to drain off whatever it is we've got that protects us."

She nodded without saying anything. I wondered if she was agreeing with me or just trying to shut me up.

"Let's eat," I said with a gusto I didn't really feel.

"Not hungry."

"Got to keep up your strength. We'll have soup. How's that sound?"

She smiled weakly. "Okay . . . soup."

I forgot and almost tried to stand up. Old habits die hard. My lower legs were hanging over the edge of the chair like a pair of sand-filled dancer's tights. I could twitch the muscles and see them ripple under the skin, but a muscle is pretty useless unless it's attached to a bone, and the bones down there were gone.

I slipped off my chair to what was left of my knees and shuffled over to the stove. The feel of those limp and useless leg muscles squishing under me was repulsive but I was getting used to it.

It hit the kids and old people first, supposedly because their bones were a little soft to begin with, then moved on to the rest of us, starting at the bottom and working its way up—sort of like a Horatio Alger success story. At least that's the way it worked in most people. There were exceptions, of course, like that newscaster. I had followed true to form: My left lower leg collapsed at the end of last month; my right went a few days later. It wasn't a terrible shock. My feet had already gone soft so I knew the legs were next. Besides, I'd heard the sound.

The sound comes in the night when all is quiet. It starts a day or two before a bone goes. A soft sound, like someone gently crinkling cellophane inside your head. No one else can hear it. Only you. I think it comes from the bone itself—from millions of tiny fractures slowly interconnecting into a mosaic that eventually causes the bone to dissolve into mush. Like an on-rushing train far, far away can be heard if you press your ear to the track, so the sound of each microfracture transmits from bone to bone until it reaches your middle ear.

I haven't heard the sound in almost four weeks. I thought I did a couple of times and broke out in a cold, shaking sweat, but no more of my bones have gone. Neither have Judy's. The average case goes from normal person to lump of jelly in three to four weeks. Sometimes it takes longer, but there's always a steady progression. Nothing more has happened to me or Judy since last month.

Somehow, someway, we're immune.

With my lower legs dragging behind me, I got to the counter of the kitchenette and kneed my way up the stepstool to where I could reach things. I filled a pot with water—at least the pressure was still up—and set it on the Sterno stove. With gas and electricity long gone, Sterno was a lifesaver.

While waiting for the water to boil I went to the window and looked out. The late afternoon March sky was full of dark gray clouds streaking to the east. Nothing moving on West 16th Street one floor below but a few windblown leaves from God-knows-where. I glanced across at the windows of George's apartment, looking for movement but finding none, then back down to the street below.

I hadn't seen anybody but George on the street for ages, hadn't seen or smelled smoke in well over two months. The last fires must have finally burned themselves out. The riots were one direct result of the viral theory. Half the city went up in the big riot last fall—half the city and an awful lot of people. Seems someone got the bright idea that if all the people going soft were put out of their misery and their bodies burned, the plague could be stopped, at least here in Manhattan. The few cops left couldn't stop the mobs. In fact a lot of the city's ex-cops had been *in* the mobs! Judy and I lost our apartment when our building went up. Luckily we hadn't any signs of softness then. We got away with our lives and little else.

"Water's boiling, Dad," Judy said from across the room.

I turned and went back to the stove, not saying anything, still thinking about how fast our nice rent-stabilized apartment house had burned, taking everything we had with it.

Everything was gone . . . furniture and futures . . . gone. All my plans. Gone. Here I stood—if you could call it that—a man with a college education, a B.S. in biology, a secure city job, and what was left? No job. Hell—no *city!* I'd had it all planned for my dancer. She was going to make it *so* big. I'd hang on to my city job with all those civil service idiots in the Department of Health, putting up with their sniping and their back-stabbing and their lousy office politics so I could keep all the fringe benefits and foot the bill while Judy pursued the dance. She was going to have it *all!* Now what? All her talent, all her potential . . . where was it going?

Going soft . . .

I poured the dry contents of the Lipton envelope into the boiling water and soon the odor of chicken noodle soup filled the room.

Which meant we'd have company soon.

I dragged the stepstool over to the door. Already I could hear their claws begin to scrape against the outer surface of the door, their tiny teeth begin to gnaw at its edges. I climbed up and peered through the hole I'd made last month at what had then been eye-level.

There they were. The landing was full of them. Gray and brown and dirty, with glinty little eyes and naked tails. Revulsion rippled down my skin. I watched their growing numbers every day now, every time I cooked something, but still hadn't got used to them.

So I did Cagney for them: "Yooou diiirty raaats!" and turned to wink at Judy on the far side of the fold-out bed. Her expression remained grim.

Rats. They were taking over the city. They seemed to be immune to the softness and were traveling in packs that got bigger and bolder with each passing day. Which was why I'd chosen this building for us: Each apartment was boxed in with pre-stressed concrete block. No rats in the walls here.

I waited for the inevitable. Soon it happened: A number of them squealed, screeched, and thrashed as the crowding pushed them at each other's throats, and then there was bedlam out there. I didn't bother to watch any more. I saw it every day. The pack jumped on the wounded ones. Never failed. They were so hungry they'd eat anything, even each other. And while they were fighting among themselves they'd leave us in peace with our soup.

Soon I had the card table between us and we were sipping the yellow broth and those tiny noodles. I did a lot of *mmm-good*ing but got no response from Judy. Her eyes were fixed on the walkie-talkie on the end table.

"How come we haven't heard from him?"

Good question—one that had been bothering me for a couple of days now. Where *was* George? Usually he stopped by every other day or so to see if there was anything we needed. And if he didn't stop by, he'd call us on the walkie-talkie. We had an arrangement between us that we'd both turn on our headsets every day at six P.M. just in case we needed to be in touch. I'd been calling over to George's place across the street at six o'clock sharp for three days running now with no result.

"He's probably wandering around the city seeing what he can pick up. He's a resourceful guy. Probably come back with something we can really use but haven't thought of."

Judy didn't flash me the anticipated smile. Instead, she frowned. "What if he went down to the research center?"

"I'm sure he didn't," I told her. "He's a trusting soul, but he's not a fool."

I kept my eyes down as I spoke. I'm not a good liar. And that very question had been nagging at my gut. What if George had been stupid enough to present himself to the researchers? If he had, he was through. They'd never let him go and we'd never see him again.

For George wasn't an immune like us. He was different. Judy and I had caught the virus—or toxin—and defeated it. We were left with terrible scars from the battle but we had survived. We *acquired* our immunity through battle with the softness agent. George was special—he had remained untouched. He'd exposed himself to infected people for months as he helped everyone he could, and was still hard all over. Not so much as a little toe had gone soft on him. Which meant—to me at least—that George had been *born* with some sort of immunity to the softness.

Wouldn't those researchers love to get their needles and scalpels into *him!*

I wondered if they had. It was possible George might have been picked up and brought down to the research center against his will. He told me once that he'd seen official-looking vans and cars prowling the streets, driven by guys wearing gas masks or the like. But that had been months ago and he hadn't reported anything like it since. Certainly no cars had been on this street in recent memory. I warned him time and again about roaming around in the daylight but he always laughed good-naturedly and said nobody'd ever catch him—he was too fast.

What if he'd run into someone faster?

There was only one thing to do.

"I'm going to take a stroll over to George's just to see if he's okay."

Judy gasped. "No, Dad! You can't! It's too far!"

"Only across the street."

"But your legs—"

"—are only half gone."

I'd met George shortly after the last riot. I had two hard legs then. I'd come looking for a sturdier building than the one we'd been burned out of. He helped us move in here.

I was suspicious at first, I admit that. I mean, I kept asking myself, *What does this guy want?* Turned out he only wanted to be friends. And so friends we became. He was soon the only other man I trusted in this whole world. And that being the case, I wanted a gun—for protection against all those other men I didn't trust. George told me he had stolen a bunch during the early lootings. I traded him some Sterno and batteries for a .38 and a pump-action 12-gauge shotgun with ammo for both. I promptly sawed off the barrel of the shotgun. If the need arose, I could clear a room real fast with that baby.

So it was the shotgun I reached for now. No need to fool with it—I kept its chamber empty and its magazine loaded with #5 shells. I laid it on the floor and reached into the rag bag by the door and began tying old undershirts around my knees. Maybe I shouldn't call them knees; with the lower legs and caps gone, "knee" hardly seems appropriate, but it'll have to serve.

From there it was a look through the peep hole to make sure the hall was clear, a blown kiss to Judy, then a shuffle into the hall. I was extra wary at first, ranging the landing up and down, looking for rats. But there weren't any in sight. I slung the shotgun around my neck, letting it hang in front as I started down the stairs one by one on hands and butt, knees first, each flabby lower leg dragging alongside its respective thigh.

Two flights down to the lobby, then up on my padded knees to the swinging door, a hard push through and I was out on the street.

Silence.

We kept our windows tightly closed against the cold and so I hadn't noticed the change. Now it hit me like a slap in the face. As a lifelong New Yorker I'd never heard—or *not* heard—the city like this. Even when there'd been nothing doing on your street, you could always hear that dull roar pulsing from the sky and the pavement and the walls of the buildings. It was the life sound of the city, the beating of its heart, the whisper of its breath, the susurrant rush of blood through its capillaries.

It had stopped.

The shiver that ran over me was not just the result of the sharp edge of the March wind. The street was deserted. A plague had been through here, but there were no contorted bodies strewn about. You didn't fall down and die on the spot with the softness. No, that would be too kind. You died by inches, by bone lengths, in back rooms, trapped, unable to make it to the street. No public displays of morbidity. Just solitary deaths of quiet desperation.

In a secret way I was glad everyone was gone—nobody around to see me tooling across the sidewalk on my rag-wrapped knees like some skid row geek.

The city looked different from down here. You never realize how cracked the sidewalks are, how *dirty*, when you have legs to stand on. The buildings, their windows glaring red with the setting sun that had poked through the clouds over New Jersey, looked half again as tall as they had when I was a taller man.

I shuffled to the street and caught myself looking both ways before sliding off the curb. I smiled at the thought of getting run down by a truck on my first trip in over a month across a street that probably hadn't seen the underside of a car since December.

Despite the absurdity of it, I hurried across, and felt relief when I finally reached the far curb. Pulling open the damn doors to George's apartment building was a chore, but I slipped through both of them and into the lobby. George's bike—a light-frame Italian model ten-speeder—was there. I didn't like that. George took that bike everywhere. Of course he could have found a car and some gas and gone sightseeing and not told me, but still the sight of that bike standing there made me uneasy.

I shuffled by the silent bank of elevators, watching my longing expression reflected in their silent, immobile chrome doors as I passed. The fire door to the stairwell was a heavy one, but I squeezed through and started up the steps—backward. Maybe there was a better way, but I hadn't found it. It was all in the arms: Sit on the bottom step, get your arms back, palms down on the step above, lever yourself up. Repeat this ten times and you've done a flight of stairs. Two flights per floor. Thank the Lord or Whatever that George had decided he preferred a second-floor apartment to a penthouse after the final power failure.

It was a good thing I was going up backward. I might never have seen the rats if I'd been faced around the other way.

Just one appeared at first. Alone, it was almost cute with its twitching whiskers and its head bobbing up and down as it sniffed the air at the bottom of the flight. Then two more joined it, then another half dozen. Soon they were a brown wave, undulating up the steps toward me. I hesitated for an instant, horrified and fascinated by their numbers and all their little black eyes sweeping toward me, then I jolted myself into action. I swung the scattergun around, pumped a shell into the chamber, and let them have a blast. Dimly through the reverberating roar of the shotgun I heard a chorus of squeals and saw flashes of flying crimson blossoms, then I was ducking my face into my arms to protect my eyes from the ricocheting shot. I should have realized the danger of shooting in a cinderblock stairwell like this. Not that it would have changed things—I still had to protect myself—but I should have anticipated the ricochets.

The rats did what I'd hoped they'd do—jumped on the dead and near-dead of their number and forgot about me. I let the gun hang in front of me again and continued up the stairs to George's floor.

He didn't answer his bell but the door was unlocked. I'd warned him about that in the past but he'd only laughed in that carefree way of his. "Who's gonna pop in?" he'd say. Probably no one. But that didn't keep me from locking mine, even though George was the only one who knew where I lived. I wondered if that meant I didn't really trust George.

I put the question aside and pushed the door open.

It stank inside. And it was empty as far as I could see. But there was this sound, this wheezing, coming from one of the bedrooms. Calling his name and announcing my own so I wouldn't get my head blown off, I closed the door behind me—locked it—and followed the sound. I found George.

And retched.

George was a blob of flesh in the middle of his bed. Everything but some ribs, some of his facial bones, and the back of his skull had gone soft on him.

I stood there on my knees in shock, wondering how this could have happened. George was *immune!* He'd laughed at the softness! He'd been walking around as good as new just last week. And now . . .

His lips were dry and cracked and blue—he couldn't speak, couldn't swallow, could barely breathe. And his eyes . . . they seemed to be just floating there in a quivering pool of flesh, begging me . . . darting to his left again and again . . . begging me . . .

For what?

I looked to his left and saw the guns. He had a suitcase full of them by the bedroom door. All kinds. I picked up a heavy-looking revolver—an S&W .357—and glanced at him. He closed his eyes and I thought he smiled.

I almost dropped the pistol when I realized what he wanted.

"No, George!"

He opened his eyes again. They began to fill with tears.

"George—I can't!"

Something like a sob bubbled past his lips. And his eyes . . . his pleading eyes . . .

I stood there a long time in the stink of his bedroom,

listening to him wheeze, feeling the sweat collect between my palm and the pistol grip. I knew I couldn't do it. Not George, the big, friendly, good-natured slob I'd been depending on.

Suddenly, I felt my pity begin to evaporate as a flare of irrational anger began to rise. I *had* been depending on George now that my legs were half gone, and here he'd gone soft on me. The bitter disappointment fueled the anger. I knew it wasn't right, but I couldn't help hating George just then for letting me down.

"Damn you, George!"

I raised the pistol and pointed it where I thought his brain should be. I turned my head away and pulled the trigger. Twice. The pistol jumped in my hand. The sound was deafening in the confines of the bedroom.

Then all was quiet except for the ringing in my ears. George wasn't wheezing anymore. I didn't look around. I didn't have to see. I have a good imagination.

I fled that apartment as fast as my ruined legs would carry me.

But I couldn't escape the vision of George and how he looked before I shot him. It haunted me every inch of the way home, down the now empty stairs where only a few tufts of dirty brown fur were left to indicate that rats had been swarming there, out into the dusk and across the street and up more stairs to home.

George . . . how could it be? He was immune!

Or was he? Maybe the softness had followed a different course in George, slowly building up in his system until every bone in his body was riddled with it and he went soft all at once. *God*, what a noise he must have heard when all those bones went in one shot! That was why he hadn't been able to call or answer the walkie-talkie.

But what if it had been something else? What if the virus theory was right and George was the victim of a more virulent mutation? The thought made me sick with dread. Because if that were true, it meant Judy would eventually end up like George. And I was going to have to do for her what I'd done for George.

But what of me, then? Who was going to end it for *me*? I didn't know if I had the guts to shoot myself. And what if my hands went soft before I had the chance?

I didn't want to think about it, but it wouldn't go away. I couldn't remember ever being so frightened. I almost considered going down to Rockefeller Center and presenting Judy and myself to the leechers, but killed that idea real quick. Never. I'm no jerk. I'm college-educated. A degree in biology! I know what they'd do to us!

Inside, Judy had wheeled her chair over to the door and was waiting for me. I couldn't let her know.

"Not there," I told her before she could ask, and I busied myself with putting the shotgun away so I wouldn't have to look her straight in the eyes.

"Where could he be?" Her voice was tight.

"I wish I knew. Maybe he went down to Rockefeller Center. If he did, it's the last we'll ever see of him."

"I can't believe that."

"Then tell me where else he can be."

She was silent.

I did Warner Oland's Chan: "Numbah One Dawtah is finally at loss for words. Peace reigns at last."

I could see that I failed to amuse, so I decided a change of subject was in order.

"I'm tired," I said. It was the truth. The trip across the street had been exhausting.

"Me, too." She yawned.

"Want to get some sleep?" I knew she did. I was just staying a step or two ahead of her so she wouldn't have to ask to be put to bed. She was a dancer, a fine, proud artist. Judy would never have to ask anyone to put her to bed. Not while I was around. As long as I was able I would spare her the indignity of dragging herself along the floor.

I gathered Judy up in my arms. The whole lower half of her body was soft; her legs hung over my left arm like weighted drapes. It was all I could do to keep from crying when I felt them so limp and formless. My dancer . . . you should have seen her in *Swan Lake*. Her legs had been so strong, so sleekly muscular, like her mother's . . .

I took her to the bathroom and left her in there. Which left me alone with my daymares. What if there really was a mutation of the softness and my dancer began leaving me again, slowly, inch by inch. What was I going to do when she was gone? My wife was gone. My folks were gone. My what few friends I'd ever had were gone. Judy was the only attachment I had left. Without her I'd break loose from everything and just float off into space. I needed her . . .

When she was finished in the bathroom I carried her out and arranged her on the bed. I tucked her in and kissed her goodnight.

Out in the living room I slipped under the covers of the fold-out bed and tried to sleep. It was useless. The fear wouldn't leave me alone. I fought it, telling myself that George was a freak case, that Judy and I had licked the softness. We were *immune* and we'd *stay* immune. Let everyone else turn into puddles of Jell-O, I wasn't going to let them suck us dry to save themselves. We were on our way to inheriting the earth, Judy and I, and we didn't even have to be meek about it.

But still sleep refused to come. So I lay there in the growing darkness in the center of the silent city and listened . . . listened as I did every night . . . as I knew I would listen for the rest of my life . . . listened for that sound . . . that cellophane crinkling sound . . .

Introduction

This is a Just Deserts story.

Horror fiction is a great way of getting even. I've been a rock fan since a summer night in 1955 when I first heard Chuck Berry's "Maybellene." In 1983 I was reading a series of interviews with some of the originators of rock and how they were ripped off by d.j.'s, record companies, and promotors—sometimes all wrapped up in a single slimy individual. I decided to get even for them.

Figuratively, of course. And with tongue set firmly in cheek. Stu Schiff bought it for one of his *Whispers* anthologies.

THE LAST "ONE MO' ONCE GOLDEN OLDIES REVIVAL"

The announcer broke in with the news—right into the middle of a song by the latest New Wave sensation, Polio.

Philip "Flip" Goodloe was gone. The father and seminal stylist of the rock 'n' roll guitar was dead at age forty-eight.

Lenny Winter leaned back and took a long draw on the Royal Jamaican delicately balanced between his pudgy thumb and forefinger. He certainly didn't mind anybody cutting Polio's music short—this New Wave crap was worse than the stuff he jockeyed twenty-five years ago. And he wasn't all that surprised about Flip.

Dead . . . the Flipper was dead. Lenny had sensed that coming last week. The only disconcerting thing was that it had happened so soon after seeing him. Fifteen or twenty years without laying eyes on Flip Goodloe, then Lenny visits him, then he's dead, all within a few days' time. Definitely disconcerting.

He listened for details about the death but there were none. Only a hushed voice repeating that the major influence on every rocker who had ever picked up an electric six-string was dead. Even guitarists who had never actually heard a Flip Goodloe record owed him a debt because, as the voice said, if you weren't directly influenced by Goodloe, you were influenced by somebody who got his licks from somebody else who got *his* licks from Flip Goodloe. "All riffs eventually lead to Goodloe," the voice said. It closed the break-in with: ". . . the exact cause of death is unknown at this time."

"I can tell you the exact cause of death," Lenny muttered to the empty room. "Smack. Flip Goodloe the hophead finally overjuiced himself."

The disc jockey—whoops, sorry, they liked to be called "radio personalities" now—yanked the Polio record and put on "Mary-Liz" from 1955, Flip's first hit record. An instant Flip Goodloe retrospective was under way.

In spite of his personal knowledge of what a jerk Flip was, Lenny Winter suffered a pang of nostalgia as the frenetic guitar notes and wailing voice poured out of the twin Bose 901s in the corners of the room. Nobody could play like the Flipper in his day. Flip didn't showboat and he didn't just doodle around the melody—he got behind his bands and pushed, driving them 'til they were cooking at white heat.

Lenny Winter put his cigar down and pulled his considerable bulk out of the recliner. He was pushing fifty-five and was at least that many pounds overweight. He waddled over to the north wall of his trophy room—one of the smaller of the eighteen rooms in his house. Where was it, now? He scanned along rows of gold records. There—the 45 with the Backgammon label. "Mary-Liz" by Flip Goodloe. A million sales, RIAA-certified. And beneath the title, the composer credit: *(P. Goodloe–L. Weinstein)*. Lenny smiled. Not too many people knew that Lenny Winter's birth certificate read "Leonard Weinstein."

He wondered how many copies would sell in the inevitable

surge of interest after Flip's death. Look how many Lennon records moved after he bought it. Lenny did not like to think of himself as one who made money off the dead, but a buck was a buck, and half of all royalties from sales and airplay of a good number of Flip's early songs belonged to Lenny and it was only fair that he got what was rightfully his. He made a mental note to call BMI in the morning.

The radio segued into Goodloe's second big hit, "Little Rocker"—another P. Goodloe–L. Weinstein composition. A gold copy of that, too, was somewhere on the wall.

Those were the days when Lenny could do no wrong. Flip had it all then, too. But he blew it. Lenny had managed to stay at or near the top. Flip had been nowhere for years.

Which was why Lenny had visited him last week—to give the Flipper another chance.

He shook his head. What a mistake that had been!

It hadn't been easy to find Flip. He had moved back to Alexandria, Virginia, his old hometown. He still played an occasional solo gig in some of the M Street clubs in D.C., but sporadically. He was unreliable. Club owners learned to expect him when they saw him. Everyone knew he was shooting shit again. No one had a phone number, but a bartender knew a girl who had gone home with him after a recent gig. Lenny found her. As expected, she was young and white. She remembered the address.

It was in a garden apartment complex that gave new meaning to the word "run-down." Waist-high weeds sprouted through cracks in the parking lot blacktop; a couple of stripped and rotting wrecks slumped amid the more functional cars; children's toys lay scattered over the dirt patch that had once been a lawn; on the buildings themselves the green of the previous coat of paint showed through cracks and chips in the current white coat, which was none too current.

This was where Flip Goodloe lived? Lenny shook his head. Flip could have had it all.

Building seven, apartment 4-D. Lenny pushed the bell button but heard no ring within. He did hear an acoustic guitar plunking away on the other side of the door, so he knocked. No answer. He knocked again, louder. The guitar kept playing, but not loud enough to drown out Lenny's pounding on the door. The player obviously heard Lenny; he was just ignoring him.

Typical.

He tried the doorknob. It turned. He went in.

A pigsty. That's what it was—a pigsty. Empty Kentucky Fried Chicken buckets caught the breeze from the door, rolling among the Styrofoam Big Mac boxes and countless candy bar wrappers littering the floor. Dust everywhere. The rug had once been red—possibly; it was hard to tell in the dim light. Cobwebs in all the ceiling corners. Clothes strewn everywhere. Acrid smoke layered out at three distinct levels in the air of the room, undulating sensuously in the draft.

And there in the middle of the room, sitting cross-legged like some black-skinned maharishi, his emaciated body naked but for a stained pair of jockey shorts, was Flip Goodloe, staring off into space while he picked and chorded an aimless melody from the Martin clutched before him. His hair was a rat's nest, looking like he had tried to weave a natural into dreadlocks but had given up halfway along.

"Flip," Lenny said, raising his voice to break through the noise. *"Flip!"*

Rheumy, red-rimmed eyes focused on Lenny through pinpoint pupils. A slow smile spread across Flip's features.

"Well, if it ain't my old friend Lenny. Been seeing you on tv pushing those moldy oldies collections. You got fat, man. You look like Porky Pig on the tube. Yeah. L. Weinstein, a.k.a. Daddy Shoog, a.k.a. Lenny Winter, former d.j., former owner of countless tiny record companies—bankrupt record companies—and now known as Mr. Golden Oldies."

Lenny bowed—not an easy trick with his girth—more to escape the naked hostility in Flip's eyes and voice than to accept the sarcastic approbation.

"Oh, yeah. I almost forgot: former collaborator. I must be the only guy in rock who collaborated with someone who's never written a single lyric or note of music in his life."

Not the only, Lenny thought. *Plenty of others.*

Flip switched to a Kingfisher voice: "Ah guess dat makes yo' de collabora*tor*, an' me de collabora*tee*."

"That's all water under the bridge, Flip," Lenny said, acutely uncomfortable. This man had no class—no class at all. "Whatever disagreements we had in the past, we can bury now. I've got a deal for you. A great deal. It'll mean your comeback. Chuck Berry came back. You can, too—bigger than ever!"

Flip's smile finally faded. "What makes you think I want a comeback?"

Lenny ignored the remark. Every has-been wants a comeback. He went on to explain the details of the ninth annual "One Mo' Once Golden Oldies Revival" tour, how it was going to be the biggest and best ever of its kind. And how he, Lenny Winter, out of the goodness of his heart, had decided to let Flip Goodloe headline the tour.

What he didn't say was that he needed Flip as headliner to put the icing on the cake, so to speak. The back-to-basics influence of the punk and New Wave groups over the past few years was having its effect, and Lenny was going to cash in on it. Lenny had always been able to pick up trends. It was his big talent. It was what had made him Daddy Shoog back in the fifties. He sensed new interest growing in old-time rock 'n' roll, especially in the unpretentious, down-and-dirty, no-holds-barred guitar style of someone like the Flipper. Lenny could feel it in his gut—Flip Goodloe leading the bill would turn a successful, reasonably profitable tour into a gold rush.

He needed Flip. And he was going to get him.

"Not interested," Flip said.

"You don't mean that. What else have you got going for you?"

"Religion, Lenny. I got religion."

Lenny kept his face straight but mentally rolled his eyes. *Who's the guru this time?*

"Born again?" he said.

"No way. I worship the great god Doolang."

"Doolang." *Swell.*

"Yeah." Flip pointed toward the ceiling. "Behold His image."

Lenny squinted into the hazy air. Hanging from a thread thumbtacked to the ceiling was a wire coat hanger twisted into an "S"-like configuration . . . like a cross between a G-clef and a dollar sign.

"Doolang?"

"You got it. The God of Aging Rockers. I already burned my offering to Him and was just warming up to sing His favorite hymn."

"Is that what I smell? What did you burn?"

"An Air Supply record." He giggled. "Know what hymn he likes best?"

Lenny sighed. "I'll bite—what?"

" 'He's So Fine.' By the Chiffons. Remember?"

Lenny thought back. Oh, yeah: *Doolang-doolang-doolang.* He laughed. "I get it."

Flip began to laugh, too. "You can also sing 'My Sweet Lord.' I'm not sure ol' Doolang knows the difference." He laughed harder. He flopped back on the floor and spread his arms and laughed from deep in his gut.

Lenny saw the tracks on Flip's arms and his own laughter

died, strangled in coils of pity and revulsion. Flip must have noticed the direction of his gaze, for he suddenly fell silent. He sat up and folded his arms across his chest, hiding the scars.

"Doolang don't mind if someone shoots up once in a while. Especially if they been blackballed out of the industry."

"Don't give me this Doolang crap!" Lenny shouted, angry with the knowledge that a hopped-up Flip Goodloe would be a liability rather than an asset. There'd be a constant risk of his getting busted making a score in K.C. or Montgomery or some other burg and that would be it for the tour. Finis. Caput. Dead. "You're screwing up your—"

Flip was on his feet in a flash, his face barely an inch from Lenny's.

"Don't you *dare* take the name of the great god Doolang in vain! Your lips aren't even worthy to speak His name in praise! You'd better watch out, L. Weinstein. Doolang's pretty pissed at you. You've screwed more rockers than anybody else in history. One day He may decide to get even!"

That did it! The Flipper was completely *meshugge*. His brain was fried. He'd mainlined once too often. Lenny pulled five C-notes from his wallet and threw them on the floor.

"Here! Buy yourself a nice load of smack, a bunch of Air Supply records, and a truckload of coat hangers. Twist the hangers into cute little curlicues, burn the records, and shoot up to your heart's content. I don't want to hear about it!"

He spun and lurched out the door, away from the stink, away from the madness, away from the sight of the man he had ruined twenty years ago.

Twenty years . . . had it been that long?

A third Goodloe song, "Goin' Home," immediately followed the second. Flip's music was starting to get on his nerves. He went back to where he had left his cigar. Smoke ran straight up in a thin wavering line from the tip. Near the ceiling it curled into a twisted shape almost like a G-clef. Lenny gave it passing notice as he knocked off the ash, then wandered around the trophy room in a pensive mood.

Flip had accused him of screwing more rockers than anyone else in history. A rotten thing to say. Sure, a lot of them *felt* screwed, but in truth they owed Lenny Winter a debt of thanks for giving them a chance in the first place. He'd pulled some fast ones—no use kidding himself—but he felt no guilt. In fact, he could not help but take a certain amount of pride in his fancy footwork.

He had realized early on the power wielded by a New York City d.j. He could make a new artist by raving about the record and playing it every half hour, or he could abort a career simply by losing the record. Those were heady days. Every agent, every manager, every P.R. man for every label was pushing gifts, trips, girls, and cash at him. He took everything they offered—except the cash.

Not to say he didn't want the dough. He wanted that most of all. But he saw the dangers from the start. For obvious reasons, you couldn't declare the money as income; but that left you open to a federal charge of income tax evasion if a scandal arose. You wouldn't just lose your job then—you could be headed for Leavenworth if the IRS boys built up a good case against you.

So cash was out for Lenny unless it could be laundered and declared. It nearly killed him to say no to all the easy money being pushed at him . . . until the spring of '55 when he came up with a revolutionary scam. It happened the day a portly black—they were called Negroes then—from a small Washington, D.C., label brought in a regional hit by someone named Flip Goodloe. It was called "Georgia-Mae" and it was special. Lenny had never heard a guitar played quite that way. It seemed to feed directly into the central nervous system. His sixth sense told him this artist and this record had almost everything needed for a big hit. Almost.

"There's just one problem," Lenny had told the company rep. "That name won't play around here."

"Y'mean 'Flip'?" the black had said.

"No. I mean 'Georgia-Mae.' It's too hick, daddy. City kids won't dig it." (Hard to believe now that he actually talked like that in those days.)

"He wrote it, he can change it. What's in a name?"

"Everything, as far as this record's concerned. Tell him to change it to something more . . . American sounding, if you get my drift." The message was clear: change it to a *white*-sounding name. "Then I can make it a biggie."

The black guy had been sharp. *"Can?* Or *will?"*

Lenny had been ready to do his silent routine and see what was offered when it struck him that he had just made a significant contribution to this Flip Goodloe's song. Fighting a burst of excitement that nearly lifted him from his chair, he spoke calmly, as if making a routine proposal.

"I want to go down as co-composer of this song and of the B-side as well. And if I make it a hit—which I will—I want half credit on his next ten releases."

The company rep had shaken his head. "Don't know about that. I don't think the Flipper will go for it."

Lenny had written "L. Weinstein" on a slip of paper, then stood up and opened the door to his office. "He will if he wants to get out of D.C.," he said as he handed the slip to the rep. "And that's the name of his new songwriting partner."

Lenny never did find out what transpired back in the offices of Backgammon Records, but four weeks later he received a promo 45 by Flip Goodloe called "Mary-Liz"—exactly the same song but for the name. And under the title was "(P. Goodloe–L. Weinstein)." Lenny began to play it two or three times an hour that very night. The record went gold before the summer. Half of all composer royalties went to Lenny. It was all legal, all aboveboard. It was, he knew, utterly brilliant.

It was not a stunt he could pull if the song came from the

Brill Building or one of the other Tin Pan Alley tune mills, but it became a standard practice for Lenny with new artists who wrote their own material. The trouble was there weren't enough of them.

Then it occurred to him: He had struck gold at the composer level. Why not get in on other levels? So he did. He started a record company and a publishing company, found an *a cappella* group with a few songs of their own, recorded them with an instrumental backup, and published their music. All without anyone having the slightest notion that the famous Lenny Winter was involved in any way at all. The record was then pushed on Lenny's show and more often than not became a hit. Lenny knew nothing about music, could not sing a note. But he knew what would sell.

When sales for the record had dried up and all the royalties were in, Lenny closed up his operation and opened up down the street under a different name. The artists came looking for their money and found an empty office.

Lenny followed the formula for years, funneling all profits through Winter Promotions, the company he had set up to finance his plans for live rock 'n' roll shows, the kind with which Alan Freed was doing hand-over-fist business in places like the Brooklyn Paramount.

"Down the Road and Around the Bend," another Flip Goodloe hit, started through the speakers.

Come *on*! Too bad about Flip being dead and all, but enough was enough.

Lenny went over to the tuner. He noticed some wires had fallen out from behind the stereo system. They were twisted into a configuration that looked something like a dollar sign. He kicked them back out of sight and twisted the tuner dial a few degrees to the left until he caught the neighboring FM station.

The opening chords of "You're Mine Mine Mine" by the Camellows filled the room.

Lenny smiled and shook his head. This must be oldies night

or something. He had recorded the Camellows on his Land-lubber label back in '58. This was their only hit. Unfortunately, Landlubber records folded before any royalties could be paid. Such a shame.

He moved along the wall to a poster from the fall of '59 proclaiming his first rock 'n' roll show. His own face—younger, leaner in the cheeks—was at the top, and below ran a list of his stars, some of them the very same acts he had recorded and deserted during the preceding years. A great line-up, even if he did say so himself.

The shows—that was where the money was! Continuous shows ten A.M. 'til midnight for a week or two straight! One horde of pimple-pussed kids after another buying tickets, streaming in with their money clutched in their sweaty fists, streaming out with programs and pictures and records in place of that money. Lenny had wanted a piece of that action.

But he had to start small. He didn't have enough to bankroll a really big show the first time out, so he found the Bixby, a medium-sized theatre in Astoria whose owners, what with the movie business in a slump and all, were interested in a little extra revenue. The place was a leftover from those Depression-era movie palaces and wasn't adequately wired for the lighting needed for a live show. No matter: A wad of bills stuffed into the pocket of the local building inspector took care of that permit. From then on it was full speed ahead. The acts were lined up, and he began the buildup on his radio show.

Opening night was a smash. Every show was packed for the first three days. He should have known then it couldn't last. Things were running too smoothly. A screwup was inevitable.

Lenny shifted his eyes to the right to where a framed newspaper photo showed his 1959 self dashing wide-eyed and fright-faced from a smoking doorway carrying an unconscious girl in his arms. That photo occupied a place of honor in his trophy room. It deserved it: It had saved his ass.

She had wandered backstage after the fourth show to meet

the great Lenny Winter, the Daddy Shoog of radio fame. She was a fifteen-year-old blonde but looked older, and was absolutely thrilled when he let her sit in his dressing room. They had a few drinks—she found Seven and Seven "really neat-tasting"—and soon she was tipsy and hot and on his lap. As his hand was sliding under her skirt and slip and up along the silky length of her inner thigh, someone yelled "Fire!" Lenny dumped her on the cot and went to look. He saw the smoke, heard the screams from the audience, and knew with icy-veined certainty that even if he got out of here alive, his career as Daddy Shoog was dead.

He glanced back into his dressing room and saw that the kid had passed out. It wouldn't do to have a minor with a load of booze in her blood found dead of smoke inhalation in his dressing room. It wouldn't do at all. So he picked her up and ran for the stage door. By some incredible stroke of luck, a *Daily News* photog had been riding by, had seen the smoke, and snapped Lenny coming out the door with his unconscious burden.

A hundred and forty-six kids died in the Astoria Bixby fire—most of them trampled by their fellow fans. Fingers of blame were pointed in every direction—at rock 'n' roll, at the building inspectors, at the fire department, at teenagers in general. Everywhere but at Lenny Winter. Lenny was safe, protected by that picture.

Because that picture made page one in the *News* and was picked up by the wire services. Lenny Winter, "known as 'Daddy Shoog' to his fans," was a hero. He had risked his life to save one of his young fans who had been overcome by smoke.

And when the payola scandal broke shortly thereafter in the winter of '60, that dear, dear photo carried him through. The Senate panels and the New York grand jury questioned everyone—even Dick Clark—but they left Daddy Shoog alone. He was a hero. You didn't bring a hero in and ask him about graft.

Looking back now, Lenny realized that it really hadn't mattered much what happened then. The whole scene was in flux. Alan Freed went down, the scapegoat for the whole payola scandal. Rock 'n' roll was changing. Even its name was being shortened to just plain "rock." Radio formats were changing, too. Lenny found himself out of the New York market in '62, and completely out of touch during the British invasion in the mid-sixties. Those were lean years, but he started coming back in the seventies with his series of "One Mo' Once Golden Oldies Revival" tours. He was no longer Daddy Shoog, but Mr. Golden Oldies. He sold mail-order collections of oldies on tv. He was a national figure again.

You can't keep a good man down.

A new song came on—"I'm on My Way" by the Lulus. A little bell chimed a sour note in the back of his brain. The Lulus had been one of his groups, too. Coincidence.

Lenny turned his attention back to the wall and spotted another framed newspaper clipping. He didn't know why he kept this one. Maybe it was just to remind himself that when Lenny Winter gets even, he gets *even*.

It was a 1962 UPI story. He could have cut it from the *Times* but he preferred the more lurid *News* version. The subject of the piece was Flip Goodloe and how he had been discovered *en flagrant* with a sixteen-year-old white girl. His career took the long slide after that. And even when it had all blown over, he had messed himself up too much with heroin to come back.

Strange how one thing leads to another, Lenny thought. Shortly before the incident described in the article, Flip had refused to give Lenny any further composer credit on his songs. He had called Lenny all sorts of awful things like a no-talent leech, a bloodsucker, a slimeball, and other more colorful street-level epithets. Lenny didn't get mad. He got even. He knew Flip's fondness for young stuff—young *white* stuff. He found a little teenage slut, paid her to get it on with Flip, then sent in the troops. She disappeared afterward, so the case never came to trial. But the morals charges had been filed and the newspaper stories had been run and Flip Goodloe was ruined.

To think: If it hadn't been for the teenybopper incident during the fire at the Bixby, Lenny might never have dreamed up the scam he pulled on Flip. Yes . . . strange how one thing leads to another.

But Flip's overdose. Maybe that was really Lenny's fault. Maybe the five hundred he had left the Flipper last week—guilt money?—had been too much cash at once. Maybe it had let him go out and get some really pure stuff. A lot of it. And maybe that's why he was dead—because of the money Lenny had left him.

The Lulus faded out, followed without commercial interruption or d.j. comment by the Pendrakes' "I'm So Crazy for You."

Another of Lenny's groups from the fifties!

He felt a tingle crawl up from the base of his spine. What was going on here? Coincidence was one thing, but this made seven songs in a row that he was connected with. Seven!

Lenny strode back to the tuner and spun the knob. Stations screeched by until the indicator came to rest in the nineties. Flip Goodloe once again shouted the chorus of "Little Rocker" from the speakers. Lenny gasped and gave the knob a vicious turn. Another screech and then the Boktones—another group on one of Lenny's short-lived labels—were singing "Hey-Hey Momma!"

Sweat broke out along Lenny's upper lip. This was crazy! It was Lenny Winter night all over the dial!

One more chance. Steadying his hand, he guided the indicator to the all-news station. The only tunes you ever heard there were commercial jingles. He found the number—

—and reeled away from the machine as the familiar opening riffs of "Mary-Liz" rammed against him.

With a quaking index finger stretched out before him, he forced himself forward and hit the power button.

Silence. Blessed silence.

He realized he was trembling. Why? It was all just a coincidence, nothing more. The Flipper's death had put the stations into a retrospective mood. They were playing old Goodloe tunes and other stuff from his era. And the all-news station . . . it was probably doing a feature on Goodloe, and Lenny had tuned in just as they were airing a sample of his work.

Sure. That was it. So why not turn the radio back on?

Why not indeed?

Because he had to go out now. Yes. Out. For some air.

Lenny fled the trophy room and went to the front hall. It was spring but still cool out here along the Long Island Sound, and he'd need a coat. He pulled the closet door open and stopped.

At first glance he thought the closet was empty. Then he saw all the coats and jackets on the floor. They'd all fallen off their hangers.

And those hangers . . . they didn't look like hangers anymore.

They hung on the closet pole in a neat row, but they had been twisted into an odd shape that was becoming too familiar . . . something like a cross between a G-clef and a dollar sign. They hung there, swaying gently, the light from the hall gleaming dully along the contorted lengths of wire. Lenny stared at them dumbly, feeling terror expand with the memory of where he had first seen that shape.

Goodloe's apartment.

Flip had been squatting under a hanger shaped just like these when Lenny had last seen him. He'd called it the great god Doolang or some such nonsense. Just a junkie feverdream— but what had happened to these?

Someone was in the house! That was the only explanation.

Some buddy of Flip's had come here to twist these things up into knots and scare him. Well, it was working. Lenny was terrified. Not of any supernatural mumbo-jumbo, but of the very idea of one of Flip's junkie friends in his house. Probably upstairs right now, waiting. He had to get out!

Lenny snatched a coat from the floor and stumbled toward the front door. He'd be safer outside. He could run around to the garage and take the car. Then he'd phone the police and have them go through the house. That was the best way, the safest way.

As the door slammed behind him, he waited for a blast of cool air. It never came. Instead, it was warm out here. The air was stale, heavy with the smell and humidity of packed bodies. And it was dark . . . darker than it should be. Where were the lights of downtown Monroe?

Pain shot through Lenny's abdomen as his intestines twisted in fear. This wasn't his front yard! This was someplace else! He turned back to his front door. It was gone, replaced by a pair of wide, flat, swinging panels, each with a small glass rectangle at eye level. Through the glass he could see what appeared to be a lighted theatre lobby with Art Deco designs on the walls, popcorn machine and all. But deserted. He pounded on the doors, but it was like pounding against the base of a skyscraper; they didn't even rattle.

He turned. A light was growing out where the apron of his driveway should have been. Something was moving in the glow. As his eyes adjusted he could see rows of theatre seats stretching away on either side, and a filthy carpet leading down to a stage where the light continued to grow.

Noise filtered in like someone turning up the volume of a record player. Music: the driving rhythm of "Mary-Liz" and Flip Goodloe himself shouting the lyrics.

With his tongue cleaving to the roof of his mouth, Lenny took a faltering step or two toward the stage. It couldn't be!

But it was. No mistaking those gyrations, or the voice, or the riffs: the Flipper.

He heard crowd noises—cheers, hoots, shouts, hands clapping—and tore his gaze from the stage. The seats around him were filled with kids jumping up and down and gyrating wildly as they listened to the music. But there was no excitement in their slack faces, or in their cold eyes. Lenny knew this place. And he recognized those kids.

It was the Bixby in Astoria! But that was impossible—the Bixby was gone—burned out back in '59 during his first rock show and torn down a few months later!

Lenny ran back to the swinging doors and slammed against them. They still wouldn't budge. He pounded on the glass but there was no one in the outer lobby to hear. There had to be another way out, another exit. He was halfway down the aisle when he smelled it.

Smoke.

A cough. Another. Then someone shouted "Fire!" and the panic began. The crowd leaped out of its seats and surged into the aisle, enveloping Lenny like a hungry amoeba. As he went down under the press of panicked bodies, he caught a glimpse of the stage. Flip Goodloe was still up there, hurling his wild riffs into the smoky air, oblivious to the flames that ringed him. Flip smiled fiercely his way, and then Lenny was down, his back slamming against the filthy carpet.

Pain. Shoes kicked at him, heels high and low dug into his face and abdomen in frantic effort to get by. Bodies fell on him. The weight atop him grew until he heard his ribs crack and shatter; but the lancinating pain from the bone splinters was overwhelmed by his hunger for air. He couldn't breathe! Stale air clogged in his lungs. The odor of old popcorn and dried chewing gum from the carpet was becalmed in his nasal passages.

Vision dimmed, tunneling down to a narrow circle of hazy

light filtering through the chaos that swirled around him. And there on the ceiling of the theatre he saw a chandelier. But this was not the tassled punch-bowl affair that had hung in the old Bixby. This was a huge fluorescent tube, glowing redly, twisted into that same shape . . . the Doolang shape . . .

Introduction

This is the companion piece to "Revival," and it appeared in another of Stu Schiff's *Whispers* collections for Doubleday.

It was born one day as I was thumbing through the *Rolling Stone Rock Almanac* and noted all the deaths, injuries, drop-outs, and plain bad luck that had befallen every single major name in rock 'n' roll during a two-year period in the late fifties. They had dropped like the proverbial flies. Most people would say, "Isn't that something," and read on.

I, of course, saw a hideous conspiracy.

THE YEARS THE MUSIC DIED

N antucket in November. Leave it to Bill to make a mockery of security.

And of me.

The Atlantic looked mean today. I watched its gray, churning surface from behind the relative safety of the double-paned picture windows. I would have liked a few more panes between me and all that water. Would have liked a few *miles* between us, in fact.

Some people are afraid of snakes, some of spiders; with me, it's water. And the more water, the worse it is. I get this feeling it wants to suck me down. Been that way since I was a kid. Bill has known about the phobia for a good twenty years. So why did he do it? Bad enough to set up the meeting on this dinky little island; but to hold it on this narrow spit of land between the head of the harbor and an uneasy ocean with no more than a hundred yards between the two was outright cruel. And a nor'easter coming. If that awful ocean ever reared up . . .

I shuddered and turned away. But there *was* no turning away in this huge barn of a room with all these picture windows facing east, west, and north. Like a goddamn goldfish bowl. There weren't even curtains I could pull closed. I felt naked and exposed here in this open pine-paneled space. Eight hours to go until dark blotted out the ocean. But then I'd still be able to *hear* it.

Why would my own son do something like this to me?

Security, Bill had said. A last-minute off-season rental of an isolated house on a summer resort island in the chill of November. The Commission members could fly in, attend the meeting, and fly out again with no one ever knowing they were here. What could be more secure?

I'm a stickler for security, too, but this was ludicrous. This was—

Bill walked into the room, carefully not looking in my direction. I studied my son a moment: a good-looking man with dark hair and light blue eyes; just forty-four but looking ten years older. A real athlete until he started letting his weight go to hell. Now he had the beginnings of a hefty spare tire around his waist. I've got two dozen years on him and only half his belly.

Something was wrong with the way he was walking . . . a little unsteady. And then I realized.

Good Lord, he's drunk!

I started to say something but Bill beat me to it.

"Nelson's here. He just called from the airport. I sent the car out for him. Harold is in the air."

I managed to say, "Fine," without making it sound choked.

My son, half-lit at a Commission meeting, and me surrounded by water—this had a good chance of turning into a personal disaster. All my peers, the heads of all the major industries in the country, were downstairs at the buffet brunch. Rockefeller was on the island, and Vanderbilt was on his way; they would complete the Commission in its present composition. Soon they'd be up here to start the agenda. Only Joe Kennedy would be missing. Again. Too bad. I've always liked Joe. But with a son in the White House, we all had serious doubts about his objectivity. It had been a tough decision, but Joe had gracefully agreed to give up his seat on the Commission for the duration of Jack's presidency.

Good thing, too. I was glad he wouldn't be here to see how Bill had deteriorated.

His son's going down in history while mine is going down the drain.

What a contrast. And yet, on the surface, there was not a single reason why Bill couldn't be where Jack Kennedy was. Both came from good stock, both had good war records and plenty of money behind them. But Jack had gone for the gold ring and Bill had gone for the bottle.

I wasn't going to begrudge Joe his pride in his son. All of us on the Commission were proud of the job Jack was doing. I remember that inner glow I felt when I heard, "Ask not what your country can do for you; ask what you can do for your country." That's *just* the way I feel. The way everybody on the Commission feels.

I heard ice rattle and turned to see Bill pouring himself a drink at the bar.

"Bill! It's not *noon* yet, for God's sake!"

Bill raised his glass mockingly.

"Happy anniversary, Dad."

I didn't know what to say to that. Today was nobody's anniversary.

"Have you completely pickled your brains?"

Bill's eyebrows rose. "How soon we forget. Six years ago today: November 8, 1957. Doesn't that ring a bell?"

"No!" I could feel my jaw clenching as I stepped toward him. "Give me that glass!"

"That was the day the Commission decided to 'do something' about rock 'n' roll."

"So what!"

"Which led to February 3, 1959."

That date definitely had a familiar ring.

"You *do* remember February 3, don't you, Dad? An airplane crash. Three singers. All dead."

I took a deep breath. "That again!"

"Not again. Still." He raised his glass. "*Salud.*" Taking a long pull on his drink, he dropped into a chair.

I stood over him. The island, the drinking . . . here was what it was all about. I've always known the crash bothered him, but never realized how much until now. What anger he must have been carrying around these past few years! Anger and guilt.

"You mean to tell me you're still blaming yourself for that?" The softness of my voice surprised me.

"Why not? My idea, wasn't it?"

"The plane crash was *nobody's* idea! How many times do we have to go over this?"

"There never seems to be a time when I *don't* go over it! And now it's November 8, 1963. Exactly six years to the day that I opened my big mouth at the Commission meeting."

"Yes, you did." *And how proud I was of you that day.* "You came up with a brilliant solution that resolved the entire crisis."

"Hah! Some crisis!"

A sudden burst of rain splattered against the north and east windows. The storm was here.

I sat down with my back to most of the windows and tried to catch Bill's eyes. "And you talk about how soon *I* forget! You had a crisis in your own home—Peter. Remember?"

Bill nodded absently.

I pressed on. Maybe I could break through this funk he was wallowing in, straighten him out before the meeting. "Peter is growing to be a fine man now and I'm proud to call him my grandson, but back in '57 he was only eleven and already thoroughly immersed in rock and roll—"

"Not 'rock *and* roll,' Dad. You've got to be the only one in the country who pronounces the 'and.' It's 'rock 'n' roll'—like one word."

"It's *three* words and I pronounce all three. But be that as it may, your house was a war zone, and you know it!"

That had been a wrenching time for the whole McCready clan, but especially for me. Peter was my only grandson then and I adored him. But he had taken to listening to those atrocious Little Richard records and combing his hair like Elvis Presley. Bill banned the music from the house but Peter was defying everyone, sneaking records home, listening to it on the radio, plunking his dimes into jukeboxes on the way home from school.

But Bill's house was hardly unique. The same thing was happening in millions of homes all over the country. Everyone but the kids seemed to have declared war on the music. Old-line disc jockeys were calling it junk noise and were having rock and roll record-smashing parties on the air; television networks were refusing to broadcast Presley below the waist; church leaders were calling it the Devil's music, cultural leaders were calling it barbaric, and a lot of otherwise mild-mannered ordinary citizens were calling it nigger music.

They should have guessed what the result of such mass persecution would be: The popularity of rock and roll *soared*.

"But the strife in your home served a useful purpose. It opened my eyes. I say with no little pride that I was probably the only man in the country who saw the true significance of what rock and roll was doing to American society."

"You *thought* you saw significance, and you were very persuasive. But I don't buy it anymore. It was only music."

I leaned back and closed my eyes. *Only music . . .*

Bill was proving to be a bigger and bigger disappointment with each passing year. I'd had such high hopes for him. I'd even started bringing him to Commission meetings to prepare him to take my seat someday. But now I couldn't see him ever sitting on the Commission. He had no foresight, no vision for the future. He couldn't be trusted to participate in the decisions the Commission had to make. Nor could I see myself leaving my controlling interest in the family business to Bill.

I have a duty to the McCready newspaper chain: My dad started it with a measly little weekly local in Boston at the turn of the century and built it to a small string. I inherited that and sweated my butt to expand it into a publishing empire that spans the country today. There was no way I could leave the McCready Syndicate to Bill in good conscience. Maybe this was a signal to start paying more attention to Jimmy. He was a full decade younger than Bill but showing a *lot* more promise.

Bill showed promise in '57, though. I'll never forget the fall meeting of the Commission that year when Bill sat in as a non-voting member. I was set to address the group on what I saw as an insidious threat to the country. I knew I was facing a tough audience, especially on the subject of music. I drew on every persuasive skill I had to pound home the fact that rock and roll was more than just music, more than just an untrained nasal voice singing banal lyrics to a clichéd melody backed by a bunch of guitar notes strung together over a drumbeat. *It had become a social force.* Music as a social force—I knew that concept was unheard-of, but the age of mass communication was here and life in America was a new game. I saw that. I had to make the Commission see it. The Commission had to learn the rules of the new game if it wanted to remain a guiding force. In 1957, rock and roll was a pivotal piece in the game.

Irritating as it was, I knew the music itself was unimportant. Its status as a threat had been created by the hysterically negative reaction from the adult sector of society. As a result, untold millions of kids under eighteen came to see it as *their* music. Everyone born before World War II seemed to be trying to take it away from them. So they were closing ranks against all the older generations. That frightened me.

It did not, however, impress the other members of the

Commission. So for weeks before our regular meeting, I hammered at them, throwing facts and figures at them, sending newspaper accounts of rock and roll riots, softening them up for my pitch.

And I was good that day. God, was I good! I can still remember my closing words:

"And gentlemen, as you all know, the upcoming generation includes the post-war baby boom, making it the largest single generation in the nation's history. If that generation develops too much self-awareness, if it begins to think of itself as a group outside the mainstream, catastrophe could result.

"Consider, gentlemen: In ten years most of them will be able to vote. If the wrong people get their ear, the social and political continuity that this Commission has sworn to safeguard could be permanently disrupted.

"The popularity of the music continues to expand, gathering momentum all the time. If we don't act now, next year may be too late! We cannot *silence* this music, because that will only worsen the division. We must find a way to *temper* rock and roll . . . make it more palatable to the older generations . . . fuse it to the mainstream. Do that, and the baby boom generation will fall in line! Do nothing and I see only chaos ahead!"

But in the ensuing discussion, it became quite clear nobody, including myself, had the foggiest notion of how to change the music.

Then someone—I forget who—made a comment about how it was too bad all these rock and roll singers couldn't give up their guitars and go into the religion business like Little Richard had just done.

Bill had piped up then: "Or the Army. I'd love to see a military barber get a hold of Elvis Presley! Can't we get him drafted?"

The room suddenly fell silent as the Commission members —all of us—shared an epiphany:

Don't go after the music—go after the ones who *make* the music! Get rid of the raucous leaders and replace them with more placid, malleable types.

Brilliant! It might never have occurred to anyone without Bill's remark!

The tinkling of the ice in Bill's glass as he took another sip dragged me back to the present, to Nantucket and the storm. In what I hoped he would take as a friendly gesture, I slapped Bill on the knee.

"Don't you remember the excitement back then after the Commission meeting? You and I became *experts* on rock and roll. We listened to all those awful records, got to know all about the performers, and then we began to zero in on them."

Bill nodded. "But I had no idea where it was going to end."

"No one did. Remember making the list? We sat around for weeks, going through the entertainment papers and picking out the singers most closely associated with the music, the leaders, the trendsetters, the originals."

I still savor the memory of that time of closeness with Bill, working together with him, both of us tingling with the knowledge that we were doing something important.

Elvis was the prime target, of course. More than anyone else, he personified everything that was rock and roll. His sneers, his gyrations, everything he did on stage was a slap in the face to the older generations. And his too-faithful renditions of colored music getting airplay all over the country, the screaming, fainting girls at his concerts, the general hysteria. Elvis had to go first.

And he turned out to be the easiest to yank from sight, really. With the Commission's vast influence, all we had to do was pass the word. In a matter of weeks, a certain healthy twenty-two-year-old Memphis boy received his draft notice. And on March 24, 1958—a landmark date I'll never forget— Elvis Presley was inducted into the U.S. Army. But *not* to hang around stateside and keep up his public profile. Oh, no. Off to West Germany. Bye-bye, Elvis Pelvis.

Bill seemed to be reading my thoughts. He said, "Too bad we couldn't have taken care of everyone like that."

"I agree, son." Bill seemed to be perking up a little. I kept up the chatter, hoping to bring him out some more. "But someone would have smelled a rat. We had to move slowly, cautiously. That was why I rounded up some of our best reporters and had them start sniffing around. And as you know, it didn't take them long to come up with a few gems."

The singers weren't my only targets. I also wanted to strike at the ones who spread the music through the airwaves. That proved easy. We soon learned that a lot of the big-time rock and roll disc jockeys were getting regular payoffs from record companies to keep their new releases on the air. We made sure that choice bits of information got to congressmen looking to heighten their public profile, and we made sure they knew to go after Alan Freed.

Oh, how I wanted Freed off the air back then. The man had gone from small-time Cleveland d.j. to big-time New York music show impresario. By 1959 he had appeared in a line of low-budget rock and roll movies out of Hollywood and was hosting a nationwide music television show. He had become "Mr. Rock 'n' Roll." His entire career was built on the music and he was its most vocal defender.

Alan Freed had to go. And payola was the key. We set the gears in motion and turned to other targets. And it was in May, only two months after Presley's induction, that the reporters turned up another spicy morsel.

"Remember, Bill? Remember when they told us that Jerry Lee Lewis had secretly married his third cousin in November of '57? Hardly a scandal in and of itself. But the girl was only fourteen. *Fourteen!* Oh, we made sure the McCready papers gave plenty of press to that, didn't we! Within days he was being booed off the stage. Yessir, Mr. Whole Lotta Shakin'/ Great Balls of Fire was an instant has-been!"

I laughed, and even Bill smiled. But the smile didn't last. "Don't stop now, Dad. Next comes 1959."

"Bill, I had nothing to do with that plane crash. I swear it."

"You told your operatives to 'get Valens and Holly off the tour.' I heard you myself."

"I don't deny that. But I meant 'off the tour'—not *dead!* We couldn't dig up anything worthwhile on them so I intended to create some sort of scandal. We discussed it, didn't we? We wanted to see them replaced by much safer types, by pseudo-crooners like Frankie Avalon and Fabian. I did *not* order any violence. The plane crash was pure coincidence."

Bill studied the ceiling. "Which just happened to lead to the replacement of Holly, Valens, and that other guy with the silly name—The Big Bopper—by Avalon, Fabian, and Paul Anka. Some coincidence!"

I said nothing. The crash *had* been an accident. The operatives had been instructed to do enough damage to the plane to keep it on the ground, forcing the three to miss their next show. Apparently they didn't do enough, and yet did too much. The plane got into the air, but never reached its destination. Tragic, unfortunate, but it all worked out for the best. I couldn't let Bill know that, though.

"I can understand why you lost your enthusiasm for the project then."

"But *you* didn't, did you, Dad? You kept right on going."

"There was a job to be done. An important one. And when one of our reporters discovered that Chuck Berry had brought that Apache minor across state lines to work in his club, I couldn't let it pass!"

Berry was one of the top names on my personal list. Strutting up there on stage, swinging his guitar around, duck-walking across back and forth, shouting out those staccato lyrics as he spread his legs and wiggled his hips, and all those white girls clapping and singing along as they gazed up at him. I tell you it made my hackles rise.

"The Mann Act conviction we got on him has crippled his career! And then later in '59 we finally spiked Alan Freed. When he refused to sign that affadavit saying he had never accepted payola, he was through! Fired from WNEW-TV, WABC-TV, and WABC radio—one right after the other!"

What a wonderful year!

"Did you stop there, Dad?"

"Yes." What was he getting at? "Yes, I believe so."

"You had nothing to do with that car crash in '60: Eddie Cochran killed, Gene Vincent crippled?"

"Absolutely not!" *Damn!* The booze certainly wasn't dulling Bill's memory! That crash had been another unfortunate, unintended mishap caused by an overly enthusiastic operative. "Anyway, it remains a fact that by the middle of 1960, rock and roll was dead."

"Oh, I don't know about that—"

"Dead as a *threat*. What had been a potent, devisive social force is now a tiny historical footnote, a brief, minor cultural aberration. Only two years after we started, Elvis was out of the service but he was certainly not the same wild man who went in. Little Richard was in the ministry, Chuck Berry was up to his ears in legal troubles, Jerry Lee Lewis was in limbo as a performer, Alan Freed was out of a job and appearing before House subcommittees."

Bill tossed off the rest of his drink and glared at me. "You forgot to mention that Buddy Holly, Richie Valens, and Eddie Cochran were dead!"

"Unfortunately and coincidentally, yes. But not by my doing. I say again: Rock and roll was dead then, and remains dead. Even Presley gave up on it after his discharge. He got sanitized and Hollywoodized and that's fine with me. More power to him. I bear him no ill will."

"There's still rock 'n' roll," Bill mumbled as he got up and stood by the bar, glass in hand.

"I disagree, son," I said quickly, hoping he wouldn't pour himself another. "I stay current on these things and I know. There's still popular music they *call* rock and roll, but it has none of the abrasive, irritating qualities of the original. Remember how some of those songs used to set your teeth on edge and make your skin crawl? That stuff is extinct."

"Some of it's still pretty bad."

"Not like it used to be. Its punch is gone. Dried up. Dead." I pointed to the radio at the end of the bar. "Turn that thing on and I'll show you."

Bill did. A newscast came on.

"Find some music."

He spun the dial until the sweet blend of a mixed duet singing "Hey, Paula" filled the room.

"Hear that? Big song. I can live with it. Find another so-called rock 'n' roll station." He did and the instrumental "Telstar" came on. "Monotonous, but I can live with that, too. Try one more." A d.j. announced the number one song in the country as a twelve-string guitar opening led into "Walk Right In."

Bill nodded and turned the radio off. "I concede the point."

"Good. And you must also concede that the wartime and post-war generations are now firmly back in the fold. There are pockets of discontent, naturally, but they are small and isolated. There is no clear-cut dividing line—*that's* what's important. Jack's doing his part in the White House. He's got them all hot for his social programs like the Peace Corps and such where their social impulses can be channeled and directed by the proper agencies. They see themselves as part of the mainstream, *involved* in the social continuum rather than separate from it.

"And we saved them, Bill—you, me, and the Commission."

Bill only stared at me. Finally, he said, "Maybe we did. But I never really understood about Buddy Holly—"

I felt like shouting, but controlled my voice. "Can't you drop that? I told you—"

"Oh, I don't mean the crash. I mean why he was so high on your list. He always struck me as an innocuous four-eyes who hiccupped his way through songs."

"Perhaps he was. But like Berry and Little Richard and Valens and Cochran, he had the potential to become a serious threat. He and the others originated the qualities that made the music so devisive. They wrote, played, and sang their own songs. That made me extremely uneasy."

Bill shook his head in bafflement. "I don't see . . ."

"All right: Let's suppose the Commission hadn't acted and had let things run their course. And now, here in '63, the wartime and post-war baby boom generation is aware of itself and a group, psychologically separate and forming its own subculture within ours. A lot of them are voting age now, and next year is an election year. Let's say one of these self-styled rock and roll singers who writes his own material gets it into his head to use his songs to influence the generation that idolizes him. Think of it: a thinly disguised political message being played over and over again, on radios, TVs, in homes, in jukeboxes, hummed, sung in the shower by all those voters. With their numbers, God knows what could happen at the polls!"

I paused for breath. It *was* a truly frightening thought.

"But that's all fantasy," I said. "The airwaves are once again full of safe, sane Tin Pan Alley tunes."

Bill smiled.

I asked, "What's so funny?"

"Just thinking. When I was in London last month I noticed that Britain seems to be going through the same kind of thing we did in '57. Lots of rock and roll bands and fans. There's one quartet of guys who wear their hair in bangs—can't remember the name now—that's selling records like crazy and packing the kids into the old music halls where they're screaming and fainting just like in Elvis Presley's heyday. And I understand they write and play and sing their own music, too."

I heard the windows at my back begin to rattle and jitter as hail mixed with the rain. I did not turn around to look.

"Forget Britain. England is already a lost cause."

"But what if their popularity spreads over here and the whole process gets going again?"

I laughed. That was a good one.

"A bunch of Limeys singing rock and roll to American kids? That'll be the day!"

But I knew that if such a thing ever came to pass, the Commission would be there to take the necessary measures.

Introduction

This was originally intended as a flashback within *The Touch*. I wanted it in the novel, but no matter which way I turned it, I couldn't get it to fit without a lot of seams showing. So I fleshed it out a little and transformed it into a freestanding story—a prequel to the novel. George Scithers bought it for *Amazing* shortly before he resigned as editor. It wound up as a finalist for the first Bram Stoker Awards.

DAT-TAY-VAO

1.

Patsy cupped his hands gently over his belly to keep his intestines where they belonged. Weak, wet, and helpless, he lay on his back in the alley looking up at the stars in the crystal sky, unable to move, afraid to call out. The one time he had yelled loud enough to be heard on the street, loops of bowel had squirmed against his hands, feeling like a pile of Mom's slippery-slick homemade sausage all gray from boiling and coated with her tomato sauce. Visions of his insides surging from the slit in his abdomen like spring snakes from a novelty can of nuts had kept him from yelling again.

No one had come.

He knew he was dying. Good as dead, in fact. He could feel the blood oozing out of the vertical gash in his belly, seeping around his fingers and trailing down his forearms to the ground. Wet from neck to knees. Probably lying in a pool of blood . . . his very own homemade marinara sauce.

Help was maybe fifty feet away and he couldn't call for it. Even if he could stand the sight of his guts jumping out of him, he no longer had the strength to yell. Yet help was there . . . the nightsounds of Quang Ngai streetlife . . . so near . . .

Nothing ever goes right for me. Nothing. Ever.

It had been such a *sweet* deal. Six keys of Cambodian brown. He could've got that home to Flatbush no sweat and then he'd have been set up real good. Uncle Tony would've known what to do with the stuff and Patsy would've been made. And he'd never be called Fatman again. Only the grunts over here called him Fatman. He'd be Pasquale to the old boys, and Pat to the younger guys.

And Uncle Tony would've called him Kid, like he always did.

Yeah. *Would have.* If Uncle Tony could see him now, he'd call him Shit-for-Brains. He could hear him now:

Six keys for ten G's? Whatsamatta witchoo? Din't I always tell you if it seems too good to be true, it usually is? Ay! Gabidose! Din't you smell no rat?

Nope. No rat smell. Because I didn't *want* to smell a rat. Too eager for the deal. Too anxious for the quick score. Too damn stupid as usual to see how that sleazeball Hung was playing me like a hooked fish.

No Cambodian brown.

No deal.

Just a long, sharp K-bar.

The stars above went fuzzy and swam around, then came into focus again.

The pain had been awful at first, but that was gone now. Except for the cold, it was almost like getting smashed and crashed on scotch and grass and just drifting off. Almost pleasant. Except for the cold. And the fear.

Footsteps . . . coming from the left. He managed to turn his head a few degrees. A lone figure approached, silhouetted against the light from the street. A slow, unsteady, almost staggering walk. Whoever it was didn't seem to be in any hurry.

Hung? Come to finish him off?

But no. This guy was too skinny to be Hung.

The figure came up and squatted flatfooted on his haunches next to him. In the dim glow of starlight and streetlight, Patsy saw a wrinkled face and a silvery goatee. The gook babbled something in Vietnamese.

God, it was Ho Chi Minh himself come to rob him. *Too late! The money's gone. All gone!*

No. Wasn't Ho. Couldn't be. Uncle Ho had died last month. This was just an old papa-san in the usual black pajamas. They all looked the same, especially the old ones. The only thing different about this one was the big scar across his right eye. Looked as if the lids had been fused closed over the socket.

The old man reached down to where Patsy guarded his intestines, and pushed his hands away. Patsy tried to scream in protest but heard only a sigh, tried to put his hands back up on his belly but they had weakened to limp rubber and wouldn't move.

The old man smiled as he singsonged in gooktalk, and pressed his hands against the open wound in Patsy's belly. Patsy screamed then, a hoarse, breathy sound torn from him by the searing pain that shot in all directions from where the old gook's hands lay. The stars really swam around this time, fading as they moved, but they didn't go out.

By the time his vision cleared, the old gook was up and turned around and weaving back toward the street. The pain, too, was sidling away.

Patsy tried again to lift his hands up to his belly, and this time they moved. They seemed stronger. He wiggled his fingers through the wetness of his blood, feeling for the edges of the wound, afraid of finding loops of bowel waiting for him.

He missed the slit on the first pass. And missed it on the second. How could that happen? It had been at least a foot long and had gaped open a good three or four inches, right there to the left of his belly button. He tried again, carefully this time . . .

. . . and found a thin little ridge of flesh.

But no opening.

He raised his head—he hadn't been able to do that before—and looked down at his belly. His shirt and pants were a bloody mess, but he couldn't see any guts sticking out. And he couldn't see any wound, either. Just a dark wet mound of flesh.

If he wasn't so goddamn fat he could see down there!

He rolled onto his side—God, he *was* stronger!—and pushed himself up to his knees to where he could slump his butt onto his heels, all the time keeping at least one hand tight over his belly. But nothing came out, or even pushed against his hand. He pulled his shirt open.

The wound was closed, leaving only a thin, purplish vertical line.

Patsy felt woozy again. *What's going on here?*

He was in a coma—that had to be it. He was dreaming this.

But everything was so *real*—the rough ground beneath his knees, the congealing red wetness of the blood on his shirt, the sounds from the street, even the smell of the garbage around him. All so real . . .

Bracing himself against the wall, he inched his way up to his feet. His knees were wobbly and for a moment he thought they'd give out on him. But they held and now he was standing.

He was afraid to look down, afraid he'd see himself still on the ground. Finally, he took a quick glance. Nothing there but two clotted puddles of blood, one on each side of where he had been lying.

He tore off the rest of the ruined shirt and began walking—very carefully at first—toward the street. Any moment now he would wake up or die, and this craziness would stop. No doubt about that. But until then he was going to play out this little fantasy to the end.

By the time he made it to his bunk—after giving the barracks guards and a few wandering night owls a story about an attempted robbery and a fight—Patsy had begun to believe that he was really awake and walking around.

It was so easy to say it had all been a dream, or maybe hallucinations brought on by acid slipped into his coffee by some wise-ass during the day. He managed to fully convince himself of that scenario a good half dozen times. And then he would look down at the scar on his belly, and at the blood on his pants.

Patsy sat on his rack in a daze.

It really happened! He just touched me and closed me up!

A hushed voice in the dark snapped him out of it.

"Hey! Fatman! Got any weed?"

It sounded like Donner from two bunks over, a steady customer.

"Not tonight, Hank," he said.

"What? Fatman's never out of stock!"

"He is tonight."

"You shittin' me?"

"Good night, Hank."

Actually, he had a bunch of bags stashed in his mattress, but Patsy didn't feel like dealing tonight. His mind was too numb to make change. He couldn't even mourn the loss of all his cash—every red cent he had saved up from almost a year's worth of chickenshit deals with guys like Donner. All he could think about, all he could see, was that old one-eyed gook leaning over him, smiling, babbling, and touching him.

He'd talk to Tram tomorrow. Tram knew everything that went on in this goddamn country. Maybe he had heard something about the old gook. Maybe he could be persuaded to look for him.

One way or another, Patsy was going to find that old gook.

He had plans for him. *Big* plans.

Somehow he managed to make it through breakfast without perking the powdered eggs and scrambling the coffee.

It hadn't been easy. He had been late getting to the mess hall kitchen. He had got up on time, but had stood in the shower staring at that purple line up and down his belly for he didn't know how long, remembering the cut of Hung's knife, the feel of his intestines in his hands.

Did it really happen?

He knew it had. Accepting it and living with it was going to be the problem.

Finally, he had pulled on his fatigues and hustled over to the kitchen. Rising long before sun-up was the only bad thing about being an army cook. The guys up front might call him a pogue but it sure beat hell out of being a stupid grunt in the field. *Anything* was better than getting shot at. Only *gavones* got sent into the field. Smart guys got mess assignments in nice safe towns like Quang Ngai.

At least smart guys with an Uncle Tony did.

Patsy smiled as he scraped hardened scrambled egg off the griddle. He had always liked to cook. Good thing, too. Because in a way, the cooking he had done for Christmas dinner last year had kept him out of the fight this year.

As always, Uncle Tony had come for Christmas dinner. At the table Pop edged around to the big question: what to do about Patsy and the draft. To everyone's surprise, he had passed his induction physical . . .

. . . another example of how nothing ever went right for him. Patsy had learned that a weight of 225 pounds would keep a guy his height out on medical deferment. He hadn't had far to go, so he gorged on everything in sight for weeks. It would have been fun if he hadn't been so desperate. But he made the weight: On the morning of his induction physical the bathroom scale read 229.

But the scale they used downtown at the Federal Building read 224.

He was in and was set to go to boot camp after the first of the year.

Pop finally came to the point: Could Uncle Tony maybe . . . ?

Patsy could still hear the disdain in Uncle Tony's voice as he spoke around a mouthful of bread.

"You some kinda peacenik or somethin'?"

No, no, Pop had said, and went on to explain how he was afraid that Patsy, being so fat and so clumsy and all, would get killed in boot camp or step on a mine his first day in the field. You know how he is.

Uncle Tony knew. Everybody knew Patsy's fugazi reputation. Uncle Tony had said nothing as he poured the thick red gravy over his lasagna, gravy Patsy had spent all morning cooking. He took a bite and pointed his fork at Patsy.

"Y'gotta do your duty, kid. I fought in the big one. You gotta fight in this here little one." He swallowed. "Say, you made this gravy, dincha? It's good. It's real good. And it gives me an idea of how we can keep you alive so you can go on making this stuff every Christmas."

So Uncle Tony pulled some strings and Patsy wound up an army cook.

He finished with the clean-up and headed downtown to the central market area, looking for Tram. He smelled the market before he got to it—the odors of live hens, *thit heo*, and roasting dog meat mingled in the air.

He found Tram in his usual spot by his cousin's vegetable stand, wearing his old ARVN fatigue jacket; and as usual he had removed his right foot at the ankle and was polishing its shoe.

"Nice shine, yes, Fatman?" he said as he looked up and saw Patsy.

"Beautiful." He knew Tram liked to shock passersby with his plastic lower leg and foot. Patsy should have been used to the gag by now, but every time he saw that foot he thought of having his leg blown off . . . "I want to find someone."

"American or gook?" He crossed his right lower leg over his left and snapped his shoed foot back into place at the ankle.

Patsy couldn't help feeling uncomfortable about a guy who called his own kind gooks.

"Gook."

"What name?"

"Uh, that's the problem. I don't know."

Tram squinted up at him.

"How I supposed to find somebody without a name?"

"Old papa-san. Looks like Uncle Ho."

Tram laughed. "All you guys think old gooks look like Ho!"

"And he has a scar across his eye"—Patsy put his index finger over his right eye—"that seals it closed like this."

2.

Tram froze for a heartbeat, then snapped his eyes back down to his prosthetic foot. He composed his expression while he calmed his whirling mind.

Trinh . . . Trinh was in town last night! And Fatman saw him!

He tried to change the subject. Keeping his eyes down, he said:

"I am glad to see you still walking around this morning. Did Hung not show up last night? I warned you—he number ten bad gook."

After waiting and hearing no reply, Tram looked up and saw that Fatman's eyes had changed. They looked glazed.

"Yes," Fatman finally said, shaking himself. "You warned me." He cleared his throat. "But about the guy I asked you about—"

"Why you want find this old gook?"

"I want to help him."

"How?"

"I want to do something for him."

"You want do something for old gook?"

Fatman's gaze wandered away as he spoke. "You might say I owe him a favor."

Tram's first thought was that Fatman was lying. He doubted the young American knew the meaning of returning a favor.

"Can you find him for me?" Fatman said.

Tram thought about that. And as he did, he saw Hung saunter out of a side street into the central market. He watched Hung's jaw drop when he spotted Fatman, watched his amber skin pale to the color of boiled bean curd as he spun and hurriedly stumbled away.

Tram knew in that instant that Hung had betrayed Fatman in a most vicious manner last night, and that Trinh had happened by and saved Fatman with the *Dat-tay-vao*.

It was all clear now.

On impulse, Tram said, "He lives in my cousin's village. I can take you to him."

"Great!" Fatman said, grinning and clapping him on the shoulder. "I'll get us a jeep!"

"No jeep," Tram said. "We walk."

"Walk?" Fatman's face lost much of its enthusiasm. "Is it far?"

"Not far. Just a few klicks on the way to Mo Duc. A fishing village. We leave now."

"Now? But—"

"Could be he not there if we wait." Which wasn't exactly true, but he didn't want to give Fatman too much time to think.

Tram watched reluctance and eagerness battle their way back and forth across the American's face. Finally:

"All right. Let's go. Long as it's not too far."

"If not too far for man with one foot, not too far for man with two."

As Tram led Fatman south toward the tiny fishing village where Trinh had been living for the past year, he wondered why he had agreed to bring the two of them together. His instincts were against it, yet he had agreed to lead the American to Trinh.

Why?

Why was a word too often on his mind, it seemed. Especially where Americans were concerned. Why did they send so many of their young men over here? Most of them were either too frightened or too disinterested to make good soldiers. And the few who were eager for the fight hadn't the experience to make them truly valuable. They did not last long.

He wanted to shout across the sea: *Send us seasoned soldiers, not your children!*

But who would listen?

And did age really matter? After all, hadn't he been even younger than these American boys in the fight against the French at Dien Bien Phu fifteen years ago? But he and his fellow Vietminh had had a special advantage on their side. They had all burned with a fiery zeal to drive the French from their land.

Tram had been a communist then. He smiled at the thought as he limped along on the artificial foot that served in place of the real one he had lost to a Cong booby trap last year. Communist . . . he had been young at Dien Bien Phu and the constant talk from his fellow Vietminh about the glories of class war and revolution had drawn his mind into their ideological camp. But after the fighting was over, after the partition, what he saw of the birth pangs of the glorious new social order almost made him long for French rule again.

He had come south then, and had remained here ever since. He had willingly fought for the South until the finger-charge booby trap had caught him at the knee; after that he found that his verve for any sort of fight had departed with his leg.

He glanced at Fatman, who sweated so profusely as he walked beside him along the twisting jungle trail. He had come to like the boy, and he could not say why. Fatman was greedy, cowardly, and selfish, and he cared for no one other than himself. Yet Tram had found himself responding to the boy's vulnerability. Something tragic behind the boy's bluff and bravado. With Tram's aid, Fatman had gone from the butt of many of the jokes around the American barracks to their favored supplier of marijuana. Tram could not deny that he had profited well by helping him gain that position. He had needed the money to supplement his meager pension from the ARVN, but that had not been his only motivation. He had felt a need to help the boy.

And he *was* a boy, no mistake about that. Young enough to be Tram's son. But Tram knew he could never raise such a son as this.

So many of the Americans he had met here were like Fatman. No values, no traditions, no heritage. Empty. Hollow creatures who had grown up with nothing expected of them. And now, despite all the money and all the speeches, they knew in their hearts that they were not expected to win this war.

What sort of parents provided nothing for their children to believe in, and then sent them halfway around the world to fight for a country they had never heard of?

And that last was certainly a humbling experience—to learn that until a few years ago most of these boys had been blithely unaware of the existence of the land that had been the center of Tram's life since he had been a teenager.

"How much further now?" Fatman said.

Tram could tell from the American's expression that he was uneasy being so far from town. Perhaps now was the time to ask.

"Where did Hung stab you?" he said.

Fatman staggered as if Tram had struck him a blow. He stopped and gaped at Tram with a gray face.

"How . . . ?"

"There is little that goes on in Quang Ngai that I don't know," he said, unable to resist an opportunity to enhance his stature. "Now, show me where."

Tram withheld a gasp as Fatman pulled up his sweat-soaked shirt to reveal the purple seam running up and down to the left of his navel. Hung had gut-cut him, not only to cause an agonizing death, but to show his contempt.

"I warned you . . ."

Fatman pulled down his shirt. "I know, I know. But after Hung left me in the alley, this old guy came along and touched me and sealed it up like magic. Can he do that all the time?"

"Not all the time. He has lived in the village for one year. He can do it some of the time every day. He will do it many more years."

Fatman's voice was a breathy whisper. "Years! But how? Is it some drug he takes? He looked like he was drunk."

"Oh, no. *Dat-tay-vao* not work if you drunk."

"*What* won't work?"

"*Dat-tay-vao* . . . Trinh has the touch that heals."

"Heals what? Just knife wounds and stuff?"

"Anything."

Fatman's eyes bulged. "You've got to get me to him!" He glanced quickly at Tram. "So I can thank him . . . reward him."

"He requires no reward."

"I've got to find him. How far to go?"

"Not much." He could smell the sea now. "We turn here."

As he guided Fatman left into thicker brush that clawed at their faces and snagged their clothes, he wondered again if he had done the right thing by bringing him here. But it was too late to turn back now.

Besides, Fatman had been touched by the *Dat-tay-vao*. Surely that worked some healing changes on the spirit as well as the body. Perhaps the young American truly wanted to pay his respects to Trinh.

3.

He will do it many more years!

The words echoed in Patsy's ears and once again he began counting the millions he'd make off the old gook. God, it was going to be so great! And so *easy!* Uncle Tony's contacts would help get the guy into the states where Patsy would set him up in a "clinic." Then he would begin to cure the incurable.

And oh God the prices he'd charge!

How much to cure someone of cancer? Who could say what price was too high? He could ask anything—*anything!*

But Patsy wasn't going to be greedy. He'd be fair. He wouldn't strip the patients bare. He'd just ask for half—half of everything they owned.

He almost laughed out loud. This was going to be *so* sweet! All he had to do was—

Just ahead of him, Tram shouted something in Vietnamese. Patsy didn't recognize the word, but he knew a curse when he heard one. Tram started running ahead. They had broken free of the suffocating jungle atop a small sandy rise. Out ahead, the sun rippled off a calm sea. A breeze off the water brought blessed relief from the heat. Below lay a miserable ville—a jumble of huts made of odd bits of wood, sheet metal, palm fronds, and mud.

One of the huts was burning. Frantic villagers were hurling sand and water at it.

Patsy followed Tram's headlong downhill run at a cautious walk. He didn't like this. He was far from town and doubted very much he could find his way back; he was surrounded by gooks and something bad was going down.

He didn't like this at all.

As he approached, the burning hut collapsed in a shower of sparks. To the side, a cluster of black pajama-clad women stood around a supine figure. Tram had pushed his way through to the center of the babbling group and now knelt beside the figure. Patsy followed him in.

"Aw, shit!" He recognized the guy on the ground. It wasn't easy. He had been burned bad and somebody had busted caps all over him, but his face was fairly undamaged and the scarred eye left no doubt that it was the same old gook who had healed him up last night. Both his eyes were closed and he looked dead, but his chest still moved with shallow respirations. Patsy's stomach lurched at the sight of all the blood and charred flesh. What was keeping him alive?

Suddenly weak and dizzy, Patsy dropped to his knees beside Tram. His millions . . . all those sweet dreams of millions and millions of easy dollars were fading away.

Nothing ever goes right for me!

"I share your grief," Tram said, looking at him with sorrowful dark eyes.

"Yeah. What happened?"

Tram glanced around at the frightened, grieving villagers. "They say the Cong bring one of their sick officers here and demand that Trinh heal him. Trinh couldn't. He try to explain that the time not right yet but they grow angry and tie him up and shoot him and set his hut on fire."

"Can't he heal himself?"

Tram shook his head slowly, sadly. "No. *Dat-tay-vao* does not help the one who has it. Only others."

Patsy wanted to cry. All his plans . . . It wasn't *fair!*

"Those shitbums!"

"Worse than shitbums," Tram said. "These Charlie say they come back soon and destroy whole village."

Patsy's anger and self-pity vanished in a cold blast of fear. He peered at the trees and bushes, feeling naked with a thousand eyes watching him. *They're coming back!* His knees suddenly felt stronger.

"Let's get back to town!" He began to rise to his feet, but Tram held him back.

"Wait. He looking at you."

Sure enough, the old gook's eyes were open and staring directly into his. Slowly, with obvious effort, he raised his charred right hand toward Patsy. His voice rasped something.

Tram translated: "He say, 'You the one.'"

"What's that mean?" Patsy didn't have time for this dramatic bullshit. He wanted out of here. But he also wanted to stay tight with Tram because Tram was the only one who could lead him back to Quang Ngai.

"I don't know. Maybe he mean that you the one he fix last night."

Patsy was aware of Tram and the villagers watching him, as if they expected something of him. Then he realized what it was: He was supposed to be grateful, show respect to the old gook. Fine. If it was what Tram wanted him to do, he would do it. Anything to get them on their way out of here. He took a deep breath and gripped the hand, wincing at the feel of the fire-crisped skin—

—electricity shot up his arm.

His whole body spasmed with the searing bolt. He felt himself flopping around like a fish on a hook, and then he was falling. The air went out of him in a rush as his back slammed against the ground. It was a moment before he could open his eyes, and when he did, he saw Tram and the villagers staring down at him with gaping mouths and wide, astonished eyes. He glanced at the old gook.

"What the hell did he do to me?"

The old gook was staring back, but it was a glassy, unfocused, sightless stare. He was dead.

The villagers must have noticed this too because some of the women began to weep.

Patsy staggered to his feet.

"What happened?"

"Don't know," Tram said with a puzzled shake of his head. "Why you fall? He not strong enough push you down."

Patsy opened his mouth to explain, then closed it. There was nothing he could say that would make sense. He shrugged.

"Let's go," he said.

He felt like hell and just wanted to be gone. It wasn't only the threat of Charlie returning; he was tired and discouraged and so bitterly disappointed he could have sat down on the ground right then and there and cried like a wimp.

"Okay. But first I help bury Trinh. You help, too."

"What? You kidding me? Forget it!"

Tram said nothing, but the look he gave Patsy said it all: It called him fat, lazy, and ungrateful.

Screw you! Patsy thought. Who cared what Tram or anybody else in this stinking sewer of a country thought! It held nothing for him anymore. All his money was gone, and his one chance for the brass ring lay dead and fried on the ground before him.

4.

As he helped dig a grave for Trinh, Tram glanced over at Fatman where he sat in the elephant grass staring morosely out to sea. Tram could sense that he was not grief-stricken over Trinh's fate. He was unhappy for himself.

So . . . he had been right about Fatman from the first: The American had come here with something in mind other than paying his respects to Trinh. Tram didn't know what it was, but he was sure Fatman had not had the best interests of Trinh or the village at heart.

He sighed. He was sick of foreigners. When would the wars end? Wars could be measured in languages here. He knew numerous Vietnamese dialects, Pidgin, French, and now English. If the North won, would he then have to learn Russian? Perhaps he would have been better off if the booby trap had taken his life instead of just his leg. Then, like Trinh, the endless wars would be over for him.

He looked down into the empty hole where Trinh's body soon would lie. Were they burying the *Dat-tay-vao* with him? Or would it rise and find its way to another? So strange and mysterious, the *Dat-tay-vao* . . . so many conflicting tales. Some said it came here with the Buddha himself, some said it had always been here. Some said it was as capricious as the wind in the choice of its instruments, while others said it followed a definite plan.

Who was to say truly? The *Dat-tay-vao* was a rule unto itself, full of mysteries that were not meant to be plumbed.

As he turned back to his digging, Tram's attention was caught by a dark blot in the water's glare. He squinted to make it out, then heard the chatter of one machine gun, then others, saw villagers begin to run and fall, felt sand kick up around him.

A Cong gunboat!

He ran for the tree where Fatman half-sat, half-crouched with a slack, terrified expression on his face. He was almost there when something hit him in the chest and right shoulder with the force of a sledgehammer, and then he was flying through the air, spinning, screaming with pain.

He landed with his face in the sand and rolled. He couldn't breathe! Panic swept over him. Every time he tried to take a breath, he heard a sucking sound from the wound in his chest wall, but no air reached his lungs. His chest felt ready to explode. Black clouds encroached on his dimming vision.

Suddenly, Fatman was leaning over him, shouting through the typhoon roaring in his ears.

"*Tram! Tram! Jesus God get up! You gotta get me outta here! Stop bleeding f'Christsake and get me out of here!*"

Tram's vision clouded to total darkness and the roaring grew until it drowned out the voice.

5.

Patsy dug his fingers into his scalp.

How was he going to get back to town? Tram was dying, turning blue right here in front of him and he didn't know enough Vietnamese to use with anyone else and didn't know the way back to Quang Ngai and the area was lousy with Charlie.

What am I gonna do?

As suddenly as they started, the AKs stopped. The cries of the wounded and the terrified filled the air in their place.

Now was the time to get out!

Patsy looked at Tram's mottled, dusky face. If he could stopper up that sucking chest wound, maybe Tram could hang on, and maybe tell him the way back to town. He slapped the heel of his hand over it and pressed.

Tram's body arched in seeming agony. Patsy felt something, too—electric ecstasy shot up his arm and spread through his body like subliminal fire. He fell back, confused, weak, dizzy.

What the hell—?

He heard raspy breathing and looked up. Air was gushing in

and out of Tram's wide-open mouth in hungry gasps; his eyes opened and his color began to lighten.

Tram's chest wasn't sucking anymore. As Patsy leaned forward to check the wound, he felt something in his hand and looked. A bloody lead slug sat in his palm. He looked at the chest where he had laid that hand and what he saw made the walls of his stomach ripple and compress, as if looking for something to throw up.

Tram's wound wasn't *there* anymore! Only a purplish blotch remained.

Tram raised his head and looked down at where the bullet had torn into him.

"The *Dat-tay-vao!* You have it now! Trinh passed it on to you! You have the *Dat-tay-vao!*"

I do? he thought, staring at the bullet rolling in his palm. *Holy shit, I do!*

He wouldn't have to get some gook back to the States to make his mint—all he had to do was get himself home in one piece.

Which made it all the more important to get the hell out of this village now.

"Let's go!"

"Fatman, you can't go. Not now. You must help. They—"

Patsy threw himself flat as something exploded in the jungle a hundred yards behind them, hurling a brown and green geyser of dirt and underbrush high into the air.

Mortar!

Another explosion followed close on the heels of the first, but this one was down by the waterline south of the village.

Tram was pointing out to sea.

"Look! They firing from boat." He laughed. "Can't aim mortar from boat!"

Patsy stayed hunkered down with his arms wrapped tight around his head, quaking with terror as the ground jittered with each of the next three explosions. Then they stopped.

"See?" Tram said, sitting boldly in the clearing and looking out to sea. "Even *they* know it foolish! They leaving. They only use for terror. Cong very good at terror."

No argument there, Patsy thought as he climbed once more to his feet.

"Get me out of here *now*, Tram. You owe me!"

Tram's eyes caught Patsy's and pinned him to the spot like an insect on a board. "Look at them, Fatman."

Patsy tore his gaze away and looked at the ville. He saw the villagers—the maimed and bleeding ones and their friends and families—looking back at him. Waiting. They said nothing, but their eyes . . .

He ripped his gaze loose. "Those Cong'll be back!"

"They need you, Fatman," Tram said. "You're the only one who can help them now."

Patsy looked again, unwillingly. Their eyes . . . calling him. He could almost feel their hurt, their need.

"No way!"

He turned and began walking toward the brush. He'd find his own way back if Tram wouldn't lead him. Better than waiting around here to get caught and tortured by Charlie. It might take him all day, but—

"Fatman!" Tram shouted. *"For once in your life!"*

That stung. Patsy turned and looked at the villagers once more, feeling their need like a taut rope around his chest, pulling him toward them. He ground his teeth. It was idiotic to stay, but . . .

One more. Just one, to see if I still have it. He could spare a couple of minutes for that, then be on his way. At least that way he'd be sure what had happened with Tram wasn't some sort of crazy freak accident. *Just one.*

As he stepped toward the villagers, he heard their voices begin to murmur excitedly. He didn't know what they were saying but felt their grateful welcome like a warm current through the draw of their need.

He stopped at the nearest wounded villager, a woman holding a bloody, unconscious child in her arms. His stomach lurched as he saw the wound—a slug had nearly torn the kid's arm off at the shoulder. Blood oozed steadily between the fingers of the hand the woman kept clenched over the wound. Swallowing the revulsion that welled up in him, he slipped his hands under the mother's to touch the wound—

—and his knees almost buckled with the ecstasy that shot through him.

The child whimpered and opened his eyes. The mother removed her hand from the wound. There was no wound. Gone, just like Tram's. She cried out in joy and fell to her knees beside Patsy, clutching his leg as she wept.

Patsy swayed. He had it! No doubt about it—he had the goddamn *Dat-tay-vao!* And it felt so *good!* Not just the pleasure it caused, but how that little gook kid was looking up at him now with his bottomless black eyes and flashing him a shy smile. He felt high, like he'd been smoking some of his best merchandise.

One more. Just one more.

He disengaged his leg from the mother and moved over to where an old woman writhed in agony on the ground, clutching her abdomen. *Belly wound . . . I know the feeling, mama-san.* He knelt and wormed his hand under hers. That burst of pleasure surged again as she stiffened and two slugs popped into his hand. Her breathing eased and she looked up at him with gratitude beaming from her eyes.

Another!

On it went. Patsy could have stopped at any time, but found he didn't want to. There didn't seem to be any doubt in the villagers' minds that he would stay and heal them all. They knew he could do it and *expected* him to do it. It was so new, such a unique feeling, he didn't want it to end. Ever. He felt a sense of belonging he had never known before. He felt protective of the villagers. But it went beyond them, beyond this little ville, seemed to take in the whole world.

Finally, it was over. Patsy stood in the clearing before the huts, looking for another wounded body. He checked his watch—only thirty minutes or so at it and there were no more villagers left to heal. They all clustered around him at a respectful distance, silently watching him. He gave himself up to the euphoria enveloping him, blending with the sound of the waves, the wind in the trees, the cries of the gulls. He hadn't realized what a beautiful place this was. If only—

A new sound intruded—the drone of a boat engine. Patsy looked out at the water and saw the Cong gunboat returning. Fear knifed through the pleasurable haze as the villagers scattered for the trees. Were the Cong going to land?

No. Patsy saw a couple of the crew crouched on the deck, heard the familiar *choonk!* of a mortar shell shooting out of its tube. An explosion quickly followed somewhere back in the jungle. Tram had been right. No way they could get any accuracy with a mortar on the rocking deck of a gunboat. Just terror tactics.

Damn those bastards! Why'd they have to come back and wreck his mood. Just when he'd been feeling good for the first time since leaving home. Matter of fact, he'd been feeling better than he could ever remember, home or anywhere else. For once, everything seemed *right*.

For once, something was going Patsy's way, and the Cong had to ruin it.

Two more wild mortar shots, then he heard gunfire start from the south and saw three new gunboats roaring up toward the first. But these were flying the old red, white, and blue. Patsy laughed and raised his fist.

"Get 'em!"

The Cong let one more shell go *choonk!* before pouring on the gas and slewing away.

Safe!

Then he heard a whine from above and the world exploded under him.

6.

. . . a voice from far away . . . Tram's . . .

"*. . . chopper coming, Fatman . . . get you away soon . . . hear it? . . . almost here . . .*"

Patsy opened his eyes and saw the sky, then saw Tram's face poke into view. He looked sick.

"Fatman! You hear me?"

"How bad?" Patsy asked.

"You be okay."

Patsy turned his head and saw a ring of weeping villagers who were looking everywhere and anywhere but at him. He realized he couldn't feel anything below his neck. He tried to lift his head for a look at himself but didn't have the strength.

"I wanna see."

"You rest," Tram said.

"Get my head up, dammit!"

With obvious reluctance, Tram gently lifted his head. As Patsy looked down at what was left of him, he heard a high, keening wail. His vision swam, mercifully blotting out sight of the bloody ruin that had once been the lower half of his body. He realized that the wail was his own voice.

Tram lowered his head and the wail stopped.

I shouldn't even be alive!

Then he knew. He was waiting for someone. Not just anyone would do. A certain someone.

A hazy peace came. He drifted into it and stayed there until the chopping thrum of a slick brought him out; then he heard an American voice.

"I thought you said he was alive!"

Tram's voice: "He is."

Patsy opened his eyes and saw the shocked face of an American soldier.

"Who are you?" Patsy asked.

"Walt Erskine. Medic. I'm gonna—"

"You're the one," Patsy said. Somehow, he bent his arm at the elbow and lifted his hand. "Shake."

The medic looked confused. "Yeah. Okay. Sure." He grabbed Patsy's hand and Patsy felt the searing electric charge. Erskine jerked back, clutching his hand. "What the hell?"

The peace closed in on Patsy again. He had held on as long as he could. Now he could embrace it. One final thought arced through his mind like a lone meteorite in a starless sky.

The *Dat-tay-vao* was going to America after all.

Introduction

Greystone Bay ("The City Horror Calls Its Own") is a shared world anthology for horror fans. I read the first volume and was interested by the possibilities—a *Thieves' World* of contemporary horror. I immediately wrote the editor, Charlie Grant, and told him that the town definitely needed a doctor and that I would gladly supply him. He agreed, told me to give it a shot, and sent me the particulars on the town of Greystone Bay.

I wound up supplying the town with *two* doctors. One is pretty straight, but the other . . . the other is Doc Johnson.

You don't mess with ol' Doc Johnson.

DOC JOHNSON

"I think you'd better take the call on oh-one," Jessie said, poking her head into the consultation room. I glanced up from the latest issue of *Cardiology* and looked at my wife. It was Monday morning and I had a grand total of three patients scheduled.

"Why?" I said.

"Because I said so."

That's what I get for hiring my wife as my nurse-receptionist, but I had to keep overhead down until I built up a decent practice and could afford a stranger . . . someone I could reprimand without paying for it later at home. I had to admit, though, that Jessie was doing a damn fine job so far. She wasn't letting the pregnancy slow her down a bit.

"Who is it?"

Jessie shrugged. "Not sure. Says she's never been here before but says her husband needs a doctor real bad."

"Got it," I said. Never turn down a patient in need. Especially one who might be able to pay.

I picked up the phone. "Hello. Dr. Reid."

"Oh, Doctor," said a woman's voice. "My husband's awful sick. Can you come see him?"

"A *house call?*" After all, I was a board-eligible internist. House calls were for GPs and family practitioners, not specialists. "What's wrong with your husband, Mrs. . . . ?"

"Mosely—Martha Mosely. My husband, Joseph, he's . . . he's just not right. Sometimes he says he wants a doctor and sometimes he says he doesn't. He says he wants one now."

"Can you be a little more specific?" If this Mosely fellow was going to end up in the hospital, I'd rather have him transported there first and *then* see him.

"I wish I could, Doctor, but I can't."

"Who's his regular doctor?"

"Doc Johnson."

Ah-ha! "And why aren't you calling him?"

"Joe won't let me. He says he doesn't ever want to see Doc Johnson again. He only wants you."

I hesitated. I didn't want to get into the house call habit, but as the new kid in town, I couldn't afford to pass up a chance to score some points.

"All right," I said. "Give me the address and I'll be out after dinner."

He doesn't ever want to see Doc Johnson again.

I thought about that as I drove out to the Mosely house. An odd thing to say. Most people in Greystone Bay swore by Johnson. You'd think he walked on water the way some of them talked. And that wasn't making it any easier for me to get started in Greystone Bay. I'd been living—quite literally—off the crumbs he left behind. Joseph Mosely appeared to be a crumb. And so I was on my way to gather him up.

I turned south off Port Boulevard onto New Hope Road, watching the houses change from post–World War II tract homes to smaller, older homes on bigger lots. The January wind slapped at the car as I drove.

This was my first winter in Greystone Bay and it was *cold*. The natives like to say that the nearness of the ocean tends to moderate the severity of the weather. Maybe that's true. According to the thermometer, it doesn't seem to get quite as cold here as it does inland, but I think the extra moisture in the air from the ocean sends the cold straight through the clothing and deep into the bone.

But the cold was locked outside the car and I was warm within. I had a bellyful of Jessie's tuna casserole, the Skylark's heater-defrost system was blowing hard and warm, snow blanketed the lawns and was banked on the curbs, but the asphalt was clean and dry. It was a beautiful, crystalline winter night for a drive. Too bad Jessie wasn't with me. Too bad this wasn't a pleasure drive. People attach such rosy nostalgia to the house call, but in this end of the twentieth century, the house is a *lousy* place to practice medicine.

I slowed the car as the numbers on the mailboxes told me I was nearing the Mosely place. There it was: 620 New Hope Road. As I pulled into the driveway, my headlamps lit up the house and grounds. I stopped the car halfway through the turn and groaned.

The Mosely house was a mess.

Every neighborhood has one. You know the type of house I mean. You drive along a street lined with immaculately kept homes, all with freshly painted siding and manicured lawns, all picture-perfect . . . except for one. There's always one house that has a front yard where even the weeds won't grow; the Christmas lights are still attached to the eaves even though it might be June; if the neighborhood is lucky, there will be only one rusting auto in the front yard, and the house's previous coat of paint will have merely peeled away, exposing much of the original color of the siding; if the neighborhood is especially cursed, there will be two or more automobile hulks in various stages of refurbishing in the front and the occupant will have started to paint the derelict home a hot pink or a particularly noxious shade of green and then quit halfway through.

The Mosely house was New Hope Road's derelict.

I turned off my engine and, black bag in hand, stepped out into the cold. No path had been dug through the snow anywhere I could see but I found a narrow path where it had been packed down by other feet before me. It led across the front lawn. At least I think it was a lawn. The glow from a nearby streetlight picked out odd bumps and rises all over the front yard. I could only guess as to what lay beneath. A blanket of snow hides a multitude of sins.

I got a closer look at the house as I carefully picked my way toward it. The front porch was an open affair and its overhang was tilted at a crazy angle. The paint on the front of the house was particularly worn and dirty on the porch up to a level of about two feet. It looked to me like a dog had spent a lot of time there but I saw no paw prints and heard no barking. The light from within barely filtered through the window shades.

The front door opened before I could knock. A thin, fiftyish woman wearing an old blue housedress and a stretched-out brown cardigan sweater stood there with her hand on the knob.

"I'm terribly sorry, Doctor," she said in a mousy voice, "but Joe's decided he don't want to see a doctor tonight."

"What?" I said, my voice hoarse with shock. "You mean to tell me I came—"

"Oh, let him in, Martha!" said a rough voice from somewhere behind her. "Long as he's here, we might as well get a look at him."

"Yes, Joe," she said, and let me in.

The air within was hot, dry, and sour-smelling. I wondered how many years it had been since they'd had the windows open. A wood stove sat in a corner to my left. What little light there was in the room came from candles and kerosene lamps.

Joseph Mosely sat in a rocker facing me. He was the same

age as his wife but thinner. His skin was stretched tight across his high forehead and cheekbones. He had a full head of lank hair and a three-day stubble of beard. There was something familiar about him. As I watched, he sipped from a four-ounce tumbler clutched in his right hand; a half-empty bottle of local-brand gin sat on a small table next to him. He was staring at me. I've seen prosthetic eyes of porcelain and glass show more warmth and human feeling than Joe Mosely's.

"If that was your idea of a joke, Mr. Mosely—"

"Don't bother trying to intimidate me, Dr. Charles Reid. It's a waste of breath. Take the man's coat, Martha."

"Yes, Joe."

Sighing resignedly, I shrugged out of my jacket and turned to hand it to her. I stopped and stared at her face. A large black and purple hematoma, a good inch and a half across, bloomed on her right cheek. Due to the way the light had been falling, I hadn't noticed it when she opened the door. But now . . . I knew from the look of it that it wasn't more than a couple of hours old.

"Better get the ice back on that bruise," he said to her from his rocker. "And careful you don't slip on the kitchen floor and hurt yourself again."

"Yes, Joe," She hung my coat on a hook next to the front door.

Clenching my teeth against the challenge that leaped into my throat, I handed her my coat and turned to her husband.

"What seems to be the problem, Mr. Mosely?"

He put the glass down. "This." He rolled up his right sleeve and showed me a healing laceration on the underside of his forearm. It ran up the arm from the wrist for about five inches or so and looked to be about ten days to two weeks old. Three silk sutures were still in place.

My anger flared. "You brought me all the way out here for a suture removal?"

"I didn't bring you anywhere. You brought yourself. And besides—" He kicked up his left foot; it looked deformed under the dirty sock. "I'm disabled."

"All right," I said, cooling with effort. "How'd you cut yourself?"

"Whittling."

I felt like asking him if he'd been using a machete, but restrained myself. "They sew it up at County General?"

"Nope."

"Then who?"

There was a pause and I looked at him. His eyes were even colder and flatter than before. "Doc Johnson."

"Why'd he leave these three sutures in?"

"He didn't. I took the rest out myself. He won't ever get near me again! Ever!" He half rose from the rocker. "I wouldn't take my *dog* to him if she was still alive!"

"Hey! Take it easy." He calmed down with another sip of gin. "So why did *you* leave the last three sutures in?"

He looked at the wound, then away. "Because there's something wrong with it."

I inspected it more closely. It looked fine. The wound edges had knitted nicely. Dr. Johnson had done a good closure. There was no redness or swelling to indicate infection.

"Looks okay to me." I opened my bag, got out an alcohol swab, and dabbed the wound. Then I took out scissors and forceps and removed those last three sutures. "There. Good as new."

"There's *still* something wrong with it!" He pulled his arm away to reach for the gin glass; he drained it, then slammed it down. "There's something in there."

I almost laughed. "Pardon me?"

"Something's *in* there! I can feel it move every now and then. The first time it moved was when I started taking the sutures out. There! Look!" He stiffened and pointed to the wound. "It's moving now!"

I looked and saw nothing the least bit out of the ordinary.
But I thought I knew what was bothering him.

"Here," I said, taking his left hand and laying the fingers
over the underside of his forearm. "Press them there. Now,
open and close your hand, making a fist. There . . . feel the
tendons moving under the skin? You've probably got a little
scar tissue building up in the deeper layers next to a tendon
sheath and it's—"

"Something's *in* there, I tell you! Doc Johnson put it there
when he sewed me up!"

I stood up. "That's ridiculous!"

"It's true! I wouldn't make up something like that!"

"Did you watch him sew you up?"

"Yes."

"Did you see him put anything in the wound?"

"No. But he's sneaky. I know he put something in there!"

"You'd better lay off the gin," I said as I closed my bag.
"You're having delusions."

"I shoulda known," he said bitterly, reaching for his bottle.
"You doctors think you've got all the answers."

I took my coat off the hook and pulled it on. "What's that
supposed to mean? And haven't you had enough of that for
one night?"

"*Damn* you!" Eyes ablaze with fury, he hurled the glass
across the room and leaped out of the rocker. "Who the hell do
you think you are to tell me when I've had enough!"

He limped toward me and then I remembered why he
looked familiar. The limp triggered it: I had seen him dozens of
times in the Port Boulevard shopping area, usually coming or
going in and out of the liquor store. He had lied to me—he
wasn't disabled enough to warrant a house call.

"You're drunk," I said, reaching for the doorknob. "Sleep it
off."

Suddenly he stopped his advance and grinned maliciously.
"Oh, I'll sleep, all right. But will *you?* Better pray nothing goes

bad with this arm here, or you'll have another malpractice case on your hands. Like the one in Boston."

My stomach wrenched into a tight ball. "How do you know about that?" I hoped I didn't look as sick as I felt.

"Checked into you. When I heard that we had this brand-new doctor in town, fresh from a big medical center in Boston, I asked myself why a young, hot-shot specialist would want to practice in the Bay? So I did some digging. I'm real good at digging. 'Specially on doctors. They got these high an' mighty ways with how they dole out pills and advice like they're better'n the rest of us. Dr. Tanner was like that. That office you're in used to be his. I dug up some *good* dirt on Tanner but he disappeared before I could rub his face in it."

"Good night," I said. I stepped out on the porch and pulled the door closed behind me.

There was nothing else to say. I thought I had left that malpractice nightmare behind me in Boston. The sudden realization that it had followed me here threatened all the hopes I'd had of finding peace in Greystone Bay. And to hear it from the grinning lips of someone like Joe Mosely made me almost physically ill.

I barely remembered the trip home. I seemed to be driving through the past, through interrogatories and depositions and sweating testimonies. I didn't really come back to the present until I parked the car and walked toward the duplex we were renting.

Jessie was standing on the front steps, wrapped in her parka with her arms folded across her chest, looking up at the stars under a full moon. Suddenly I felt calm. This was the way I had found her when we first met—standing on a rooftop gazing up at the night sky, looking for Jupiter. She owned two telescopes that she used regularly, but she's told me countless times that a true amateur astronomer never tires of naked-eye stargazing.

She smiled as she saw me walk up. "How was the house call?"

I put on an annoyed expression. "Unnecessary." I wouldn't tell her about tonight. At least one of us should rest easy. I patted her growing belly. "How we doing in there?"

"You mean the Tap Dance Kid? Active as ever." She turned back to the stars and frowned.

"What's the matter?" I said.

"I don't know. Something weird about the stars out here."

I looked up. They looked all right to me, except that there was a hell of a lot more of them than I'd ever seen in Boston.

Jessie slipped an arm around me and seemed to read my expression without looking at me.

"Yeah. I said *weird*. They don't look right. I could get out a star map and I know everything would look fine. But something's just not right up there. The perspective's somehow different. Only another stargazer would notice. Something's wrong."

I had heard that expression too many times tonight.

"The baby wants to go in," I said. "He's cold."

"*She's* cold."

"Anything you say."

I had trouble sleeping that night. I kept reliving the malpractice case and how I wound up scapegoat for a couple of department heads at the medical center. After all, I was only a resident and they had national reputations. I was sure they were sleeping well tonight while I lay here awake.

I kept seeing the plaintiff attorney's hungry face, hearing his voice as he tore me apart. I'm a good doctor, a caring one who knows internal medicine inside and out, but you wouldn't have thought so after that lawyer was through with me. He got a third of the settlement and I got the word that I shouldn't apply for a position on the staff of the medical center when my residency was up. I suppose the Bigshots didn't want me around as a reminder of the case.

Jessie wanted me to fight them for an appointment but I knew better. Every hospital staff application has a question that reads: "Have you ever been denied staff privileges at any other hospital?" If you answer *Yes*, they want to know all the particulars. If you say *No* and later they find out otherwise, your ass is grass.

Discretion is the better part of valor, I always say. I knew they would turn me down, and I didn't want to answer yes to that question for the rest of my life, so I packed up and left when my residency was over. The medical center reciprocated by giving me good recommendations.

Jessie says I'm too scared of making waves. Jessie's probably right. She usually is. I know I couldn't have made it through the trial without her. She stuck by me all the way.

She's right about the waves, though. All I want to do is live in peace and quiet and practice the medicine I've been trained for. That's all. I don't need a Porsche or a mansion. Just Jessie and our kids and enough to live comfortably. That's all I want. That's all I've ever wanted.

Wednesday afternoon, two days after the Mosely house call, I was standing outside Doc Johnson's house, ringing his bell.

"Stop by the house this afternoon," he had said on the phone a few hours ago. "Let's get acquainted."

I had been in town seven months now and this was the first time he had spoken to me beyond a nod and a good-morning while passing in the hall at County General. I couldn't use the excuse that my office was too busy for me to get away, so I accepted. Besides, I was curious as to why he wanted to see me.

I saw Joe Mosely on my way over. He was coming out of the liquor store and he spotted me waiting at the light. He looked terrible. I wasn't sure if it was just the daylight or if he was actually thinner than the other night. His cheeks looked more sunken, his eyes more feverish. But his smile hadn't changed. The way he grinned at me had tied my stomach into a knot that was just now beginning to unravel.

I tried not to think of Joe Mosely as I waited for someone to answer my ring. I inspected my surroundings. The Johnson house was as solid as they come, with walls built of the heavy gray native granite that rimmed the shore in these parts. There was little mortar visible. Someone had taken great pains to mate each stone nook and cranny against its neighbor. The resultant pattern was like the flip side of one of those thousand-piece Springbok jigsaw puzzles that Jessie liked to diddle with. From the front steps here high on North Hill I had a clear view of the beach and the ocean, all the way down to Blind Point and beyond.

I wouldn't mind getting used to this, I thought.

I thought about Doc Johnson, too. I'd heard that he was a widower with no children, that his family came over here with Greystone Bay's original settlers back in the seventeenth century. Doctors apparently came and went pretty regularly around the Bay, but "the Doc"—that's what the natives called him—was as constant as the moon, always available, always willing to come out to the house if you were too sick to go to him. If you were a regular patient of the Doc's he never let you down. They talked like he'd always been here and always would be. His practice seemed to encompass the whole town. That was impossible, of course. No one man could care for 20,000 people. But to hear folks talk—and to listen to the grumbling of the few other struggling doctors in town—that was the way it was.

The handle rattled and Doc Johnson opened the door himself. He was a portly man in his sixties with a full, friendly, florid face and lots of white hair combed straight back. He was wearing a white shirt, open at the collar, white duck pants, and a blue blazer with a gold emblem on the breast pocket. He looked more like a yacht club commodore than a doctor.

"Charles!" he said, shaking my hand. "So good of you to come! Come in out of the chill and I'll make you a drink!"

It wasn't as chilly as it had been the past few days but I was glad to step into the warmth of his home. He fixed me an excellent vodka gimlet with a dash of Cointreau and showed me around the house which one of his ancestors had built a couple of centuries ago. We made small talk during the tour until we ended up in his study before a fire. He was a gracious, amiable host and I took an immediate liking to him.

"Let's talk shop a minute," he said to me after we settled into chairs and I refused a refill on the gimlet. "I like to feel out a new doctor in town on his philosophy of medicine." His eyes penetrated mine. "Do you have one?"

I thought about that. Since starting med school I'd been so involved in learning whatever there was to know about medicine that I hadn't given much consideration to a philosophical approach. I was tempted to say *Keeping my head above water* but thought better of it. I decided to go Hippocratic.

"I guess I'd start with 'Above all else do no harm.'"

He smiled. "An excellent start. But how would triage fit into your philosophy, Horatio?"

"Horatio?"

"I'm an avid reader. You will forgive me a literary reference once in a while, won't you? That was to *Hamlet*. A strained reference, I'll grant you, but *Hamlet* nonetheless."

"Of course. But triage . . . ?"

"Under certain circumstances we have to choose those who will get care and those who won't. In disasters, for instance: We must ignore those whom we judge to be beyond help in order to aid those who are salvageable."

"Of course. That's an accepted part of emergency care."

"But aren't you doing harm by withholding care?"

"Not if a patient is terminal. Not if the outcome will remain unchanged no matter what you do."

"Which means we must place great faith in our judgment, then, correct?"

I nodded. "Yes, I suppose so." What was he getting at?

"And what if one must amputate a gangrenous limb in order to preserve the health of the rest of the body? Isn't that doing harm of sorts to the diseased limb?"

I said, "I suppose you could look at it that way, but if the health of the good tissue is threatened by the infected limb, and you can't cure the infection, then the limb's got to go."

"Precisely. It's another form of triage: The diseased limb must be lopped off and discarded. Sometimes I find that triage must be of a more active sort where radical decisions must be made. Medicine is full of life-and-death decisions, don't you think?"

I nodded once more. This was a baffling conversation.

"I understand you had the pleasure of meeting the estimable Joseph Mosely the other night."

The abrupt change of subject left me reeling for a second.

"I don't know if I'd call it a pleasure," I said.

"There'd be something seriously wrong with you if you did. A despicable excuse for a human being. Truly a hollow man, if you'll excuse the Yeats reference—or is that Eliot? No matter. It fits Joe Mosely well enough: no heart, no soul. An alcoholic who abused his children mercilessly. I patched up enough cuts and contusions on his battered boys, and I fear he battered his only daughter in a far more loathsome way. They all ran away as soon as they were able. So now he abuses poor Martha when the mood suits him, and that is too often. Last summer I had to strap up three broken ribs on that poor woman. But she won't press charges against him. Love's funny, isn't it? Did you notice his mangled foot? That happened when he was working at the shoe factory. Talk is that he stuck his foot in that machine on purpose, only he stuck it in further than he intended and did too good a job of injuring himself. Anyway, he got a nice settlement out of it, which is what he wanted, but he drank it up in no time.

"And did you notice the lack of electricity? The power company caught him tampering with the meter and cut him off. I've heard he's blackmailing a few people in town. And he steals anything that's not nailed down. That cut on his arm I sewed up? That was the first time in all these years I'd ever had a chance to actually treat him. He tried to tell me he did it whittling. Ha! Never yet seen a right-handed man cut himself in the right arm with a knife. No, he did that breaking into a house on Accardo Street. Did it on storm-window glass. Read in the *Gazette* how they found lots of blood at the scene and were checking ERs in the area to see if anybody had been sewn up. That was why he came to me. I tell you, he will make the world a brighter place by departing it."

"You didn't report him to the police?"

"No," he said levelly. "And I don't intend to. The courts won't give him his due. And calling the police is not my way of handling the likes of Joe Mosely."

I had to say it. "Joe Mosely says you put something in the laceration when you sewed it up."

I watched Doc Johnson's face darken. "I hope you will consider the source and not repeat that."

"Of course not," I said. "I only mentioned it now because you were the accused."

"Good." He cleared his throat. "There's some things you should know about the Bay. We like it quiet here. We don't like idle chatter. You'll find that things have a way of working themselves out in their own way. You don't get outsiders involved if you can help it."

"Like me?"

"That's up to you. You can be an insider if you want to be. 'Newcomer' and 'insider' aren't mutually exclusive terms in Greystone Bay. A town dies if it doesn't get *some* new blood.

But discretion is all-important. As a doctor in town you may occasionally see something out of the ordinary. You could take it as it comes and deal with it, and leave it at that, and that would bring you closer to the inside. Or, you could talk about it a lot or maybe even submit a paper on it to something like the *New England Journal of Medicine*, and that would push you out. *Far* out. Soon you'd have to pack up and move away." He stood up and patted my shoulder. "I like you, Charles. This town needs more doctors. I'd like to see you make it here."

"I'd like to stay here."

"Good! I do my own sort of triage on incoming doctors. If I think they'll work out, I send them my overflow." He sighed. "And believe me, I'm getting ready to increase my overflow. I'd like to slow down a bit. Not as young as I used to be."

"I'd appreciate that," I said.

He gave me a calculating look. "Okay. We'll see. But first—" He glanced out the window. "Well, here it comes!" He motioned me over to the big bay window. "Look out there!"

I stepped to his side and looked out at the Atlantic—or rather, where the Atlantic had been. The horizon was gone, lost in a fog bank that was even now rolling into the bay itself.

Doc Johnson pointed south. "If you watch, you'll see Blind Pew disappear."

"Excuse me?"

He laughed. "Another reference, my boy. I've called Blind Point 'Blind Pew' ever since I read *Treasure Island* when I was ten. You remember Blind Pew, don't you?"

N. C. Wyeth's moonlit painting of the character suddenly flashed before my eyes. That painting had always given me the chills. "Of course. But where's the fog coming from?"

"The Gulf Stream. For reasons known only to itself, it swings in here a couple of times a winter. The warm air from the stream hits the cold air on the land and then we have fog. Oh, my, do we have *fog!*"

As I watched, I saw lacy fingers of mist begin to rise from the snow in the front yard.

"Yes, sir!" he said, rubbing his hands together and smiling. "This one's going to be a beauty!"

Mrs. Mosely called me Friday night.

"You've got to come out and see Joe," she said.

"No, thank you," I told her. "Once was quite enough."

"I think he's dying!"

"Then get him over to County General."

"He won't let me call an ambulance. He won't let me near him!"

"Then I'm sorry—"

"*Please*, Dr. Reid!" Her voice broke into a wail. "If not for him, then for me! I'm frightened!"

Something in her voice got to me. And I remembered that bruise on her cheek. "Okay," I said reluctantly. "I'll be over in a half hour."

I knew I'd regret it.

The fog was still menacingly thick, and worse at night than during the day. At least you could pick out shadows in daylight. At night the headlights bounced off the fog instead of penetrating it. It was like driving through cotton.

When I finally got to the Mosely place, the air seemed cooler and the fog appeared to be thinning. Somewhere above, moonlight struggled to get through. Maybe that predicted cold front from the west was finally moving in.

Martha Mosely opened the door for me. "Thank you for coming, Dr. Reid. I don't know what to do! He won't let me touch him or go near him! I'm at my wit's end!"

"Where is he?"

"In bed." She led me to a room in the back and stood at the door clutching her hands between her breasts as I entered.

By the light of the room's single flickering candle I could see

Joe Mosely lying naked on the bed, stretched out like a corpse. In fact, for a moment I thought he was dead—he looked emaciated and his breathing was so shallow I couldn't see his chest move. Then he turned his head a few degrees in my direction.

"So, it's you." His lips barely moved. The eyes were the only things alive in his face.

"Yeah. Me. What can I do for you?"

"First, you can close the door—with that woman on the other side." Before I could answer, I heard the door close behind me. I was alone in the room with Mosely. "And second, you can keep your distance."

"What's the matter? Anything hurt?"

"No pain. But I'm a dead man. It's Doc Johnson's doing. I told you he put something in that cut."

His words were disturbing enough, but his completely emotionless tone made them even more chilling. It was as if whatever emotions he possessed had been drained away along with his vitality.

"You need to be hospitalized."

"No use. I'm already gone. But let me tell you about Doc Johnson. He did this to me. He's got his own ways and he follows his own rules. I've tailed him up onto South Hill a few times but I always lost him. Don't know what he goes there for, but it can't be for no good."

I took out my stethoscope as he raved quietly. When he saw it, his voice rose in pitch.

"Don't come near me. Just keep away."

"Don't be ridiculous. I'm here. I might as well see if I can do anything for you." I put the earpieces in my ears and went down on one knee beside the bed.

"Don't. Keep back."

I pressed the diaphragm over his heart to listen—

—and felt his chest wall give way like a stale soda cracker. My left hand disappeared up to the wrist inside his chest cavity. And it was *cold* in there! I yanked it out and hurled myself away from the bed, not stopping until I came up against the bedroom wall.

"Now you've done it," he said in that passionless voice.

As I watched, yellow mist began to stream out of the opening in his chest. It slid over his ribs and down to the sheet under him, and from there down to the floor, like the mist from dry ice in water.

I looked at Mosely's face and saw the light go out of his eyes. He was gone.

A wind began blowing outside, whistling under the doors and banging the shutters. I glanced out the window on the far side of the room and saw the fog begin to swirl and tear apart. Suddenly there came a crash from the front room. I pulled myself up and opened the bedroom door. A freezing wind hit me in the face with the force of a gale, tearing the door from my grip and swirling into the room. I saw Martha Mosely get up from the sofa and struggle to close the front door against the rage of the wind.

The bedroom window shattered under the sudden impact and now the wind howled through the house.

The yellow mist from Mosely's chest cavity caught the wind and rode it out the window, slipping along the floor and up the wall and over the sill in streaks that gleamed in the growing moonlight.

Then the mist was gone and the fog was gone and I was alone in the room with the wind and Joe Mosely's empty shell.

And then Mosely's shell began to crumble, caving in on itself piece by piece, almost in slow motion like a miniature special-effects building in a Japanese monster movie, fracturing into countless tiny pieces which in turn disintegrated into a gray, dust-like powder. This too was caught by the wind and carried out into the night.

Joe Mosely was gone, leaving behind not so much as a depression in the bedcovers.

The front door finally closed behind Martha's efforts and I heard the bolt slide home. She walked up to the bedroom door but did not step inside.

"Joe's gone, isn't he?" she said in a low voice.

I couldn't speak. I opened my mouth but no words would come out. I simply nodded as I stood there trembling.

She stepped into the room then and looked at the bed. She looked at the broken window, then at me. With a sigh she sat on the edge of the bed and ran her hand over the spot where her husband had lain.

My home phone rang at eight o'clock the next morning. It didn't disturb my sleep. I had been awake all night. Part of the time I'd spent lying rigid in bed; most had been spent here in the kitchen with all the lights on, waiting for the sun.

It was an awful wait. When I wasn't reliving the scene in the Mosely bedroom I was hearing voices. If it wasn't Joe Mosely telling me that Doc Johnson had put something in his wound, it was Doc Johnson himself talking about making life-and-death decisions, talking about triage with literary references.

I hadn't told Jessie a thing about it. She'd think I was ready for a straitjacket. And if by some chance she *did* believe it, she'd want to pack up and get out of town. But where to? There was the baby to think about.

I had spent the time since dawn going over my options. And when the phone rang, I had no doubt as to who was calling.

"I understand Joe Mosely is gone," Doc Johnson said without preamble.

I said, "Yes."

. . . a hollow man . . .

"Any idea where?"

"Out the window," I said. My voice sounded half dead to me. "Beyond that, I don't know."

. . . calling the police is not my way of handling the likes of Joe Mosely . . .

"Seen anything lately worth writing to any of the medical journals about?"

"Not a thing."

. . . the diseased limb has to be lopped off and discarded . . .

"Just another day in Greystone Bay," Doc Johnson said.

"Oh, I hope not." I could not hide the tremor in my voice.

. . . sometimes triage has to be of a more active sort where radical decisions must be made . . .

He chuckled. "Charles, my boy, I think you'll do all right here. As a matter of fact, I'd like to refer a couple of patients to your office today. They've got complicated problems that require more attention than I can give them at this time. I'll assure them that they can trust you implicitly. Can you take them on?"

I paused. Even though my mind was made up, I took a deep breath and held it, waiting for some argument to come out of the blue and swing me the other way. Finally, I could hold my breath no longer.

"Yes," I said. "Thank you."

"Charles, I think you're going to do just fine in Greystone Bay!"

Introduction

Alan Ryan came up to me during the Friday night autograph party at the 1985 World Fantasy Convention in Tucson and said, "Doctors and Halloween: See if you can write a story around that." I took up the challenge and flipped through my notebook when I got back to Jersey. I came across an idea I had scribbled down at the height of the Atlanta child murders mystery: "Child killer faced with ghosts of his victims." I hadn't been able to develop that idea into anything worthwhile but now I saw it as "Incompetent doctor faced by ghosts of all the victims of his negligence." Nah. Same problem as the original: no second level.

Then I cross-pollinated the first and second premises and the story wrote itself.

I knew from the start that "Buckets" would be extremely unpopular with a fair number, perhaps even a majority, of readers. I won't kid you: That made me hesitate. But I decided to go ahead anyway. Besides offering the reader our best, and staying true to our craft, writers have few obligations. So when an opportunity arises to provide a voice for those who have none, we shouldn't turn away.

As you will see, "Buckets" leaves no room for a neutral stance. But given the premise, how else could it be written?

BUCKETS

"**M**y, aren't you an early bird!"

Dr. Edward Cantrell looked down at the doe-eyed child in the five-and-dime Princess Leia costume on his front doorstep and tried to guess her age. A beautiful child of about seven or eight, with flaxen hair and scrawny little shoulders drawn up as if she were afraid of him, as if he might bite her. It occurred to him that today was Wednesday and it was not yet noon. Why wasn't she in school? Never mind. It was Halloween and it was none of his business why she was getting a jump on the rest of the kids in the trick-or-treat routine.

"Are you looking for a treat?" he asked her.

She nodded slowly, shyly.

"Okay! You got it!" He went to the bowl behind him on the hall table and picked out a big Snickers. Then he added a dime to the package. It had become a Halloween tradition over the years that Dr. Cantrell's place was where you got dimes when you trick-or-treated.

He thrust his hand through the open space where the screen used to be. He liked to remove the storm door screen on

Halloween; it saved him the inconvenience of repeatedly opening the door against the kids pressing against it for their treats; and besides, he worried about one of the little ones being pushed backward off the front steps. A lawsuit could easily follow something like that.

The little girl lifted her silver bucket.

He took a closer look. No, not silver — shiny stainless steel, reflecting the dull gray overcast sky. It reminded him of something, but he couldn't place it at the moment. Strange sort of thing to be collecting Halloween treats in. Probably some new fad. Whatever became of the old pillowcase or the shopping bag, or even the plastic jack-o'-lantern?

He poised his hand over the bucket, then let the candy bar and dime drop. They landed with a soft *squish*.

Not exactly the sound he had expected. He leaned forward to see what else was in the bucket but the child had swung around and was making her way down the steps.

Out on the sidewalk, some hundred feet away along the maple-lined driveway, two older children waited for her. A stainless-steel bucket dangled from each of their hands.

Cantrell shivered as he closed the front door. There was a new chill in the air. Maybe he should put on a sweater. But what color? He checked himself over in the hall mirror. Not bad for a guy looking fifty-two in the eye. That was Erica's doing. Trading in the old wife for a new model twenty years younger had had a rejuvenating effect on him. Also, it made him work at staying young-looking — like three trips a week to the Short Hills Nautilus Club and watching his diet. He decided to forgo the sweater for now.

He almost made it back to his recliner and the unfinished New York *Times* when the front bell rang again. Sighing resignedly, he turned and went back to the front door. He didn't mind tending to the trick-or-treaters, but he wished Erica were here to share door duty. Why did she have to pick today for her monthly spending spree in Manhattan? He knew she loved Bloomingdale's—in fact, she had once told him that after she died she wanted her ashes placed in an urn in the lingerie department there—but she could have waited until tomorrow.

It was two boys this time, both about eleven, both made up like punkers with orange and green spiked hair, ripped clothes, and crude tattoos, obviously done with a Bic instead of a real tattooer's pen. They stood restlessly in the chill breeze, shifting from one foot to the other, looking up and down the block, stainless-steel buckets in hand.

He threw up his hands. "Whoa! Tough guys, eh? I'd better not mess around with the likes of—!"

One of the boys glanced at him briefly, and in his eyes Cantrell caught a flash of such rage and hatred—not just for him, but for the whole world—that his voice dried away to a whisper. And then the look was gone as if it had never been and the boy was just another kid again. He hastily grabbed a pair of Three Musketeers and two dimes, leaned through the opening in the door, and dropped one of each into their buckets.

The one on the right went *squish* and the one on the left went *plop*.

He managed to catch just a glimpse of the bottom of the bucket on the right as the kid turned. He couldn't tell what was in there, but it was red.

He was glad to see them go. *Surly pair*, he thought. Not a word out of either of them. And what was in the bottom of that bucket? Didn't look like any candy he knew, and he considered himself an expert on candy. He patted the belly that he had been trying to flatten for months. More than an expert—an *aficionado* of candy.

Further speculation was forestalled by a call from Monroe Community Hospital. One of his postpartum patients needed a laxative. He okayed a couple of ounces of milk of mag. Then the nurse double-checked his pre-op orders on the hysterecto-my tomorrow.

He managed to suffer through it all with dignity. It was Wednesday and he always took Wednesdays off. Jeff Sewell was supposed to be taking his calls today, but all the floors at the hospital had the Cantrell home phone number and they habitually tried here first before they went hunting for whoever was covering him.

He was used to it. He had learned ages ago that there was no such thing as a day off in Ob-Gyn.

The bell rang again, and for half a second Cantrell found himself hesitant to answer it. He shrugged off the reluctance and pulled open the door.

Two mothers and two children. He sucked in his gut when he recognized the mothers as longtime patients.

This is more like it!

"Hi, Dr. Cantrell!" the red-haired woman said with a big smile. She put a hand atop the red-haired child's head. "You remember Shana, don't you? You delivered her five years ago next month."

"I remember *you*, Gloria," he said, noting her flash of pleasure at having her first name remembered. He never forgot a face. "But Shana here looks a little bit different from when I last saw her."

As both women laughed, he scanned his mind for the other's name. Then it came to him:

"Yours looks a little bigger, too, Diane."

"She sure does. What do you say to Dr. Cantrell, Susan?"

The child mumbled something that sounded like "Ricky Meat" and held up an orange plastic jack-o'-lantern with a black plastic strap.

"That's what I like to see!" he said. "A real Halloween treat holder. Better than those stainless-steel buckets the other kids have been carrying!"

Gloria and Diane looked at each other. "Stainless-steel buckets?"

"Can you believe it?" he said as he got the two little girls each a Milky Way and a dime. "My first three Halloween customers this morning carried steel buckets for their treats. Never seen anything like it."

"Neither have we," Diane said.

"You haven't? You should have passed a couple of boys out on the street."

"No. We're the only ones around."

Strange. But maybe they had cut back to the street through the trees as this group entered the driveway.

He dropped identical candy and coins into the identical jack-o'-lanterns and heard them strike the other treats with a reassuring rustle.

He watched the retreating forms of the two young mothers and their two happy kids until they were out of sight. *This is the way Halloween should be*, he thought. Much better than strange hostile kids with metal buckets.

And just as he completed the thought, he saw three small white-sheeted forms of indeterminate age and sex round the hedge and head up the driveway. Each had a shiny metal bucket in hand.

He wished Erica were here.

He got the candy bars and coins and waited at the door for them. He had decided that before he parted with the goodies he was going to find out who these kids were and what they had in their little buckets. Fair was fair.

The trio climbed to the top step of the stoop and stood there waiting, silently watching him through the eye holes of their sheets.

Their silence got under his skin.

Doesn't anybody say "Trick or treat?" anymore?

"Well, what have we here?" he said with all the joviality he could muster. "Three little ghosts! The Ghostly Trio!"

One of them—he couldn't tell which—said, "Yes."

"Good! I like ghosts on Halloween! You want a treat?"

They nodded as one.

"Okay! But first you're gonna have to earn it! Show me what you've got in those buckets and I'll give you each a dime and a box of Milk Duds! How's that for a deal?"

The kids looked at each other. Some wordless communication seemed to pass between them, then they turned and started back down the steps.

"Hey, kids! Hey, wait!" he said quickly, forcing a laugh. "I was only kidding! You don't have to show me anything. Here! Just take the candy."

They paused on the second step, obviously confused.

Ever so gently, he coaxed them back. "C'mon, kids. I'm just curious about those buckets, is all. I've been seeing them all day and I've been wondering where they came from. But if I frightened you, well, hey, I'll ask somebody else later on." He held up the candy and the coins and extended his hand through the door. "Here you go."

One little ghost stepped forward but raised an open hand—a little girl's hand—instead of a bucket.

He could not bear to be denied any longer. He pushed open the storm door and stepped out, looming over the child, craning his neck to see into that damn little bucket. The child squealed in fright and turned away, crouching over the bucket as if to protect it from him.

What are they trying to hide? What's the matter with them? And what's the matter with me?

Really. Who *cared* what was in those buckets?

He cared. It was becoming an obsession with him. He'd go crazy if he didn't find out.

Hoping nobody was watching—nobody who'd think he was a child molester—he grabbed the little ghost by the shoulders and twisted her toward him. She couldn't hide the bucket from him now. In the clear light of day he got a good look into it.

Blood.

Blood with some floating bits of tissue and membrane lay maybe an inch and a half deep in the bottom.

Startled and sickened, he could only stand there and stare at the red, swirling liquid. As the child tried to pull the bucket away from him, it tipped, spilling its contents over the front of her white sheet. She screamed—more in dismay than terror.

"Let her go!" said a little boy's voice from beside him. Cantrell turned to see one of the other ghosts hurling the contents of its bucket at him. As if in slow motion, he saw the sheet of red liquid and debris float toward him through the air, spreading as it neared. The warm spray splattered him up and down and he reeled back in revulsion.

By the time he had wiped his eyes clear, the kids were halfway down the driveway. He wanted to chase after them, but he had to get out of these bloody clothes first. He'd be taken for a homicidal maniac if someone saw him running after three little kids looking like this.

Arms akimbo, he hurried to the utility room and threw his shirt into the sink. *Why?* his mind cried as he tried to remember whether hot or cold water set a stain. He tried cold and began rubbing at the blood in the blue oxford cloth.

He scrubbed hard and fast to offset the shaking of his hands. What a horrible thing for anyone to do, but especially *children!* Questions tumbled over each other in confusion: What could be going through their sick little minds? And where had they gotten the blood?

But most of all, *Why me?*

Slowly the red color began to thin and run, but the bits of tissue clung. He looked at them more closely. *Damn if that doesn't look like . . .*

Recognition triggered an epiphany. He suddenly understood everything.

He now knew who those children were—or at least who had put them up to it—and he understood why. He sighed with relief as anger flooded through him like a cleansing flame. He much preferred being angry to being afraid.

He dried his arms with a paper towel and went to call the cops.

"Right-to-lifers, Joe! Has to be them!"

Sergeant Joe Morelli scratched his head. "You sure, Doc?"

Cantrell had known the Morelli family since Joe's days as a security guard at the Mall, waiting for a spot to open up on the Monroe police force. He had delivered all three of Joe's kids.

"Who else could it be? Those little stainless-steel buckets they carry—the ones I told you about—they're the same kind we use in D and C's, and get this: We used to use them in abortions. The scrapings from the uterus slide down through a weighted speculum into one of those buckets."

And it was those bloody scrapings that had been splattered all over him.

"But why you, Doc? I know you do abortions now and then—all you guys do—but you're not an abortionist per se, if you know what I'm saying."

Cantrell nodded, not mentioning Sandy. He knew the subject of Joe's youngest daughter's pregnancy two years ago was still a touchy subject. She had only been fifteen but he had taken care of everything for Joe with the utmost discretion. He now had a devoted friend on the police force.

A thought suddenly flashed through Cantrell's mind:

They must know about the women's center! But how could they?

It was due to open tomorrow, the first of the month. He had been so careful to avoid any overt connection with it, situating it downtown and going so far as to set it up through a corporate front. Abortions might be legal, but it still didn't sit well with a lot of people to know that their neighbor ran an abortion mill.

Maybe that was it. Maybe a bunch of sicko right-to-lifers had connected him with the new center.

"What gets me," Joe was saying, "is that if this is real abortion material like you say, where'd they get it?"

"I wish I knew." The question had plagued him since he had called the police.

"Well, don't you worry, Doc," Joe said, slipping his hat over his thinning hair. "Whatever's going on, it's gonna stop. I'll cruise the neighborhood. If I see any kids, or even adults with any of these buckets, I'll ID them and find out what's up."

"Thanks, Joe," he said, meaning it. It was comforting to know a cop was looking out for him. "I appreciate that. I'd especially like to get this ugly business cleared up before the wife and I get home from dinner tonight."

"I don't blame you," he said, shaking his head. "I know I wouldn't want Marie to see any buckets of blood."

The trick-or-treaters swelled in numbers as the afternoon progressed. They flowed to the door in motley hordes of all shapes, sizes, and colors. A steady stream of Spocks, Skywalkers, Vaders, Indiana Joneses, Madonnas, Mötley Crües, Twisted Sisters, and even a few ghosts, goblins, and witches.

And always among them were one or two kids with steel buckets.

Cantrell bit his lip and repressed his anger when he saw them. He said nothing, did not try to look into their buckets, gave no sign that their presence meant anything to him, pretended they were no different from the other kids as he dropped candies and coins into the steel buckets among the paper sacks and pillowcases and jack-o'-lanterns, all the while praying that Morelli would catch one of the little bastards crossing the street and find out who was behind this bullshit.

He saw the patrol car pull into the drive around 4:00. Morelli finally must have nailed one of them! *About time!* He had to leave for the women's center soon and wanted this thing settled and done with.

"No luck, Doc," Joe said, rolling down his window. "You must have scared them off."

"Are you crazy?" His anger exploded as he trotted down the walk to the driveway. "They've been through here all afternoon!"

"Hey, take it easy, Doc. If they're around, they must be hiding those buckets when they're on the street, because I've been by here about fifty times and I haven't seen one steel bucket."

Cantrell reined in his anger. It would do no good to alienate Joe. He wanted the police force on his side.

"Sorry. It's just that this is very upsetting."

"I can imagine. Look, Doc. Why don't I do this: Why don't I just park the car right out at the curb and watch the kids as they come in. Maybe I'll catch one in the act. At the very least, it might keep them away."

"I appreciate that, Joe, but it won't be necessary. I'm going out in a few minutes and won't be back until much later tonight. However, I do wish you'd keep an eye on the place—vandals, you know."

"Sure thing, Doc. No problem."

Cantrell watched the police car pull out of the driveway, then he set the house alarm and hurried to the garage to make his getaway before the doorbell rang again.

The Midtown
Women's Medical Center

Cantrell savored the effect of the westering sun glinting off the thick brass letters over the entrance as he walked by. Red letters on a white placard proclaimed "Grand Opening Tomorrow" from the front door. He stepped around the side of the building into the alley, unlocked the private entrance, and stepped inside.

Dark, quiet, deserted. *Damn!* He had hoped to catch the

contractor for one last check of the trim. He wanted everything perfect for the opening.

He flipped on the lights and checked his watch. Erica would be meeting him here in about an hour, then they would pick up the Klines and have drinks and dinner at the club. He had just enough time for a quick inspection tour.

So clean, he thought as he walked through the waiting room—the floors shiny and unscuffed, the carpet pile unmatted, the wall surfaces unmarred by chips or finger smudges. Even the air smelled new.

This center—*his* center—had been in the planning stages for three years. Countless hours of meetings with lawyers, bankers, planning boards, architects, and contractors had gone into it. But at last it was ready to go. He planned to work here himself in the beginning, just to keep overhead down, but once the operation got rolling, he'd hire other doctors and have them do the work while he ran the show from a distance.

He stepped into Procedure Room One and looked over the equipment. Dominating the room was the Rappaport 206, a state-of-the-art procedure table with thigh and calf supports on the stirrups, three breakaway sections, and fully motorized tilts in all planes—Trendelenburg, reverse Trendelenburg, left and right lateral.

Close by, the Zarick suction extractor—the most efficient abortion device on the market—hung gleaming on its chrome stand. He pressed the "on" button to check the power but nothing happened.

"It won't work tonight," said a child's voice behind him, making him almost scream with fright.

He spun around. Fifteen or twenty kids stood there staring at him. Most were costumed, and they all carried those goddamn steel buckets.

"All right!" he said. "This does it! I've had just about enough! I'm getting the police!"

He turned to reach for the phone but stopped after one step. More kids were coming in from the hall. They streamed in slowly and silently, their eyes fixed on him, piercing him. They filled the room, occupying every square foot except for the small circle of space they left around him and the equipment. And behind them he could see more, filling the hall and the waiting room beyond. A sea of faces, all staring at him.

He was frightened now. They were just kids, but there were so damn many of them! A few looked fifteen or so, and one looked to be in her early twenties, but by far most of them appeared to be twelve and under. Some were even toddlers! What sort of sick mind would involve such tiny children in this?

And how did they get in? All the doors were locked.

"Get out of here," he said, forcing his voice into calm, measured tones.

They said nothing, merely continued to stare back at him.

"All right, then. If you won't leave, *I* will! And when I return—" He tried to push by a five-year-old girl in a gypsy costume. Without warning she jabbed her open hand into his abdomen with stunning force, driving him back against the table.

"Who are you?" This time his voice was less calm, his tones less measured.

"You mean you don't recognize us?" a mocking voice said from the crowd.

"I've never seen any of you before today."

"Not true," said another voice. "After our fathers, you're the second most important man in our lives."

This was insane! "I don't know *any* of you!"

"You should." Another voice—were they trying to confuse him by talking from different spots in the room?

"*Why?*"

"Because you killed us."

The absurdity of the statement made him laugh. He straightened from the table and stepped forward. "Okay. That's it. This isn't the least bit funny."

A little boy shoved him back, roughly, violently. His strength was hideous.

"M-my wife will be here s-soon." He was ashamed of the stammer in his voice, but he couldn't help it. "She'll call the police."

"Sergeant Morelli, perhaps?" This voice was more mature than the others—more womanly. He found her and looked her in the eye. She was the tall one in her early twenties, dressed in a sweater and skirt. He had a sudden crazy thought that maybe she was a young teacher and these were her students on a class trip. But these kids looked like they spanned all grades from pre-school to junior high.

"Who are you?"

"I don't have a name," she said, facing him squarely. "Very few of us do. But this one does." She indicated a little girl at her side, a toddler made up like a hobo in raggedy clothes with burnt cork rubbed on her face for a beard. An Emmett Kelly dwarf. "Here, Laura," she said to the child as she urged her forward. "Show Dr. Cantrell what you looked like last time he saw you."

Laura stepped up to him. Behind the makeup he could see that she was a beautiful child with short dark hair, a pudgy face, and big brown eyes. She held her bucket out to him.

"She was eleven weeks old," the woman said, "three inches long, and weighed fourteen grams when you ripped her from her mother's uterus. She was no match for you and your suction tube."

Blood and tissue swirled in the bottom of her bucket.

"You don't expect me to buy this, do you?"

"I don't care what you buy, Doctor. But this is Sandra Morelli's child—or at least what her child would look like now if she'd been allowed to be born. But she wasn't born. Her mother had names all picked out—Adam for a boy, Laura for a girl—but her grandfather bullied her mother into an abortion and you were oh-so-willing to see that there were no problems along the way."

"This is absurd!" he said.

"Really?" the woman said. "Then go ahead and call Sergeant Morelli. Maybe he'd like to drive down and meet his granddaughter. The one you killed."

"I killed no one!" he shouted. *"No one!* Abortion has been legal since 1974! Absolutely legal! And besides—she wasn't really alive!"

What's the matter with me? he asked himself. *I'm talking to them as if I believe them!*

"Oh, yes," the woman said. "I forgot. Some political appointees decided that we weren't people and that was that. Pretty much like what happened to East European Jews back in World War II. We're not even afforded the grace of being called embryos or fetuses. We're known as 'products of conception.' What a neat, dehumanizing little phrase. So much easier to scrape the 'products of conception' into a bucket than a person."

"I've had just about enough of this!" he said.

"So?" a young belligerent voice said. "What're y'gonna do?"

He knew he was going to do nothing. He didn't want to have another primary-grade kid shove him back against the table again. No kid that size should be that strong. It wasn't natural.

"You can't hold me responsible!" he said. "They came to me, asking for help. They were pregnant and they didn't want to be. My God! *I* didn't make them pregnant!"

Another voice: "No, but you sure gave them a convenient solution!"

"So blame your mothers! *They're* the ones who spread their legs and didn't want to take responsibility for it! How about *them?*"

"They are not absolved," the woman said. "They shirked their responsibilities to us, but the vast majority of them are each responsible for only one of us. You, Dr. Cantrell, are responsible for *all* of us. Most of them were scared teenagers, like Laura's mother, who were bullied and badgered into 'terminating' us. Others were too afraid of what their parents would say so they snuck off to women's medical centers like this and lied about their age and put us out of their misery."

"Not all of them, sweetheart!" he said. He was beginning to feel he was on firmer ground now. "Many a time I've done three or four on the same woman! Don't tell me *they* were poor, scared teenagers. Abortion was their idea of birth control!"

"We know," a number of voices chorused, and something in their tone made him shiver. "We'll see them later."

"The point is," the woman said, "that you were always there, always ready with a gentle smile, a helpful hand, an easy solution, a simple way to get them off the hook by getting rid of us. And a bill, of course."

"If it hadn't been me, it would have been someone else!"

"You can't dilute your own blame. Or your own responsibility," said a voice from behind his chair. "Plenty of doctors refuse to do abortions."

"If you were one of those," said another from his left, "we wouldn't be here tonight."

"The *law* lets me do it. The Supreme Court. So don't blame me. Blame those Supreme Court justices."

"That's politics. We don't care about politics."

"But I believe in a woman's right to control her own life, to make decisions about her own body!"

"We don't care *what* you believe. Do you think the beliefs of a terrorist matter to the victims of his bombs? Don't you understand? This is *personal*!"

A little girl's voice said, "I could have been adopted, you

know. I would've made someone a good kid. But I never had the chance!"

They all began shouting at once, about never getting Christmas gifts or birthday presents or hugs or tucked in at night or playing with matches or playing catch or playing house or even playing doctor—

It seemed to go on endlessly. Finally the woman held up her bucket. "All their possibilities ended in here."

"Wait a goddamn minute!" he said. He had just discovered a significant flaw in their little show. "Only a few of them ended up in buckets! If you were up on your facts, you'd know that no one uses those old D and C buckets for abortions anymore." He pointed to the glass trap on the Zarick suction extractor. "This is where the products of conception wind up."

The woman stepped forward with her bucket. "They carry this in honor of me. I have the dubious distinction of being your first victim."

"You're not *my* victims!" he shouted. "The law—"

She spat in his face. Shocked and humiliated, Cantrell wiped away the saliva with his shirt sleeve and pressed himself back against the table. The rage in her face was utterly terrifying.

"The *law?*" she hissed. "Don't speak of legalities to me! Look at me! I'd be twenty-two now and this is how I'd look if you hadn't murdered me. Do a little subtraction, Doctor: 1974 was a lot less than twenty-two years ago. I'm Ellen Benedict's daughter—or at least I would have been if you hadn't agreed to do that D and C on her when she couldn't find a way to explain her pregnancy to her impotent husband!"

Ellen Benedict! God! How did they know about Ellen Benedict? Even *he* had forgotten about her!

The woman stepped forward and grabbed his wrist. He was helpless against her strength as she pressed his hand over her left breast. He might have found the softness beneath her sweater exciting under different circumstances, but now it elicited only dread.

"Feel my heart beating? It was beating when your curette ripped me to pieces. I was only four weeks old. And I'm not the only one here you killed before 1974—I was just your first. So you can't get off the hook by naming the Supreme Court as an accomplice. And even if we allowed you that cop-out, other things you've done since '74 are utterly abominable!" She looked around and pointed into the crowd. "There's one! Come here, honey, and show your bucket to the doctor."

A five- or six-year-old boy came forward. He had blond bangs and the biggest, saddest blue eyes the doctor had ever seen. The boy held out his bucket.

Cantrell covered his face with his hands. "I don't want to see!"

Suddenly he felt his hands yanked downward with numbing force and found the woman's face scant inches from his own.

"*Look*, damn you! You've seen it before!"

He looked into the upheld bucket. A fully formed male fetus lay curled in the blood, its blue eyes open, its head turned at an unnatural angle.

"This is Rachel Walraven's baby as you last saw him."

The Walraven baby! Oh, God, not that one! How could they know?

"What you see is how he'd look now if you hadn't broken his neck after the abortifacient you gave his mother made her uterus dump him out."

"He couldn't have survived!" he shouted. He could hear the hysteria edging into his voice. "He was pre-viable! Too immature to survive! The best neonatal ICU in the world couldn't have saved him!"

"Then why'd you break my neck?" the little boy asked.

Cantrell could only sob—a single harsh sound that seemed to rip itself from the tissues inside his chest and burst free into the air. What could he say? How could he tell them that he had miscalculated the length of gestation and that no one had been more shocked than he at the size of the infant that had dropped into his gloved hands. And then it had opened its eyes and stared at him and my God it seemed to be trying to breathe! He'd done late terminations before where the fetus had squirmed around awhile in the bucket before finally dying, but this one—!

Christ! he remembered thinking, *what if the damn thing lets out a cry?* He'd get sued by the patient and be the laughing stock of the staff. Poor Ed Cantrell—can't tell the difference between an abortion and a delivery! He'd look like a jerk!

So he did the only thing he could do. He gave its neck a sharp twist as he lowered it into the bucket. The neck didn't even crack when he broke it.

"Why have you come to me?" he said.

"Answer us first," a child's voice said. "Why do you do it? You don't need the money. Why do you kill us?"

"I told you! I believe in every woman's right to—"

They began to boo him, drowning him out. Then the boos changed to a chant: *"Why? Why? Why? Why?"*

"Stop that! Listen to me! I told you why!"

But still they chanted, sounding like a crowd at a football game: *"Why? Why? Why? Why?"*

Finally he could stand no more. He raised his fists and screamed. "All right! Because I can! Is that what you want to hear? I do it because I *can!*"

The room was suddenly dead silent.

The answer startled him. He had never asked himself *why* before. "Because I can," he said softly.

"Yes," the woman said with equal softness. "The ultimate power."

He suddenly felt very old, very tired. "What do you want of me?"

No one answered.

"Why have you come?"

They all spoke as one: "Because today, this Halloween, this night . . . *we* can."

"And we don't want this place to open," the woman said.

So that was it. They wanted to kill the women's center before it got started—*abort* it, so to speak. He almost smiled at the pun. He looked at their faces, their staring eyes. *They mean business*, he thought. And he knew they wouldn't take no for an answer.

Well, this was no time to stand on principle. Promise them anything, then get the hell out of here to safety.

"Okay," he said, in what he hoped was a meek voice. "You've convinced me. I'll turn this into a general medical center. No abortions. Just family practice for the community."

They watched him silently. Finally a voice said, "He's lying."

The woman nodded. "I know." She turned to the children. "Do it," she said.

Pure chaos erupted as the children went wild. They were like a berserk mob, surging in all directions. But silent. So silent.

Cantrell felt himself shoved aside as the children tore into the procedure table and the Zarick extractor. The table was ripped from the floor and all its upholstery shredded. Its sections were torn free and hurled against the walls with such force that they punctured through the plasterboard.

The rage in the children's eyes seemed to leak out into the room, filling it, thickening the air like an onrushing storm, making his skin ripple with fear at its ferocity.

As he saw the Zarick start to topple, he forced himself forward to try to save it but was casually slammed against the wall with stunning force. In a semi-daze, he watched the Zarick raised into the air; he ducked flying glass as it was slammed onto the floor, not just once, but over and over until it was nothing more than a twisted wreck of wire, plastic hose, and ruptured circuitry.

And from down the hall he could hear similar carnage in the other procedure rooms. Finally the noise stopped and the room was packed with children again.

He began to weep. He hated himself for it, but he couldn't help it. He just broke down and cried in front of them. He was frightened. And all the money, all the plans . . . destroyed.

He pulled himself together and stood up straight. He would rebuild. All this destruction was covered by insurance. He would blame it on vandalism, collect his money, and have the place brand-new inside of a month. These vicious little bastards weren't going to stop him.

But he couldn't let them know that.

"Get out, all of you," he said softly. "You've had your fun. You've ruined me. Now leave me alone."

"We'll leave you alone," said the woman who would have been Ellen Benedict's child. "But not yet."

Suddenly they began to empty their buckets on him, hurling the contents at him in a continuous wave, turning the air red with flying blood and tissue, engulfing him from all sides, choking him, clogging his mouth and nostrils.

And then they reached for him . . .

Erica knocked on the front door of the center for the third time and still got no answer.

Now where can he be? she thought as she walked around to the private entrance. She tried the door and found it unlocked. She pushed in but stopped on the threshold.

The waiting room was lit and looked normal enough.

"Ed?" she called, but he didn't answer. Odd. His car was out front. She was supposed to meet him here at five. She had taken a cab from the house—after all, she didn't want Ginger dropping her off here; there would be too many questions.

This was beginning to make her uneasy.

She glanced down the hallway. It was dark and quiet.

Almost quiet.

She heard tiny little scraping noises, tiny movements, so soft that she would have missed them if there had been any other sound in the building. The sounds seemed to come from the first procedure room. She stepped up to the door and listened to the dark. Yes, they were definitely coming from in there.

She flipped on the light . . . and felt her knees buckle.

The room was red—the walls, the ceiling, the remnants of the shattered fixtures, all dripping with red. The clots and the coppery odor that saturated the air left no doubt in Erica's reeling mind that she was looking at blood. But on the floor—the blood-puddled linoleum was littered with countless shiny, silvery buckets. The little rustling sounds were coming from them. She saw something that looked like hair in a nearby bucket and took a staggering step over to see what was inside.

It was Edward's head, floating in a pool of blood, his eyes wide and mad, looking at her. She wanted to scream but the air clogged in her throat as she saw Ed's lips begin to move. They were forming words but there was no sound, for there were no lungs to push air through his larynx. Yet still his lips kept moving in what seemed to be silent pleas. But pleas for what?

And then he opened his mouth wide and screamed— silently.

Introduction

"Traps" was also a finalist for the first Bram Stoker Awards.

Alan Rogers called me up one day in 1986 and asked if I had a story I could send him for *Night Cry*. I didn't have anything going at the time, but told him I'd keep him in mind.

It was fall then, and I started hearing these little scratchings on the far side of my bedroom ceiling . . .

Most of "Traps" is true.

Except the ending.

TRAPS

Skippy Super Chunk peanut butter was the best bait. Hank smeared it on the pedals of the four traps he'd bought. They were Victors. Something about the way the big red V in their logo formed itself around the shape of a mouse's head gave him a feeling that they knew what they were about.

Not that he took any pleasure in killing mice. He may not have had the bumper sticker, but he most certainly did brake for animals. He didn't like killing anything. Even ants. Live and let live was fine with him, but he drew the line at the threshold of his house. They could live long and prosper out *there*, he would live in *here*. When they came inside, it was war.

He'd had a few in the basement of their last house and caught them all with Skippy-baited Victors. But he always felt guilty when he found one of the little things dead in the trap, so frail and harmless-looking with its white underbelly and little pink feet and tail. The eyes were always the worst—shiny black and guileless, wide open and looking at him, almost saying, *Why? I don't eat much.*

Hank knew he could be a real sentimental jerk at times.

He consoled himself with the knowledge that the mouse didn't feel any pain in the trap. Better than those warfarin poisons where they crawl off to their nest and slowly bleed to death. With a trap, the instant the nibbling mouse disturbs the baited pedal, *wham!* the bow snaps down and breaks its neck. It's on its way to mouse heaven before it knows what hit it.

Hank was doing this on the sly. Gloria wouldn't be able to sleep a wink if she thought there were mice overhead in the ceiling. And the twins, God, they'd want to catch them and make them pets and give them names. With the trip to Disney World just three days off, all they could talk about was Mickey and Minnie. They'd never forgive him for killing a mouse. Best to set the traps before they came home in the afternoon and dispose of the little carcasses in the morning after everyone was gone. Luckily, this was his slack season and he had some time at home to take care of it.

He wondered how the mice were getting in. He knew they were up there because he'd heard them last night. Something had awakened him at about 2:30 this morning—a noise, a bad dream, he didn't remember what—and as he was lying there spooned against Gloria he heard little claws scraping on the other side of the ceiling. It sounded like two or three of them under the insulation, clawing on the plasterboard, making themselves a winter home. He was ticked. This was a brand-new two-story colonial, just built, barely lived in for six months, and already they had uninvited guests. And in the attic no less.

Well, they were in a woodsy area and it was fall, the time of year when woodsy things start looking for winter quarters. He wished them all a safe and warm winter. But not in this house.

Before setting the traps, he fitted a bolt on the attic door. The house had one of those swing-down attic doors in the hall ceiling right outside their bedroom. It had a pull cord on this side and a folding ladder on the upper side. The twins had been fascinated with it since they moved in. The attic had always been off-limits to them, but you never knew. He had visions of one of them pulling the ladder down, climbing up there, and touching one of the traps. Instant broken finger. So he screwed a little sliding bolt in place to head off that trauma at the pass.

He took the four traps up to the attic and gingerly set the bows. As he stood on the ladder and spaced them out on the particleboard flooring around the opening, he noticed an odd odor. The few times he had been up here before, the attic had been filled with the clean smell of plywood and kiln-dried fir studs. Now there was a sour tint to the air. Vaguely unpleasant. Mouse B.O.? He didn't know. He just knew that something about it didn't set well with him.

He returned to the second floor, bolted the ceiling door closed, and hit the switch that turned off the attic light. Everything was set, and well before Gloria and the girls got home.

Kate crawled into Hank's lap as he leaned back in the recliner and watched the six o'clock *Eyewitness News*.

"Let's read Mickey's book," she said.

That was all Kim had to hear. She ran in from the kitchen like a shot.

"Me too! Me too!"

"Just three days and we'll be in Disney World!" Hank said.

So with his two pale blond seven-year-old darlings snuggled up against him, Hank opened up "Mickey's book" for the nightly ritual of the past two weeks. Not a book actually, just a brochure touting all the park's attractions. But it had become a Holy Book of sorts for the twins and they never tired of paging through it. This had to be their twentieth guided tour in as many days and their blue eyes were just as wide and full of wonder this time as the first.

Hank had come to see Disney World as a religious experience for seven-year-olds. Moslems had Mecca, Catholics had the Vatican, Japanese had Mount Fuji. Kids had Disney World on the East Coast and Disneyland on the West. Katie and Kim would start out on their first pilgrimage Thanksgiving morning.

He hugged them closer, absorbing their excitement. This was what life was all about. And he was determined to show them the best time of their lives. The sky was the limit. Any ride, any attraction, he didn't care how many times they wanted to go on it, he'd take them. Four days of fantasy at Mickey's Place with no real-world intrusions. No *Time*, no *Daily News*, no Eyewitness Special Reports, no background noise about wars or floods or muggings or bombings or mousetraps.

Nothing about mousetraps.

The snap of the trap woke Hank with a start. It was faint, muffled by the intervening plasterboard and insulation. He must have been subconsciously attuned to it, because he heard it and Gloria didn't.

He checked the clock—12:42—and tried to go back to sleep. Hopefully, that was the end of that.

He was just dozing back off when a second trap sprang with a muffled snap. Two of them. Sounded like he had a popular attic.

He didn't know when he got to sleep again. It took a while.

When Hank had the house to himself again the next morning, he pulled down the ceiling door and unfolded the ladder. Halfway up, he hesitated. This wasn't going to be pleasant. He knew when he stuck his head up through that opening he'd be eye-level with the attic floor—and with the dead mice. Those shiny reproachful little black eyes . . .

He took a deep breath and stepped up a couple of rungs.

Yes, two of the traps had been sprung and two sets of little black eyes were staring at him. Eyes and little else. At first he thought it was a trick of the light, of the angle, but as he hurried the rest of the way up, he saw it was true.

The heads were still in the traps, but the bodies were gone. Little bits of gray fur were scattered here and there, but that was it. Sort of gave him the creeps. Something had eaten the dead mice. Something bigger than a mouse. A discomforting thought.

And that odor was worse. He still couldn't identify it, but it was taking on a stomach-turning quality.

He decided it was time for an inspection tour of the grounds. His home was being invaded. He wanted to know how.

He found the little buggers' route of invasion on the south side of the house. He had two heating-cooling zones inside, with one unit in the basement and one in the attic. The compressor blowers for both were outside on the south side. The hoses to the upstairs unit ran up the side of the house to the attic through an aluminum leader.

That was how they were getting in.

There wasn't much space in the leader, but a mouse can squeeze through the tiniest opening. The rule of thumb—as all mouse experts knew—was that if it can get its head through, the rest of the body can follow. They were crawling into the leader, climbing up along the hoses inside, and following them into the attic. Simple.

But what had eaten them?

Up above the spot where the hoses ran through the siding, he noticed the triangular gable vent hanging free on its right side. Something had pulled it loose. As he watched, a squirrel poked its head out, looked at him, then scurried up onto the roof. It ran a few feet along the edge, jumped onto an overhanging oak branch, and disappeared into the reddening leaves.

Great! He was collecting a regular menagerie up there!

So much for the joys of a wooded lot. Gloria and he had chosen this semi-rural development because they liked the seclusion of an acre lot and the safety for the twins of living on a cul-de-sac. They both had grown up in New Jersey, and Toms River seemed like as good a place as any to raise kids. The house was expensive but they were a two-income family —she a teacher and he a CPA—so they went for it.

So far, theirs was the only house completed in this section, although two new foundations had just started. It would be nice to have neighbors. Until recently, the only other building in sight had been a deserted stone church of unknown age and long-forgotten denomination a few hundred yards south of here. The belfry of that old building had concerned him for a while—bats, you know. Very high rabies rate. But he spoke to the workmen when they bulldozed it down last week to start another cul-de-sac, and they told him they hadn't seen a single bat. Lots of animal droppings up there, but no bats.

He wondered: Would a squirrel eat a couple of dead mice? He thought they only ate nuts and berries. Maybe this one was a carnivore. Didn't matter. One way or another, something had to be done about that gable vent. He went to get the ladder.

He had everything taken care of by the time Gloria and the girls got home from their respective schools.

He'd tacked the gable vent back into place. He couldn't see how that squirrel had pulled it free, but it wouldn't get it out now. He also plugged up the upper and lower ends of the hose leader with an aeresol foam insulation he picked up at Rickel's. It occurred to him as he watched the mustard-colored gunk harden into a solid Styrofoam plug that he was cutting off the mouse exit as well as the mouse entryway. Hopefully, they were all out for the day. When they came back they'd be locked out and would have to go somewhere else. And even more hopefully, the squirrel hadn't left a friend in the attic behind the resecured gable vent.

Hank hardly slept at all that night. He kept listening for the snap of a trap, hoping he wouldn't hear it, yet waiting for it. Hours passed. The last time he remembered on the clock radio LED was 3:34. He must have fallen asleep after that.

Dawn was just starting to bleach out the night when the snap came. He came wide awake with the sound. The clock said 5:10. But the noise didn't end with that single snap. Whatever was up there began to thrash. He could hear the wooden base of the trap slapping against the attic flooring. Something bigger than a mouse, maybe a squirrel, was caught but still alive. He heard another snap and a squeal of pain. God, it was alive and hurt! His stomach turned.

Gloria rolled over, a silhouette in the growing light.

"Djoo hear somin?" she mumbled, still nine-tenths asleep.

Suddenly the attic went still.

"Nothing," he said. "Some animals fighting outside. Go back to sleep."

She did. He couldn't.

He approached the attic door with dread. He did *not* want to go up there. What if it was still alive? What if it was weak and paralyzed but still breathing? He'd have to kill it. He didn't know if he could do that. But he'd have to. It would be the only humane thing to do. How? Drown it? Smother it in a plastic bag? He began to sweat.

This was crazy. He was wimping out over a rodent in his attic. Enough already! He flipped the attic light switch, slipped the bolt, and pulled on the cord. The door angled down on its hinges.

But it didn't come down alone. Something came with it, flying right at his face.

He yelled like a fool in a funhouse and batted it away. Then he saw what it was: one of the mousetraps. At first glance it looked empty, but when he went to pick it up, he saw what was in it and almost tossed his cookies.

A fury little forearm, no longer than the last two bones on his pinky finger, was caught under the bow. It looked like it once might have been attached to a squirrel, but now it ended in a ragged bloody stump where it had been chewed off just below the shoulder.

Where the hell was the rest of it?

Visions of the squirrel chewing off its own arm swam around him until he remembered that auto-amputation only occurred with arresting traps, the kind that were chained down. Animals had been known to chew off a limb to escape those. The squirrel could have dragged the mousetrap with it.

But it hadn't.

Hank stood at the halfway point on those steps a long while. He finally decided he had wasted enough time. He clenched his teeth, told himself it was dead, and poked his head up. He started and almost fell off the stairs when he turned his head and found the squirrel's tail only two inches from his nose. It was caught in the bow of another trap—the second snap he had heard this morning. But there was no body attached.

This was getting a bit gory. He couldn't buy a squirrel chewing off its arm and then its tail. If anything, it would drag the tail trap after it until it got stuck someplace.

Nope. Something had eaten it. Something that didn't smell too good, because the attic was really beginning to stink.

He ducked down the ladder, grabbed the flashlight he always kept in the night table, then hurried back up to the attic. The light from the single bulb over the opening in the floor didn't reach very far. And even with daylight filtering in through the gable vents, there were lots of dark spots. He wanted the flashlight so he could get a good look along the inside of the eaves and into all the corners.

He searched carefully, and as he moved through the attic he

had a vague sense of another presence, a faint awareness of something else here, a tantalizing hint of furtive movement just out of his range of vision.

He shook it off. The closeness up here, the poor lighting, the missing animal carcasses—it had all set his imagination in motion. He gave the attic a thorough going over and found nothing but a few droppings. Big droppings. Bigger than something a mouse or squirrel would leave. Maybe possum-sized. Or raccoon-sized.

Was that the answer? A possum or a coon? He didn't know much about them, but he'd seen them around in the woods, and he knew every time he put turkey or chicken scraps in the garbage, something would get the lid off the trash can and tear the Hefty bag apart until every last piece of meat was gone. Raccoons were notorious for that. If they'd eat leftover chicken, why not dead mice and squirrels?

Made sense to him. But how was it getting in? A check of the gable vent he'd resecured yesterday gave him the answer. It had been pulled free again. Well, he'd fix that right now.

He went down to his workshop and got a hammer and some heavy nails. He felt pretty good as he pounded them into the edges of the vent, securing it from the *inside*. He knew what he was up against now and knew something that big would be easy to keep out. No raccoon or possum was going to pull this vent free again. And just to be sure, he went over to the north side and reinforced the gable vent there.

That was it. His house was his own again.

Wednesday night was chaotic. Excitement was at a fever pitch with the twins packing their own little suitcases full of stuffed animals and placing them by the front door so they'd be all set to go first thing in the morning.

Hank helped Gloria with the final packing of the big suitcases and they both fell into bed around midnight. He had little trouble getting off to sleep. There probably weren't any mice left, there weren't any squirrels, and he was sure no raccoon or possum was getting in tonight. So why stay awake listening?

The snap of a trap woke him around 3:30. No thrashing, no slapping, just the snap. Another mouse. A second trap went off ten minutes later. Then a third. *Damn!* He waited. The fourth and final trap sprang at 4:00 A.M.

Hank lay tense and rigid in bed and wondered what to do. Everybody would be up at first light, just a couple of hours from now, getting ready for the drive to Newark Airport. He couldn't leave those mouse carcasses up there all the time they were away—they'd rot and the whole house would be stinking by the time they got back.

He slipped out of bed and grabbed the flashlight.

"What's wrong?" Gloria asked, awakened by the movement.

"Just getting some water," he whispered.

She rolled over and he closed the bedroom door behind him. He didn't waste any time. He had to get up there and get rid of the dead mice before the girls woke up. These damn animals were really getting on his nerves. He pulled the door down and hurried up.

Hank stood on the ladder and gaped at the traps. All four had been sprung but lay empty on the flooring around him, the peanut butter untouched. No mice heads, no bits of fur. What could have tripped them without getting caught? It was almost like a game.

He looked around warily. He was standing in a narrow cone of light. The rest of the attic was dark. Very dark. The sense of something else up here with him was very strong now. So was the odor. It was worse than ever.

Imagination again.

He waved the flashlight around quickly but saw no

scurrying or lurking shapes along the eaves or in the corners. He made a second sweep, more slowly this time, more careful. He crouched and moved all along the edges, bumping his head now and again on a rafter, his flashlight held ahead of him like a gun.

Finally, when he was satisfied nothing of any size was lurking about, he checked the gable vent.

It had been yanked loose again. Some of the nails had pulled free, and those that hadn't had ripped through the vent's plastic edge.

He was uneasy now. No raccoon was strong enough to do this. He didn't know many *men* who could do it without a crowbar. This was getting out of hand. He suddenly wanted to get downstairs and bolt the attic door behind him. He'd call a professional exterminator as soon as they got back from Orlando.

He spun about, sure that something had moved behind him, but all was still, all was dark but for the pool of light under the bulb. Yet . . .

Quickly now, he headed back toward the light, toward the ladder, toward the empty traps. As he sidled along, he checked in the corners and along the eaves one last time, and wondered how and why the traps had been sprung. He saw nothing. Whatever it was, if it had come in, it wasn't here anymore. Maybe the attic light had scared it off. If that was the case, he'd leave the light on all night. All *week*.

His big mistake was looking for it along the floor.

It got him as he came around the heating unit. He saw a flash movement as it swung down from the rafters—big as a rottweiler, brown scruffy fur, a face that was all mouth with huge countless teeth, four clawed arms extended toward him as it held on to the beams above with still two more limbs—and that was all. It engulfed his head and lifted him off the floor in one sweeping motion. For a few spasming seconds his fingers tore futilely at its matted fur and his legs kicked and writhed silently in the air. As life and consciousness fled that foul smothering unbearable agony, he sensed the bottomless pit of its hunger and thought helplessly of the open attic door, of the ladder going down, and of Gloria and the twins sleeping below.

Introduction

I finally broke into *The Magazine of Fantasy & Science Fiction* with this story. I had been trying sporadically for years to no avail. Ed Ferman would say nice things about the stories but he never took one until "Muscles."

I haven't the faintest idea where this story or the protagonist came from, why I chose Times Square for a setting or 1963 as the period. But it all fell together effortlessly.

The Times Square here is that of my adolescence, a fascinating place for a kid from Jersey. But that was before its naughty sleaze evolved into the grim, glowering sleaze of today.

I hadn't had *F&SF* in mind while writing it, but it seemed perfect for Ed Ferman when I finished it.

Happily, he agreed.

MUSCLES

He was dry. His mind was a vast open plain, barren of the slightest sprig of an idea. It worried him no little bit.

Jay finished his coffee and sandwich at his desk, then sat there tapping a pencil on his blotter. He looked around the empty office. This was getting serious. He needed a lead story for next week's edition and he was completely blank.

He picked up the current issue of *The Light* lying open on his desk, exposing the weekly eye injury on page three. That was one of his rules: Every issue had to have an eye injury on page three, preferably with a photo. Page five was reserved for the weekly UFO story. The dependable appearance of features like those kept the regulars coming back week after week. But it was page one that caught the impulse buyers, and they were the gravy. He closed it over and scanned the front page.

FOUND IN SIBERIA:
TWO-HEADED BABY SPEAKS
ENGLISH AND RUSSIAN!

There followed an eyewitness account of the left head speaking Russian and the right head answering in English (talk about internationalism!) along with a photo of a two-headed baby from the freak file.

Jay frowned. Another of his rules was that freaks were a last resort for the front page. The fact that this week's lead was about a freak was testimony to the aridity of his current dry spell. But you had to go for the gross when you were competing against something as juicy as the Profumo scandal in the dailies.

He got up and walked around the tiny office. He stopped at the front page of the March 15, 1959, issue that was framed on the wall. He had only just started with *The Light* then, but he had made his mark with that one. Even today, it was still considered a masterpiece.

SECRET VATICAN PAPERS REVEAL:
RICHIE VALENS WOULD
HAVE BEEN NEXT POPE

He shook his head at the memory. Boy, had that ever sold papers! The text had been the usual bullshit about secret information leaked by a deep contact who would talk only to *The Light*. A source in a place like the Vatican was a safe bet because the Vatican was so secretive anyway and would naturally be expected to deny a story like that. Of course, the old standby was anywhere behind the Iron Curtain. No way anyone could prove you right or wrong when the story came from Siberia.

Look at me! he thought. Standing here reminiscing about 1959 like it was the good old days. Hell, it was only four years ago! He was acting like a has-been at thirty!

He needed some air, a walk, a change of scenery. Anything but these lousy walls. He pulled on his coat and headed for the elevator. He knew where he wanted to go.

*   *   *

Ah, sleaze. There was something in the air here in Times Square that did something for Jay. Not any one particular thing. The amalgam stimulated him—a benny for his soul. And the Square looked especially sleazy today, buffeted by a chill wind under a low gray sky that promised rain or snow or a mix.

He wandered past the Tango Palace ("Continuous Dancing from 2 P.M. to 4 A.M. to the Type of Music You Love / Presenting Beautiful Girls to Dance With") and past the Square Theatre showing a double bill of *The Immoral Mr. Teas* and *Wild Women of Wongo* and the Garden Theatre with a double of *B-O-I-N-N-N-G!* and *Goldilocks and the Three Bares* and past Hubert's Museum and Flea Circus. He had been to the Tango Palace a number of times—through the plain door and up the stairs to where the music was not the type he loved and neither were the women—and had seen the movies twice each and knew the attractions of Hubert's by heart. But he never got tired of the aura of the Square. The regulars here were living by their wits on the edge of the law, on the far side of truth, justice, and the American way. The skells, the sky-grifters, the street-hawkers and streetwalkers all worked as hard at their trades as any straight, but they didn't want it straight. They wanted it their way. Jay could not deny a feeling of kinship.

Lighted headlines were crawling around the Times Building —something about Kennedy and Khrushchev. A guy in cowboy boots and a Stetson was giving Jay the eye. Jay ignored both. A lot of women had told him he looked like Anthony Perkins and maybe it was true. He was tall, very slim, had dark brown hair and an angular face. The look was useful in attracting women, but it had its drawbacks in the fact that it attracted certain men, too. It also proved a little unpopular a couple of years ago when *Psycho* was such a hit.

Jay crossed the street and slowed when he came to Harold's Mondo Emporium. There was a small crowd of about half a dozen guys filing by a ticket window. Harold's Mondo was a relative newcomer on the Square, a smaller, poor man's version of Hubert's Museum and Flea Circus. Hubert's had been on the Square since 1929. Ernie Rawson had opened up Harold's just last year. He had sounded like he was going under when Jay had spoken to him a couple of weeks ago. Now he was going like gangbusters with the lunchtime crowd.

Jay showed his press card to the ticket girl and wandered inside to look around. Same old junk as Hubert's: a taxidermied two-headed cow, a snake charmer, a belly dancer, pickled punks (the trade's charming name for bottled embryos—$25 each from Del Rio, Texas), a closed-off section with a separate admission which, if Jay remembered correctly, had housed "Sexology" lectures by a professor from the Sorbonne (uh-huh) the last time he was in. Now it said simply, "Supergirl." That was where everyone was going.

Jay spotted Ernie and came up behind him.

"I'm from DC Comics," he said in a gruff voice. "Where can I find the owner of this establishment?"

Ernie whirled, wide-eyed, then laughed. "Jay! How goes it?" He was a plump, stubby man with a plump, stubby cigar jammed into a corner of his mouth. He was grinning like an idiot.

"You look like a man who just won the Irish Sweepstakes, Ernie. What's going on?"

"Great new attraction! Wanna see uh?"

Jay tried to appear disinterested, but he had been hoping for an invitation. "All right. Maybe there's a story in her."

"Is dere ever! See uh first, den I'll tell yiz."

He stood in the back with Ernie and watched this Supergirl. She had curly red hair, fair, lightly freckled skin, and she was *built*, not just in her D-cup halter, but in her shoulders, arms, and legs. Muscles. The girl was loaded with them. And her skimpy two-piece Supergirl costume showed them all. Not bulging bodybuilder-type muscles, but thick sleek cords running under the skin. She was oiled like the Mr. Universe guys so that the light played off all the highlights when she flexed. She was good, too. She knew how to work the crowd. She'd smile, banter, do her lifts, bend her bars. She'd been around. It could have all been an elaborate scam, but the guys in the crowd didn't seem to mind. Just looking at her was worth the ticket price.

"Here comes da blow-off," Ernie said. "Wait'll yiz see dis!"

It was good. Supergirl pulled a drape off a pressing bench, got two medium-sized volunteers from the audience, and had them each sit on an end of an iron bar supported over the bench. When they were set, she lay back on the bench (with her crotch toward the audience, natch) and bench-pressed the two guys. As the audience went wild, Ernie pulled Jay outside.

"She terrif, or what?"

"She's good, all right," Jay said. "But there's not much of a story in a strong-woman act."

"Don't count on dat. Wait'll yiz hear about uh gettin' raped tree years ago."

"Raped?" This was getting interesting now. Jay couldn't imagine anyone doing anything to that lady without her permission. "Who did it—Man Mountain Dean?"

"A ghost, she said. An' anyways, she weren't musculuh back den. Maybe you seen uh at Hubert's. She was da snake dancer back in 'sixty."

"Tell you the truth, Ernie," Jay said, "I didn't get much of a look at her face." Those muscles had fascinated him. He'd never seen anything like them on a woman before . . . the way they moved under her skin . . . "But what's this about a ghost raping her?"

"Dat's what she said back den. Hollered about it to da cops, den clammed up soon as da papers came sniffin'. Quit uh job an' disappeared. Couple of weeks ago she shows up in my office wit all dese muscles an' dis act. I mean, is she dynamite or what? And if you can give me some good press on uh, I can up da ticket price and still be packin' 'em in. And should dat come to be da case, I'd be willing to maybe find a way to—"

Jay held up a hand. "Don't say it, Ernie. Either the story's worth writing or it's not." He had his journalistic integrity.

"Okay, okay. Just meet uh an' talk to uh an' see whatcha tink."

"Will do. Which way to the dressing room?" Jay was looking forward to this.

Now that she was swathed in a terry-cloth bathrobe, Jay realized that she was kind of pretty. Not beautiful, but pretty in a girlish, nice-smile way. She was pushing thirty, maybe a little hard around the edges, but there was a trace of vulnerability in those blue eyes that appealed to Jay. He wanted to get to know her.

"Dis is Jay," Ernie said. "He's a reportuh. Wants a few woids."

She gave Jay an appraising look. "As long as it's only words he wants, otherwise the two of you can take off."

Jay smiled at her. "Just words, I assure you, Miss . . ." He curved the end of the word up into a question.

"Hansen." She returned the smile. "Olivia Hansen. You can call me Liv."

She seemed interested. Maybe she liked skinny guys.

"I wancha ta give him a good story, Liv," Ernie said. "About da rape an' ev'ryding."

Suddenly the smile disappeared. Liv's expression became fierce. She lifted Ernie off the floor by his lapels and tossed him against the wall.

"I told you never to mention that!" she shouted as Ernie bounced off the wall and cowered away from her. "Didn't I? *Didn't* I?"

"Yeah, Liv, but—"

"No buts!" She turned toward Jay. "What paper you from?"

"*The Light.*"

"Oh, that's great! Just great! 'Flying Saucer Men Stick Needles in Woman's Eyes!' I can't stand it!" She snatched a beige raincoat off a hook and pulled it on over the robe. "You really are low, Ernie."

"Where y'goin?" Ernie said as she headed for the door.

"None of your business!"

"You got a two o'clock show!"

"I'll be back."

And then she was gone.

"She betta come back," Ernie said, squaring his shoulders inside his rumpled jacket and trying to look like he was really the boss. He smiled wanly at Jay. "Dey all tink dey're staws."

Jay nodded absently. He was thinking. He gauged Ernie's weight at a compact 170. Liv had handled him easily.

"Strong girl."

"Yeah," he said, smoothing his lapels.

"She coming back?"

"Sure. She always goes out between shows." He sighed. "I tink da broad's a man-hatuh. She got uh share of stage-door Johnnies, an' I see uh go off wit one from time to time, but dey neva come back. Prob'ly a dyke."

Jay thought about those muscular arms and legs wrapped around another woman . . . what a waste.

"But look," Ernie was saying. "Tonight's uh oily night. She's troo at eight-toity. Whyncha come back den an'—"

Jay shrugged. "I don't see much of a story here, Ernie. Sorry."

"Maybe I can talk to uh, make uh come aroun'."

"Sure, Ernie. Let me know." He waved good-bye.

Jay headed up to 42nd Street and followed it east to the Daily News Building. He checked the morgue files for stories about a "ghost rape." Sure enough, there it was. A little story in the lower left corner of page six. Olivia Hansen's name in print, but no direct quotes. The story looked like it was culled from a police report. Jay thought of Olivia up on that stage with those sleek, shining muscles and felt a growing arousal. He idly wondered if maybe he had some fruity tendencies that muscles could get to him like this, but reminded himself that they were on a woman. That was the important thing. A *good-looking* woman. With muscles . . .

Back to the files: He checked back a few more years and found two other similar reports: another "ghost rape" and a "monster rape." Both in the Times Square area.

The juices began flowing as he headed for the street. By the time he reached his office, he was excited. He had his story: Something prowled Times Square at odd intervals, ravaging women. Its victims said it was hideous, ghostlike. What was it? A man? Or something else? Was it perhaps the living ex-crescence of all the sleaze, disease, perversion, and depravity of Times Square? The embodied concentrate of the lost hopes, shattered dreams, wretched, wrecked lives of those who haunted the Square?

Oooh, that sounded *good*! And it wasn't so farfetched, was it? After all, the White House had been occupied by an Irish Catholic for the past couple of years. What could be more farfetched than that?

The readers would eat it up! All he needed was that final touch to give it the needed ring of authenticity that would enable him to drag it out for two or three issues—personal testimony. He needed to talk to Olivia Hansen.

It hadn't been easy to get her out of the cold and into Clancy's. Jay had used every ounce of persuasive skill he owned and fervent promises of no talk of her past, just her present and immediate future, to cajole her into having one lousy drink with him before she went home. She hadn't removed her raincoat, just sat there opposite him in a rear booth and answered in monosyllables as she sipped her drink. He had poured on the charm and pushed the Anthony Perkins boyishness to the limit to stretch one drink into two, and then into three. She was beginning to loosen up.

"I don't usually drink," she said. There was a growing slur to her words as she sipped her screwdriver. Yes, she was getting very loose. "Bad for the muscles."

"Hey, Paula" was playing on the juke. The vodka in the screwdrivers had relaxed the anger lines in her face, making her softer, prettier. There was even more vulnerability in her eyes, and a faint tang of sweat in the air. Jay found it exciting as all hell.

"Tell me about the muscles."

"What about them?"

"Why have them?"

"I gotta be strong." Her expression was suddenly fierce. "Strong enough to keep any man from doing just what he wants with me ever again!"

Jay took a deep breath. *Here goes nothing.* "You mean the rape?"

"Hey! I thought you weren't going to mention that!"

"I didn't bring it up—you did."

She calmed into silence.

"Want to talk about it?" Jay said softly.

"*No!*" She shook her head violently, then began to talk about it. "It was awful! Horrible! I was in my dressing room at Hubert's, getting ready to go on with my snake dance when he—it—appeared out of nowhere. I mean, one minute I was alone in the room with all the lights on and the next minute he was there and everything went dark and cold."

"What he look like?"

She shuddered and Jay wondered uneasily what it took to get a shudder out of a girl who used to dance wrapped up in a boa constrictor.

"I only got a glance at him before everything went dark but he was old and greasy and unshaven and dirty and his skin wasn't right, like it wasn't human, and he was cold, so goddamn cold, and the things he did to me and the things he made me do, *the things he made me do!*" She sobbed and Jay thought she was going to lose it. "I was powerless, completely powerless!" She took a deep, shuddering breath. "But that'll never happen again." He saw her flexing her muscles under her coat. "No one'll ever do something like that to me again! Ever!"

"But how come you clammed up about it back then? Maybe they could have caught this creep."

She shook her head slowly. "The way he comes and goes? Nobody'll ever catch him. And besides, everyone was looking at me like I was crazy or trying a publicity stunt. It was insult to injury. I didn't need it."

As the jukebox began "Walk Like a Man," she glanced at the Schlitz clock on the wall.

"God! I've got to get home! The kid'll be starving!"

Kid? Jay saw his story fading away as she rose to her feet. He had to say something here, and quickly. "I didn't know you were married."

"I'm not. Never was. Baby's father was . . . well, we were just talking about him."

Jay was stunned. She got pregnant from the rape and kept the kid! What a headline! *Son of the Times Square Spook!* God! He could run this for months! He could make Profumo and Christine Keeler look like the Knights of Columbus!

"Uh, why . . .?" He didn't know how to phrase it.

"What was I to do? Risk an abortion and maybe die? Besides, it wasn't Baby's fault. He didn't do anything to me. And after carrying him for nine months I . . . I couldn't give him up. I'm his mother, after all."

This was one weird lady, but she would be so *easy* to write about. The quotables just poured out of her! He couldn't let her go. He needed more time to work on her. If he could somehow get a picture of this kid—

"Let me take you home," he said quickly.

"I don't need your protection."

Jay smiled. "I was hoping you'd protect *me!*"

She laughed and Jay realized that it was the first time she had done that all evening.

"Okay. It's only a few blocks. We can walk."

Jay used the walk to make contact with her. First he took her elbow as they crossed the street, then he kept a grip on her arm, then his arm was around her shoulders. By the time they reached her apartment house, she was leaning against him.

This was working out fine, he thought as he followed her up the stairs to the third floor. A little romance here, along with a line about helping protect other innocent women from this rapist spook by going public in *The Light*, and she'd come around for sure.

It was a two-room apartment—a front room, a back room, and a kitchen. Liv went immediately to the back room, leaving Jay by the door. The front room looked like a gym—barbells and dumbbells all about. A padded pressing bench occupied the spot where most people put a couch.

Liv returned from the back room. "Baby's sleeping."

"You leave him alone here all day? How old is he?"

She took off her coat, then loosened the tie on the terry-cloth bathrobe underneath. "One and a half. He sleeps all day and most of the night. I check on him between shows."

The bathrobe was off now, revealing her Supergirl bikini, and her muscles. Ah, those muscles. Her breasts bobbed under the fabric as she walked over to him. She put her hands on his chest and looked up at him. He could tell the vodka had worked its magic.

"I need someone tonight. Want to stay?"

Jay ran his fingers up her biceps, over her deltoids and traps, and down to her lats. He pulled her close.

"I couldn't say no even if I wanted to."

He realized with a pang that it was probably the first completely honest statement he had made all night.

She led him into the dark of the rear room. In the borrowed light from the front he dimly saw a bed against the wall and a crib in the far corner. He heard a rustle from the crib and saw the kid pull himself to his feet and look at them over the rail.

"He's awake," he whispered.

"That's okay. We'll be in the dark here and he won't know what we're doing."

Jay glanced at the crib again. He couldn't make out any of the kid's features, just a shadow, craning his head and neck over the rail and staring at them. He didn't like the idea of an audience, even if it was just a single one-and-a-half-year-old, but then Liv had his shirt open and was kissing his chest, and he forgot all about the kid.

She was crying, sobbing gently under him.

"What's wrong?"

"Nothing! That was so good. Sometimes I just need that. I tell myself I don't, but sometimes I just do. And that was so good."

It *had* been good, Jay thought. *He* had been good. Damn good! At the end there, he had thought she was going to crush him. Even now she still had her arms and legs wrapped around him as he lay weak and limp atop her.

"You don't have to cry."

"Yes, I do. 'Cause I'm sorry."

"Sorry? You kidding? That was wonderful!"

"Oh, good. That makes me feel a little better."

Jay was trying to figure out what she was getting at when he heard a noise over by the crib. He glanced up. The crib was empty.

"I think your baby's out."

He felt her arms and legs tighten about him.

"I know."

He sensed movement along the floor, coming toward the bed, then a little face popped up over the edge of the mattress, only inches away, and looked at him. He cried out in shock at the huge, dark, staring eyes and wide slit of a mouth crowded with teeth that would have been more at home in a shark. As the kid's teeth angled toward his throat, he struggled to get up.

"Let me go!"

Liv's arms and legs tightened around him even more, locking him against her, helpless.

"I'm sorry," she said with a sob, "but Baby needs you, too."

Introduction

This story had been perking around in my brain for years. I'd even tried out a 5,000-word version of it in the mid-seventies, but the result was so full of holes it was useless. I forgot about it.

Then I got a letter from John Betancourt announcing that he, George Scithers, and Darrell Schweitzer were reviving *Weird Tales* and would I like to contribute. "Ménage à Trois" came to mind as a perfect story for them: It was contemporary yet seemed in tune with the more Gothic traditions of that venerable magazine. The new version turned out twice as long as the old, with all the holes plugged and a Gothic Revival motif running through the house.

Weird Tales accepted it immediately. The check for payment, however, arrived unsigned. I held it a few days, figuring maybe the signature of Farnsworth Wright was supposed to appear, but nothing happened. So I sent it back and settled for a more mundane endorsement.

Detective Burke, by the way, may seem familiar. He first appeared in "The Cleaning Machine."

MÉNAGE À TROIS

Burke noticed how Grimes, the youngest patrolman there, was turning a sickly shade of yellow-green. He motioned him closer. "You all right?"

Grimes nodded. "Sure. Fine." His pitiful attempt at a smile was hardly reassuring. "Awful hot in here, but I'm fine."

Burke could see that he was anything but. The kid's lips were as pale as the rest of his face and he was dripping with sweat. He was either going to puke or pass out or both in the next two minutes.

"Yeah. Hot," Burke said. It was no more than seventy in the hospital room. "Get some fresh air out in the hall."

"Okay. Sure." Now the smile was real—and grateful. Grimes gestured toward the three sheet-covered bodies. "I just never seen anything like this before, y'know?"

Burke nodded. He knew. This was a nasty one. Real nasty. He swallowed the sour-milk taste that puckered his cheeks. In his twenty-three years with homicide he had seen his share of crime scenes like this, but he never got used to them. The splattered blood and flesh, the smell from the ruptured *intestines, the glazed eyes in the slack-jawed faces—who could get used to that? And three lives, over and gone for good.*

"Look," he told Grimes, "why don't you check at the nurses' desk and find out where they lived. Get over there and dig up some background."

Grimes nodded enthusiastically. "Yes, sir."

Burke turned back to the room. Three lives had ended in there this morning. He was going to have to find out what those lives had been until now if he was ever going to understand this horror. And when he did get all the facts, could he ever really understand? Did he really want to?

Hot, sweaty, and gritty, Jerry Pritchard hauled himself up the cellar stairs and into the kitchen. Grabbing a beer from the fridge, he popped the top and drained half the can in one long, gullet-cooling swallow. Lord, that was *good!* He stepped over to the back door and pressed his face against the screen in search of a vagrant puff of air, anything to cool him off.

"Spring cleaning," he muttered, looking out at the greening rear acreage. "Right." It felt like August. Who ever heard of eighty degrees in April?

He could almost see the grass growing. The weeds, too. That meant he'd probably be out riding the mower around next week. Old lady Gati had kept him busy all fall getting the grounds perfectly manicured; the winter had been spent painting and patching the first and second floors; April had been designated basement clean-up time; and now the grounds needed to be whipped into shape again.

An endless cycle. Jerry smiled. But that cycle meant job security. And job security meant he could work and eat here during the day and sleep in the gatehouse at night, and never go home again.

He drained the can and gave it a behind-the-back flip into the brown paper bag sitting in the corner by the fridge.

Home . . . the thought pursued him. There had been times

when he thought he'd never get out. Twenty-two years in that little house, the last six of them pure hell after Dad got killed in the cave-in of No. 8 mine. Mom went off the deep end then. She had always been super-religious, herding everyone along to fire-and-brimstone Sunday prayer meetings and making them listen to Bible readings every night. Dad had kept her in check somewhat, but once he was gone, all the stops were out. She began hounding him about how her only son should join the ministry and spread the Word of God. She submerged him in a Bible-besotted life for those years, and he'd almost bought the package. She had him consulting the Book upon awakening, upon retiring, before eating, before going off to school, before buying a pair of socks, before taking a leak, until common sense got a hold of him and he realized he was going slowly mad. But he couldn't leave because he was the man of the house and there was his younger sister to think of.

But Suzie, bless her, ran off last summer at sixteen and got married. Jerry walked out a week later. Mom had the house, Dad's pension, her Bible, and an endless round of prayer meetings. Jerry stopped by once in a while and sent her a little money when he could. She seemed to be content.

Whatever makes you happy, he thought. He had taken his own personal Bible with him when he left. It was still in his suitcase in the gatehouse. Some things you just didn't throw away, even if you stopped using them.

The latest in a string of live-in maids swung through the kitchen door with old lady Gati's lunch dishes on a tray. None of the others had been bad-looking, but this girl was a knockout. "Hey, Steph," he said, deciding to put off his return to the cellar just a little bit longer. "How's the Dragon Lady treating you?"

She flashed him a bright smile. "I don't know why you call her that, Jerry. She's really very sweet."

That's what they all say, he thought, and then *wham!* they're out. Stephanie Watson had been here almost six weeks—a record in Jerry's experience. Old lady Gati went through maids like someone with hay fever went through Kleenex. Maybe Steph had whatever it was old lady Gati was looking for.

Jerry hoped so. He liked her. Liked her a *lot*. Liked her short tawny hair and the slightly crooked teeth that made her easy smile seem so genuine, liked her long legs and the way she moved through this big old house with such natural grace, like she belonged here. He especially liked the way her blue-flowered-print shift clung to her breasts and stretched across her buttocks as she loaded the dishes into the dishwasher. She excited him, no doubt about that.

"You know," she said, turning toward him and leaning back against the kitchen counter, "I still can't get over the size of this place. Seems every other day I find a new room."

Jerry nodded, remembering his first few weeks here last September. The sheer height of this old three-storied Gothic mansion had awed him as he had come through the gate to apply for the caretaker job. He had known it was big—everybody in the valley grew up within sight of the old Gati house on the hill—but had never been close enough to appreciate *how* big. The house didn't really fit with the rest of the valley. It wasn't all that difficult to imagine that a giant hand had plucked it from a faraway, more populated place and dropped it here by mistake. But the older folks in town still talked about all the trouble and expense mine owner Karl Gati went through to have it built.

"Yeah," he said, looking at his calloused hands. "It's big, all right."

He watched her for a moment as she turned and rinsed out the sink, watched the way her blond hair moved back and forth across the nape of her neck. He fought the urge to slip his arms around her and kiss that neck. That might be a mistake. They had been dating since she arrived here—just movies and something to eat afterward—and she had been successful so far in holding him off. Not that that was so hard to do. Growing up under Mom's watchful Pentacostal eye had prevented him from developing a smooth approach to the opposite sex. So far, his limited repertoire of moves hadn't been successful with Steph.

He was sure she wasn't a dumb innocent—she was a farm girl and certainly knew what went where and why. No, he sensed that she was as attracted to him as he to her but didn't want to be a pushover. Well, okay. Jerry wasn't sure why that didn't bother him too much. Maybe it was because there was something open and vulnerable about Steph that appealed to a protective instinct in him. He'd give her time. Plenty of it. Something inside him told him she was worth the wait. And something else told him that she was weakening, that maybe it wouldn't be too long now before . . .

"Well, it's Friday," he said, moving closer. "Want to go down to town tonight and see what's playing at the Strand?" He hated to sound like a broken record—movie-movie-movie—but what else was there to do in this county on weekends if you didn't get drunk, play pool, race cars, or watch tv?

Her face brightened with another smile. "Love it!"

Now why, he asked himself, should a little smile and a simple yes make me feel so damn good?

No doubt about it. She did something to him.

"Great! I'll—"

A deep, guttural woman's voice interrupted him. "Young Pritchard! I wish to see you a moment!"

Jerry shuddered. He hated what her accent did to the r's in his name. Setting his teeth, he followed the sound of her voice through the ornate, cluttered dining room with its huge needlepoint carpet and bronze chandeliers and heavy furniture. Whoever had decorated this house must have been awful depressed. Everything was dark and gloomy. All the furniture and decorations seemed to end in points.

He came to the semi-circular solarium where she awaited him. Her wheelchair was in its usual position by the big bay windows where she could look out on the rolling expanse of the south lawn.

"Ah, there you are, young Pritchard," she said, looking up and smiling coyly. She closed the book in her hands and laid it on the blanket that covered what might have passed for legs in a nightmare. The blanket had slipped once and he had seen what was under there. He didn't want another look. Ever. He remembered what his mother had always said about deformed people: that they were marked by God and should be avoided.

Old lady Gati was in her mid-sixties maybe, flabby without being fat, with pinched features and graying hair stretched back into a severe little bun at the back of her head. Her eyes were a watery blue as she looked at him over the tops of her reading glasses.

Jerry halted about a dozen feet away but she motioned him closer. He pretended not to notice. She was going to want to touch him again. God, he couldn't stand this!

"You called, ma'am?"

"Don't stand so far away, young Pritchard." He advanced two steps in her direction and stopped again. "Closer," she said. "You don't expect me to shout, do you?"

She didn't let up until he was standing right next to her. Except for these daily chats with Miss Gati, Jerry loved his job.

"There," she said. "That's better. Now we can talk more easily."

She placed a gnarled, wrinkled hand on his arm and Jerry's flesh began to crawl. Why did she always have to touch him?

"The basement—it is coming along well?"

"Fine," he said, looking at the floor, out the window, anywhere but at her hungry, smiling face. "Just fine."

"Good." She began stroking his arm, gently, possessively. "I hope this heat wave isn't too much for you." As she spoke she used her free hand to adjust the blanket over what there was of her lower body. "I really should have Stephanie get me a lighter blanket."

Jerry fought the urge to jump away from her. He had become adept at masking the revulsion that rippled through his body every time she touched him. And it seemed she *had* to touch him whenever he was in reach. When he first got the caretaker job, he took a lot of ribbing from the guys in town down at the Dewkum Inn. (Lord, what Mom would say if she ever saw him standing at a bar!) Everybody knew that a lot of older, more experienced men had been passed over for him. His buddies had said that the old lady really wanted him for stud service. The thought nauseated him. Who knew if she even had—

No, that would never happen. He needed this job, but there was nothing he needed *that* badly. And so far, all she had ever done was stroke his arm when she spoke to him. Even that was hard to take.

As casually as he could, he moved out of reach and gazed out the window as if something on the lawn had attracted his attention. "What did you want me to—"

Stephanie walked into the room and interrupted him.

"Yes, Miss Gati?"

"Get me a summer blanket, will you, dear?"

"Yes, ma'am." She flashed a little smile at Jerry as she turned, and he watched her until she was out of sight. Now if only it were Steph who couldn't keep her hands off him, he wouldn't—

"She appeals to you, young Pritchard?" Miss Gati said, her eyes dancing.

He didn't like her tone, so he kept his neutral. "She's a good kid."

"But does she *appeal* to you?"

He felt his anger rising, felt like telling her it was none of her damn business, but he hauled it back and said, "Why is that so important to you?"

"Now, now, young Pritchard, I'm only concerned that the two of you get along well. But not *too* well. I don't want you taking little Stephie away from me. I have special needs, and as you know, it took me a long time to find a live-in maid with Stephie's special qualities."

Jerry couldn't quite buy that explanation. There had been something in her eyes when she spoke of Steph "appealing" to him, a hint that her interest went beyond mere household harmony.

"But the reason I called you here," she said, shifting the subject, "is to tell you that I want you to tend to the roof in the next few days."

"The new shingles came in?"

"Yes. Delivered this morning while you were in the basement. I want you to replace the worn ones over my room tomorrow. I fear this heat wave might bring us a storm out of season. I don't want my good furniture ruined by leaking water."

He guessed he could handle that. "Okay. I'll finish up today and be up on the roof tomorrow. How's that?"

She wheeled over and cut him off as he tried to make his getaway. "Whatever you think best, young Pritchard."

Jerry pulled free and hurried off, shuddering.

Marta Gati watched young Pritchard's swift exit.
I repulse him.
There was no sorrow, no self-pity attached to the thought. When you were born with twig-like vestigial appendages for legs and only half a pelvis, you quickly became used to rejection—you learned to read it in the posture, to sense it behind the eyes. Your feelings soon became as calloused as a miner's hands.

He's sensitive about my little Stephie, she thought. Almost protective. He likes her. He's attracted to her. *Very* attracted.

That was good. She wanted young Pritchard to have genuine feelings for Stephie. That would make it so much better.

Yes, her little household was just the way she wanted it now. It had taken her almost a year to set it up this way. Month after month of trial and error until she found the right combination. And now she had it.

Such an arrangement would have been impossible while Karl was alive. Her brother would never have hired someone with as little experience as young Pritchard as caretaker, and he would have thought Stephie too young and too frail to be a good live-in maid. But Karl was dead now. The heart attack had taken him quickly and without warning last June. He had gone to bed early one night complaining of what he thought was indigestion, and never awoke. Marta Gati missed her brother and mourned his loss, yet she was reveling in the freedom his passing had left her.

Karl had been a good brother. Tyrannically good. He had looked after her as a devoted husband would an ailing wife. He had never married, for he knew that congenital defects ran high in their family. Out of their parents' four children, two—Marta and Gabor—had been horribly deformed. When they had come to America from Hungary, Karl invested the smuggled family fortune in the mines here and, against all odds, had done well. He saw to it that Lazlo, the younger brother, received the finest education. Lazlo now lived in New York where he tended to Gabor.

And Marta? Marta he had kept hidden away in this remote mansion in rural West Virginia where she had often thought she would go insane with boredom. At least she had been able to persuade him to decorate the place. If she had to stay here, she had a right to be caged in surroundings to her taste. And her taste was Gothic Revival.

Marta loved this house, loved the heavy wood of the tables, the carved deer legs of the chairs, the elaborate finials atop the cabinets, the ornate valances and radiator covers, the trefoil arches on her canopy bed.

But the decor could only carry one so far. And there were only so many books one could read, television shows and rented movies one could watch. Karl's conversational capacity had been limited in the extreme, and when he had spoken, it was on business and finance and little else. Marta had wanted to be out in the world, but Karl said the world would turn away from her, so he'd kept her here to protect her from hurt.

But Marta had found a way to sneak out from under his overprotective thumb. And now with Karl gone, she no longer had to sneak out to the world. She could bring some of the world into the house.

Yes, it was going to be so nice here.

"Tell me something," Steph said as she rested her head on Jerry's shoulder. She was warm against him in the front seat of his old Fairlane 500 convertible and his desire for her was a throbbing ache. After the movie—a Burt Reynolds car-chase flick, but without Burt Reynolds—he had driven them back here and parked outside the gatehouse. The top was down and they were snuggled together in the front seat watching the little stars that city people never see, even on the clearest of nights.

"Anything," he whispered into her hair.

"How did Miss Gati get along here before she had me?"

"A lady from town used to come in to clean and cook, but she never stayed over. You're the first live-in who's lasted more than a week since I've been working here. The old lady's been real choosy about finding someone after the last live-in . . . left."

Jerry decided that now was not the time to bring up the last maid's death. Steph was from the farmlands on the other side of the ridge and wouldn't know about her. Constance Granger had been her name, a quiet girl who went crazy wild. She had come from a decent, churchgoing family, but all of a sudden she became a regular at the roadside taverns, taking up with a different man every night. Then one night she became hysterical in a motel room—with two men, if the whispers could be believed—and began screaming at the top of her lungs. She ran out of the room jaybird naked and got hit by a truck.

Jerry didn't want to frighten Steph with that kind of story, not now while they were snug and close like this. He steered the talk elsewhere.

"Now you tell me something. What do you think of working for old lady Gati?"

"She's sweet. She's not a slave driver and the pay is good. This is my first job since leaving home and I guess I'm kinda lucky it's working out so well."

"You miss home?"

He felt her tense beside him. She never talked about her home. "No. I . . . didn't get along with my father. But I get along just fine with Miss Gati. The only bad thing about the job is the house. It gives me the creeps. I get nightmares every night."

"What about?"

She snuggled closer, as if chilled despite the warmth of the night. "I don't remember much by morning, all I know is that they're no fun. I don't know how Miss Gati lived here alone after the last maid left. Especially her without any legs. I'd be frightened to death!"

"She's not. She tried out girl after girl. No one satisfied her till you came along. She's a tough one."

"But she's not. She's nice. A real lady. You know, I make her hot chocolate every night and she insists I sit down and have a cup with her while she tells me about her family and how they lived in 'the old country.' Isn't that nice?"

"Just super," Jerry said.

He lifted her chin and kissed her. He felt her respond, felt her catch some of the fervor running through him like fire. He let his hand slip off her shoulder and come to rest over her right breast. She made no move to push him away as his fingers began caressing her.

"Want to come inside?" he said, glancing toward the door of the gatehouse.

Steph sighed. "Yes." She kissed him again, then pulled away. "But no. I don't think that would be such a good idea, Jerry. Not just yet. I mean, I just met you six weeks ago."

"You know all there is to know. I'm not hiding anything. Come on."

"I want to . . . you know I do, but not tonight. It's time for Miss Gati's hot chocolate. And if I want to keep this job, I'd better get up to the house and fix it for her." Her eyes searched his face in the light of the rising moon. "You're not mad at me, are you?"

"Nah!" he said with what he hoped was a reassuring grin. How could he look into those eyes and be mad? But he sure as hell *ached*. "Crushed and heartbroken, maybe. But not mad."

She laughed. "Good!"

There's plenty of time, he told the ache deep down inside. And we'll be seeing a lot of each other.

"C'mon. I'll walk you up to the house."

On the front porch, he kissed her again and didn't want to let go. Finally, she pushed him away, gently. "She's calling me. Gotta go. See you tomorrow."

Reluctantly, Jerry released her. He hadn't heard anything but knew she had to go. He wondered if her insides were as churned up as his own.

"Hurry and drink your chocolate before it gets cold," Marta Gati said as Stephie returned from down the hall.

Stephie smiled and picked up her cup from the bedside table. *A lovely child*, Marta thought. *Simply lovely.*

Her own cup was cradled in her hands. It was a little too sweet for her taste, but she made no comment. She was propped up on her bed pillows. Stephie sat in a chair pulled up to the side of the bed.

"And what did you and young Pritchard do tonight?" Marta said. "Anything special?" She watched Stephie blush as she sipped her chocolate.

Marta took a sip of her own to hide the excitement that swept through her. *They're in love!* This was perfect. "How was the movie?" she managed to say in a calm voice.

Stephie shrugged. "It was okay, I guess. Jerry likes all those cars racing around and crashing."

"Don't you?"

She shrugged. "Not really."

"But you go because young Pritchard likes them. And you like him, don't you?"

She shrugged shyly. "Yes."

"Of course you do. And he likes you. I can tell. I just hope he hasn't taken any liberties with you."

Stephie's color deepened. Marta guessed she wanted to tell her it was none of her damn business but didn't have the nerve. "No," Stephie said. "No liberties."

"Good!" Marta said. "I don't want you two running off and getting married. I need the both of you here. Now, finish your chocolate and get yourself to bed. Never let it be said I kept you up too late."

Stephie smiled and drained her cup.

Yes, Marta thought. *A lovely girl.*

The gatehouse was one room and a bathroom, furnished with a small desk, a chair, a bureau, and a hide-a-bed that folded up into a couch during the day. A sort of unattached motel room. But since he took his meals up at the house, it was all that Jerry needed.

The lights had been off for nearly an hour but he was still awake, rerunning his favorite fantasy, starring the voracious Steph and the inexhaustible Jerry. Then the door opened without warning and Steph stood there with the moonlight faintly outlining her body through the light cotton nightgown she wore. She said nothing as she came forward and crawled under the single sheet that covered him.

After that, no words were necessary.

Dawn light sneaking through the spaces between the venetian blinds on the gatehouse window woke Jerry. He was alone. After she had worn him out, Steph had left him. He sat on the edge of the hide-a-bed and cradled his head in his hands. In the thousand times he had mentally bedded Steph since her arrival, he had always been the initiator, the aggressor. Last night had been nothing at all like the fantasies. Steph had been in complete control—demanding, voracious, insatiable, a wild woman who had left him drained and exhausted. And hardly a word had passed between them. Throughout their lovemaking she had cooed, she had whimpered, she had moaned, but she had barely spoken to him. It left him feeling sort of . . . used.

Still trying to figure out this new, unexpected side to Steph, he walked up to the house for breakfast. The sun was barely up and already the air was starting to cook. It was going to be another hot one.

As he came in the back door he saw Steph heading out of the kitchen toward the dining room with old lady Gati's tray.

"Be with you in a minute," she called over her shoulder.

He waited by the swinging door and caught her as she came through. He slipped his arms around her waist and kissed her.

"Jerry, no!" she snapped. "Not here—not while I'm working!"

He released her. "Not your cheerful old self this morning, are you?"

"Just tired, I guess." She turned toward the stove.

"I guess you should be."

"And what's that supposed to mean?"

"Well, you had an unusually active night. At least I hope it was unusual."

Steph had been about to crack an egg on the edge of the frying pan. She stopped in mid-motion and turned to face him.

"Jerry . . . what on earth are you talking about?"

She looked genuinely puzzled, and that threw him. "Last night . . . at the gatehouse . . . it was after three when you left."

Her cranky scowl dissolved into an easy smile. "You must really be in a bad way!" She laughed. "Now you're believing your own dreams!"

Jerry was struck by the clear innocence of her laughter. For a moment, he actually doubted his memory—but only for a moment. Last night had been real. Hadn't it?

"Steph . . ." he began, but dropped it. What could he say to those guileless blue eyes? She was either playing some sort of game, and playing it very well, or she really didn't remember. Or it really never happened. None of those choices was the least bit reassuring.

He wolfed his food as Steph moved in and out of the kitchen, attending to old lady Gati's breakfast wants. She kept glancing at him out of the corner of her eye, as if checking up on him. Was this a game? Or had he really dreamed it all last night?

Jerry skipped his usual second cup of coffee and was almost relieved to find himself back in the confines of the cellar. He threw himself into the job, partly because he wanted to finish it, and partly because he didn't want too much time to think about last night. By lunchtime he was sweeping up the last of the debris when he heard the sound.

It came from above. The floorboards were squeaking. And

something else as well—the light sound of feet moving back and forth, rhythmically. It continued as he filled a cardboard box with the last of the dirt, dust, and scraps of rotten wood from the cellar. He decided to walk around the south side of the house on his way to the trash bins. The sound seemed to be coming from there.

As he passed the solarium, he glanced in and almost dropped the box. Steph was waltzing around the room with an invisible partner in her arms. Swirling and dipping and curtsying, she was not the most graceful dancer he had ever seen, but the look of pure joy on her face made up for whatever she lacked in skill.

Her expression changed abruptly to a mixture of surprise and something like anger when she caught sight of him gaping through the window. She ran toward the stairs, leaving Miss Gati alone. The old lady neither turned to watch her go, nor looked out the window to see what had spooked her. She just sat slumped in her wheelchair, her head hanging forward. For a second, Jerry was jolted by the sight: She looked dead! He pressed his face against the solarium glass for a closer look, and was relieved to see the gentle rise and fall of her chest. Only asleep. But what had Steph been doing waltzing around like that while the old lady napped?

Shaking his head at the weirdness of it all, he dumped the box in the trash area and returned to the house through the back door. The kitchen was empty, so he made his way as quietly as possible to the solarium to see if Steph had returned. He found all quiet—the music off and old lady Gati bright and alert, reading a book. He immediately turned back toward the kitchen, hoping she wouldn't spot him. But it was too late.

"Yes, young Pritchard?" she said, rolling that *r* and looking up from her book. "You are looking for something?"

Jerry fumbled for words. "I was looking for Steph to see if she could fix me a sandwich. Thought I saw her in here when I passed by before."

"No, dear boy," she said with a smile. "I sent her up to her room for a nap almost an hour ago. Seems you tired her out last night."

"Last night?" He tensed. What did she know about last night?

Her smile broadened. "Come now! You two didn't think you could fool me, did you? I know she sneaked out to see you." Something about the way she looked at him sent a sick chill through Jerry. "Surely you can fix something yourself and let the poor girl rest."

Then it hadn't been a dream! But then why had Steph pretended—?

He couldn't figure it. "Yeah. Sure," he said dully, his thoughts jumbled. "I can make a sandwich." He turned to go.

"You should be about through with the basement by now," she said. "But even if you're not, get up to the roof this afternoon. The weatherman says there's a sixty percent chance of a thunderstorm tonight."

"Basement's done. Roof is next."

"Excellent! But don't work *too* hard, young Pritchard. Save something for Stephie."

She returned to her book.

Jerry felt numb as he walked back to the kitchen. The old lady hadn't touched him once! She seemed more relaxed and at ease with herself than he could ever remember—a cat-that-had-swallowed-the-canary sort of self-satisfaction. And she hadn't tried to lay a single finger on him!

The day was getting weirder and weirder.

Replacing the shingles on the sloping dormer surface outside old lady Gati's bedroom had looked like an easy job from the ground. But the shingles were odd, scalloped affairs that she had ordered special from San Francisco to match the originals on the house, and Jerry had trouble keeping them aligned on the curved surface. He could have used a third hand, too. What would have been an hour's work for two men had already taken Jerry three in the broiling sun, and he wasn't quite finished yet.

While he was working, he noted that the wood trim on the upper levels was going to need painting soon. That was going to be a hellish job, what with the oculus windows, the ornate friezes, cornices, brackets, and keystones. Some crazed woodcarver had had a field day with this stuff—probably thought it was "art." But Jerry was going to be the one to paint it. He'd put that off as long as he could, and definitely wouldn't do it in summer.

He pulled an insulated wire free of the outside wall to fit in the final shingles by the old lady's window. It ran from somewhere on the roof down to the ground—directly *into* the ground. Jerry pulled himself up onto the parapet above the dormer to see where the wire originated. He followed it up until it linked into the lightning rod on the peak of the attic garret. *Everything* connected with this house was ornate—even the lightning rods had designs on them!

He climbed back down, pulled the ground wire free of the dormer, and tacked the final shingles into place. When he reached the ground, he slumped on the bottom rung of the ladder and rested a moment. The heat from the roof was getting to him. His tee-shirt was drenched with perspiration and he was reeling with fatigue.

Enough for today. He'd done the bulk of the work. A hurricane could hit the area and that dormer would not leak. He could put the finishing touches on tomorrow. He lowered the ladder to the ground, then checked the kitchen for Steph. She wasn't there. Just as well. He didn't have the energy to pry an explanation out of her. Something was cooking in the oven, but he was too bushed to eat. He grabbed half a six-pack of beer from the fridge and stumbled down to the gatehouse. Hell with dinner. A shower, a few beers, a good night's sleep, and he'd be just fine in the morning.

It was a long ways into dark, but Jerry was still awake. Tired as he was, he couldn't get to sleep. As thunder rumbled in the distance, charging in from the west, and slivers of ever-brightening light flashed between the blinds, thoughts of last night tumbled through his mind, arousing him anew. Something strange going on up at that house. Old lady Gati was acting weird, and so was Steph.

Steph . . . he couldn't stop thinking about her. He didn't care what kind of game she was playing, she still meant something to him. He'd never felt this way before. He—

There was a noise at the door. It opened and Steph stepped inside. She said nothing as she came forward, but in the glow of the lightning flashes from outside, Jerry could see her removing her nightgown as she crossed the room. He saw it flutter to the floor and then she was beside him, bringing the dreamlike memories of last night into the sharp focus of the real and now. He tried to talk to her but she would only answer in a soft, breathless "uh-huh" or "uh-uh" and then her wandering lips and tongue wiped all questions from his mind.

When it was finally over and the two of them lay in a gasping tangle of limbs and sheets, Jerry decided that now was the time to find out what was going on between her and old lady Gati, and what kind of game she was playing with him. He would ask her in a few seconds . . . or maybe in a minute . . . soon . . . thunder was louder than ever outside but that wasn't going to bother him . . . all he wanted to do right now was close his eyes and enjoy the delicious exhaustion of this afterglow a little longer . . . only a little . . . just close his eyes for a few seconds . . . no more . . .

"Sleep well, my love."

Jerry forced his eyes open. Steph's face hovered over him in the flashing dimness as he teetered on the brink of unconsciousness. She kissed him lightly on the forehead and whispered, "Good night, young Pritchard. And thank you."

It was as if someone had tossed a bucket of icy water on him. Suddenly Jerry was wide awake. *Young Pritchard?* Why had she said that? Why had she imitated old lady Gati's voice that way? The accent, with its roll of the *r*, had been chillingly perfect.

Steph had slipped her nightgown over her head and was on her way out. Jerry jumped out of bed and caught her at the door.

"I don't think that was funny, Steph!" She ignored him and pushed the screen door open. He grabbed her arm. "Hey, look! What kind of game are you playing? What's it gonna be tomorrow morning? Same as today? Pretend that nothing happened tonight?" She tried to pull away but he held on. "Talk to me, Steph! What's going on?"

A picture suddenly formed in his mind of Steph going back to the house and having hot chocolate with old lady Gati and telling her every intimate detail of their lovemaking, and the old lady getting excited, *feeding* off it.

"What's going *on!*" Involuntarily, his grip tightened on her arm.

"You're hurting me!" The words cut like an icy knife. The voice was Steph's, but the tone, the accent, the roll of the *r*s, the inflection—all were perfect mimicry of old lady Gati, down to the last nuance. But she had been in pain. It couldn't have been rehearsed!

Jerry flipped the light switch and spun her around. It was Steph, all right, as achingly beautiful as ever, but something was wrong. The Steph he knew should have been frightened. The Steph before him was changed. She held herself differently. Her stance was haughty, almost imperious. And there was something in her eyes—a strange light.

"Oh, sweet Jesus! What's happened to you?"

He could see indecision flickering through her eyes as she

regarded him with a level stare. Outside, it began to rain. A few scattered forerunner drops escalated to a full-scale torrent in a matter of seconds as their eyes remained locked, their bodies frozen amid day-bright flashes of lightning and the roar of thunder and wind-driven rain. Then she smiled. It was like Steph's smile, but it wasn't.

"Nothing," she said in that crazy mixed voice.

And then he thought he knew. For a blazing instant, it was clear to him: "You're not Steph!" In the very instant he said it he disbelieved it, but then her smile broadened and her words turned his blood to ice:

"Yes, I am . . . for the moment." The voice was thick with old lady Gati's accent, and it carried a triumphant note. "What Stephie sees, *I* see! What Stephie feels, *I* feel!" She lifted the hem of her nightgown. "Look at my legs! Beautiful, aren't they?"

Jerry released her arm as if he had been burned. She moved closer but Jerry found himself backing away. Steph was crazy! Her mind had snapped. She thought she was old lady Gati! He had never been faced with such blatant madness before, and it terrified him. He felt exposed, vulnerable before it. With a trembling hand, he grabbed his jeans from the back of the chair.

Marta Gati looked out of Stephie's eyes at young Pritchard as he struggled into his trousers, and she wondered what to do next. She had thought him asleep when she had kissed him good night and made the slip of calling him "young Pritchard." She had known she couldn't keep her nightly possession of Stephie from him for too long, but she had not been prepared for a confrontation tonight. She would try for sympathy first.

"Do you have any idea, young Pritchard," she said, trying to make Stephie's voice sound as American as she could, "what it is like to be trapped all your life in a body as deformed as mine? To be repulsive to other children as a child, to grow up watching other girls find young men and go dancing and get married and know that at night they are holding their man in their arms and feeling all the things a woman should feel? You have no idea what my life has been like, young Pritchard. But through the years I found a way to remedy the situation. Tonight I am a complete woman—*your* woman!"

"Stephanie!" young Pritchard shouted, fear and disbelief mingling in the strained pallor of his face. "Listen to yourself! You sound crazy! What you're saying is impossible!"

"No! Not impossible!" she said, although she could understand his reaction. A few years ago, she too would have called it impossible. Her brother Karl had devoted himself to her and his business. He never married, but he would bring women back to the house now and then when he thought she was asleep. It would have been wonderful if he could have brought a man home for her, but that was impossible. Yet it hadn't stopped her yearnings. And it was on those nights when he and a woman were in the next bedroom that Marta realized she could sense things in Karl's women. At first she thought it was imagination, but this was more than mere fantasy. She could feel their passion, feel their skin tingling, feel them exploding within. And one night, after they both had spent themselves and fallen asleep, she found herself in the other woman's body—actually lying in Karl's bed and seeing the room through her eyes!

As time went on, she found she could enter their bodies while they slept and actually take them over. She could get up and walk! A sob built in her throat at the memory. To *walk*! That had been joy enough at first. Then she would dance by herself. She had wanted so much all her life to dance, to waltz, and now she could! She never dared more than that until Karl died and left her free. She had perfected her ability since then.

"It will be a good life for you, young Pritchard," she said. "You won't even have to work. Stephie will be my maid and housekeeper during the day and your lover at night." He shook his head, as if to stop her, but she pressed on. "And when you get tired of Stephie, I'll bring in another. And another. You'll have an endless stream of young, willing bodies in your bed. You'll have such a *good* life, young Pritchard!"

A new look was growing in his eyes: belief.

"It's really you!" he said in a hoarse whisper. "Oh, my dear sweet Lord, it's really you in Steph's body! I . . . I'm getting out of here!"

She moved to block his way and he stayed back. He could have easily overpowered her, but he seemed afraid to let her get too near. She couldn't let him go, not after all her work to set up a perfect household.

"No! You mustn't do that! You must stay here!"

"This is sick!" he cried, his voice rising in pitch as a wild light sprang into his eyes. "This is the Devil's work!"

"No-no," she said soothingly. "Not the Devil. Just me. Just something—"

"Get away from me!" he said, backing toward his dresser. He spun and pulled open the top drawer, rummaged through it, and came up with a thick book with a cross on its cover. "Get away, Satan!" he cried, thrusting the book toward her face.

Marta almost laughed. "Don't be silly, young Pritchard! I'm not evil! I'm just doing what I have to do. I'm not hurting Stephie. I'm just borrowing her body for a while!"

"Out, demon!" he said, shoving the Bible almost into her face. "*Out!*"

This was getting annoying now. She snatched the book from his grasp and hurled it across the room. "Stop acting like a fool!"

He looked from her to the book and back to her with an awed expression. At that moment there was a particularly loud crash of thunder and the lights went out. Young Pritchard cried out in horror and brushed past her. He slammed out the door and ran into the storm.

Marta ran as far as the doorway and stopped. She peered through the deluge. Even with the rapid succession of lightning strokes and sheets, she could see barely a dozen feet. He was nowhere in sight. She could see no use in running out into the storm and following him. She glanced at his keys on the bureau and smiled. How far could a half-naked man go in a storm like this?

Marta crossed the room and sat on the bed. She ran Stephie's hand over the rumpled sheets where less than half an hour ago the two of them had been locked in passion. Warmth rose within her. *So good.* So good to have a man's arms around you, wanting you, needing you, *demanding* you. She couldn't give this up. Not now, not when it was finally at her disposal after all these years.

But young Pritchard wasn't working out. She had thought any virile young man would leap at what she offered, but apparently she had misjudged him. Or was a stable relationship within her household just a fool's dream? She had so much to learn about the outside world. Karl had kept her so sheltered from it.

Perhaps her best course was the one she had taken with the last housekeeper. Take over her body when she was asleep and drive to the bars and roadhouses outside of town. Find a man—two men, if she were in the mood—and spend most of the night in a motel room. Then come back to the house, clean her up, and leave her asleep in her bed. It was anonymous, it was exciting, but it was somehow . . . empty.

She would be more careful with Stephie than with the last housekeeper. Marta had been ill one night but had moved into the other body anyway. She had lost control when a stomach spasm had gripped her own body. The pain had drawn her back to the house, leaving the woman to awaken between two strangers. She had panicked and run out into the road.

Yes, she had to be very careful with this one. Stephie was so sensitive to her power, whatever it was. She only had to become drowsy and Marta could slip in and take complete control, keeping Stephie's mind unconscious while she controlled her body. A few milligrams of a sedative in her cocoa before bedtime and Stephie's body was Marta's for the night.

But young Pritchard wasn't working out. At least not so far. There was perhaps a slim chance she could reason with him when he came back. She had to try. She found him terribly attractive. But where could he be?

Sparks of alarm flashed through her as she realized that her own body was upstairs in the house, lying in bed, helpless, defenseless. What if that crazy boy—?

Quickly, she slid onto the bed and closed her eyes. She shut out her senses one by one, blocking off the sound of the rain and thunder, the taste of the saliva in her mouth, the feel of the bedclothes against her back . . .

. . . and opened her eyes in her own bedroom in the house. She looked around, alert for any sign that her room had been entered. Her bedroom door was still closed, and there was no moisture anywhere on the floor.

Good! He hasn't been in here!

Marta pushed herself up in bed and transferred to the wheelchair. She wheeled herself out to the hall and down to the elevator, cursing its slow descent as it took her to the first floor. When it finally stopped, she propelled herself at top speed to the foyer where she immediately turned the dead bolt on the front door. She noted with satisfaction that the slate floor under her chair was as dry as when she had walked out earlier as Stephie. She was satisfied that she was alone in the house.

Safe!

She rolled herself into the solarium at a more leisurely pace. She knew the rest of the doors and windows were secure— Stephie always locked up before she made the bedtime chocolate. She stopped before the big bay windows and watched the storm for a minute. It was a fierce one. She gazed out at the blue-white, water-blurred lightning flashes and wondered what she was going to do about young Pritchard. If she couldn't convince him to stay, then surely he would be in town tomorrow, telling a wild tale. No one would believe him, of course, but it would start talk, fuel rumors, and that would make it almost impossible to get help in the future. It might even make Stephie quit, and Marta didn't know how far her power could reach. She'd be left totally alone out here.

Her fingers tightened on the armrests of her wheelchair. She couldn't let that happen.

She closed her eyes and blocked out the storm, blocked out her senses . . .

. . . and awoke in Stephie's body again.

She leaped to the kitchenette and pulled out the drawers until she found the one she wanted. It held three forks, a couple of spoons, a spatula, and a knife—a six-inch carving knife.

It would have to do.

She hurried out into the rain and up the hill toward the house.

Jerry rammed his shoulder against the big oak front door again but only added to bruises the door had already put there. He screamed at it.

"In God's name—open!"

The door ignored him. What was he going to do? He had to get inside! Had to get to that old lady! Had to wring the Devil out of her! Had to find a way in! Make her give Steph back!

His mother had warned him about this sort of thing. He could almost hear her voice between the claps of thunder: *Satan walks the earth, Jerome, searching for those who forsake the Word. Beware—he's waiting for you!*

Jerry knew the Devil had found him—in the guise of old lady Gati! What was happening to Steph was all his fault!

He ran back into the downpour and headed around toward

the rear. Maybe the kitchen door was unlocked. He glanced through the solarium windows as he passed. His bare feet slid to a halt on the wet grass as he stopped and took a better look.

There she was: old lady Gati, the Devil herself, zonked out in her wheelchair.

The sight of her sitting there as if asleep while her spirit was down the hill controlling Steph's body was more than Jerry could stand. He looked around for something to hurl through the window, and in the next lightning flash he spotted the ladder next to the house on the lawn. He picked it up and charged the solarium like a jousting knight. Putting all his weight behind the ladder, he rammed it through the center bay window. The sound of shattering glass broke the last vestige of Jerry's control. Howling like a madman, he drove the ladder against the window glass again and again until every pane and every muntin was smashed and battered out of the way.

Then he climbed in.

The shards of glass cut his bare hands and feet but Jerry barely noticed. His eyes were on old lady Gati. Throughout all the racket, she hadn't budged.

Merciful Lord, it's true! Her spirit's left her body!

He stumbled over to her inert form and stood behind her, hesitating. He didn't want to touch her—his skin crawled at the thought—but he had to put an end to this. Now. Swallowing the bile that sloshed up from his stomach, Jerry wrapped his fingers around old lady Gati's throat. He flinched at the feel of her wrinkles against his palms, but he clenched his teeth and began to squeeze. He put all his strength into it—

—and then let go.

He couldn't do it.

"God, give me strength!" he cried, but he couldn't bring himself to do it. Not while she was like this. It was like strangling a corpse! She was barely breathing as it was!

Something tapped against the intact bay window to the right.

Jerry spun to look—a flash from outside outlined the grounding wire from the lightning rods as it swayed in the wind and slapped against the window. It reminded him of a snake—

A *snake!* And suddenly he knew: *It's a sign! A sign from God!*

He ran to the window and threw it open. He reached out, wrapped the wire around his hands, and pulled. It wouldn't budge from the ground. He braced a foot against the window-sill, putting his back and all his weight into the effort. Suddenly, the metal grounding stake pulled free and he staggered back, the insulated wire thrashing about in his hands . . . just like a snake.

He remembered that snake handlers' church back in the hills his mother had dragged him to one Sunday a few years ago. He had watched in awe as the men and women would grab water moccasins and cottonmouths and hold them up, trusting in the Lord to protect them. Some were bitten, some were not. Ma had told him it was all God's will.

God's will!

He pulled the old lady's wheelchair closer to the window and wrapped the wire tightly around her, tying it snugly behind the backrest of the chair, and jamming the grounding post into the metal spokes of one of the wheels.

"This is your snake, Miss Gati," he told her unconscious form. "It's God's will if it bites you!"

He backed away from her until he was at the entrance to the solarium. Lightning flashed as violently as ever, but none came down the wire. He couldn't wait any longer. He had to find Steph. As he turned to head for the front door, he saw someone standing on the south lawn, staring into the solarium. It was old lady Gati, wearing Steph's body. When she looked through the broken bay window and saw him there, she screamed and slumped to the ground.

"Steph!" What was happening to her?

Jerry sprinted across the room and dove through the shattered window onto the south lawn.

Marta awoke in her own body, panicked.

What has he done to me?

She felt all right. There was no pain, no—

My arms! Her hands were free but she couldn't move her upper arms! She looked down and saw the black insulated wire coiled tightly around her upper body, binding her to the chair. She tried to twist, to slide down on the chair and slip free, but the wire wouldn't give an inch. She tried to see where it was tied. If she could get her hands on the knot . . .

She saw the wire trailing away from her chair, across the floor and out the window and up into the darkness.

Up! To the roof! The lightning rods!

She screamed, "Nooooo!"

Jerry cradled Steph's head in his arm and slapped her wet face as hard as he dared. He'd hoped the cold pounding rain and the noise of the storm would have brought her around, but she was still out. He didn't want to hurt her, but she had to wake up.

"Steph! C'mon, Steph! You've got to wake up! Got to fight her!"

As she stirred, he heard old lady Gati howl from the solarium. Steph's eyes fluttered, then closed again. He shook her. "Steph! Please!"

She opened her eyes and stared at him. His spirits leaped.

"That's it, Steph! Wake up! It's me—Jerry! You've got to stay awake!"

She moaned and closed her eyes, so he shook her again.

"Steph! Don't let her take you over again!"

As she opened her eyes again, Jerry dragged her to her feet. "Come on! Walk it off! Let's go! You've *got* to stay awake!"

Suddenly, her face contorted and she swung on him.

Something gleamed in her right hand as she plunged it toward his throat. Jerry got his forearm up just in time to block it. Pain seared through his arm and he cried out.

"Oh, God! It's you!"

"*Yes!*" She slashed at him again and he backpedaled to avoid the knife. His bare feet slipped on the grass and he went down on his back. He rolled frantically, fearing she would be upon him, but when he looked up, she was running toward the house, toward the smashed bay window.

"No!"

He couldn't let her get inside and untie the old lady's body. Steph's only hope was a lightning strike.

Please, God, he prayed. *Now! Let it be now!*

But though bolts crackled through the sky almost continuously, none of them hit the house. Groaning with fear and frustration, Jerry scrambled to his feet and sprinted after her. He had to stop her!

He caught her from behind and brought her down about two dozen feet from the house. She screamed and thrashed like an enraged animal, twisting and slashing at him again and again with the knife. She cut him along the ribs as he tried to pin her arms and was rearing back for a better angle on his chest when the night turned blue-white. He saw the rage on Steph's face turn to wide-eyed horror. Her body arched convulsively as she opened her mouth and let out a high-pitched shriek of agony that rose and cut off like a circuit being broken—

—only to be taken up by another voice from within the solarium. Jerry glanced up and saw old lady Gati's body juttering in her chair like a hooked fish while blue fire played all about her. Her hoarse cry was swallowed and drowned as her body exploded in a roiling ball of flame. Fire was everywhere in the solarium. The very air seemed to burn.

He removed the knife from Steph's now limp hand and dragged her to a safer distance from the house. He shook her. "Steph?"

He could see her eyes rolling back and forth under the lids. Finally, they opened and stared at him uncomprehendingly.

"Jerry?" She bolted up to a sitting position. "Jerry! What's going on?"

His grip on the knife tightened as he listened to her voice, searching carefully for the slightest hint of an accent, the slightest roll of an *r*. There wasn't any he could detect, but there was only one test that could completely convince him.

"My name," he said. "What's my last name, Steph?"

"It's Pritchard, of course. But—" She must have seen the flames flickering in his eyes because she twisted around and cried out. "The house! It's on fire! Miss Gati—!"

She had said it perfectly! The real Steph was back! Jerry threw away the knife and lifted her to her feet. "She's gone," he told her. "Burnt up. I saw her."

"But how?"

He had to think fast—couldn't tell her the truth. Not yet. "Lightning. It's my fault. I must have messed up the rods when I was up on the roof today!"

"Oh, God, Jerry!" She clung to him and suddenly the storm seemed far away. "What'll we do?"

Over her shoulder, he watched the flames spreading throughout the first floor and lapping up at the second through the broken bay window. "Got to get out of here, Steph. They're gonna blame me for it and God knows what'll happen."

"It was an accident! They can't blame you for that!"

"Oh, yes, they will!" Jerry was thinking about the ground wire wrapped around the old lady's corpse. No way anyone would think that was an accident. "I hear she's got family in New York. They'll see me hang if they can, I just know it! I've got to get out of here." He pushed her to arm's length and stared at her. "Come with me?"

She shook her head. "I can't! How—?"

"We'll make a new life far from here. We'll head west and

won't stop till we reach the ocean." He could see her wavering. "Please, Steph! I don't think I can make it without you!"

Finally, she nodded.

He took her hand and pulled her along behind him as he raced down the slope for the gatehouse. He glanced back at the old house and saw flames dancing in the second-floor windows. Somebody down in town would see the light from the fire soon and then half the town would be up here to either fight it or watch it being fought. They had to be out of here before that.

It's gonna be okay, he told himself. They'd start a new life out in California. And someday, when he had the nerve and he thought she was ready for it, he'd tell her the truth. But for now, as long as Steph was at his side, he could handle anything. Everything was going to be all right.

Patrolman Grimes looked better now. He was back from the couple's apartment and stood in the hospital corridor with an open notebook, ready to recite.

All right," Burke said. "What've we got?"

"We've got a twenty-three-year-old named Jerome Pritchard. Came out here from West Virginia nine months ago."

"I mean drugs—crack, angel dust, needles, fixings."

"No, sir. The apartment was clean. The neighbors are in absolute shock. Everybody loved the Pritchards and they all seem to think he was a pretty straight guy. A real churchgoer —carried his own Bible and never missed a Sunday, they said. Had an assembly line job and talked about starting night courses at UCLA as soon as he made the residency requirement. He and his wife appeared to be real excited about the baby, going to Lamaze classes and all that sort of stuff."

"Crack, I tell you!" Burke said. "Got to be!"

"As far as we can trace his movements, sir, it seems that after the baby was delivered at 10:06 this morning, he ran out of here like a bat out of hell, came back about an hour later carrying his Bible and a big oblong package, waited until the

baby was brought to the mother for feeding, then . . . well, you know."

"Yeah. I know." The new father had pulled a 10-gauge shotgun from that package and blown the mother and kid away, then put the barrel against his own throat and completed the job. "But why, dammit!"

"Well . . . the baby did have a birth defect."

"I know. I saw. But there are a helluva lot of birth defects a damn sight worse. Hell, I mean, her legs were only withered a little!"

Introduction

Another Just Deserts story.

I never would have written this one if not for Dave Schow. We were conversing aimlessly at the 1986 World Fantasy Convention in Providence when he mentioned an anthology he was pitching to the publishers. The title was *Silver Scream* and was to contain horror stories dealing with "the Hollywood experience." Dave knew my feelings about the way *The Keep* had been treated on the screen. Would I be interested in contributing? I said most definitely. (See? Business really does get done at these conventions.)

"Cuts" is probably one of the nastiest stories I've ever written. I wanted to do a toned-down rewrite but Dave threatened me with bodily harm if I touched it. So I didn't.

CUTS

I t started in Milo's right foot. He awoke in the dark of his bedroom with a pins-and-needles sensation from the lower part of his calf to the tips of his toes. He sat up, massaged it, walked around the bedroom. Nothing helped. Finally, he took a Darvocet and went back to bed. He managed to get to sleep but was awake again by dawn, this time with both feet tingling. In the wan light, he inspected his lower legs.

A thin, faintly red line around each leg about three inches up from the ankle. Milo snapped on the night table light for a closer look. He touched the line. It was more than a line—an indentation, actually, like something left after wearing a pair of socks too tight at the top. But it felt as if the constricting band were still there.

He got up and walked around. It felt a little funny to stand on partially numb feet but he couldn't worry about it now. In just a couple of hours he was doing a power breakfast at the Polo with Regenstein from TriStar and he had to be sharp. He padded into the kitchen to put on the coffee.

* * *

As he wove through L.A.'s morning commuter traffic, Milo envied the drivers with their tops down. He would have loved to have his 380 SL opened up to the bright early morning sun. Truthfully, he would have been glad for an open window. But for the sake of his hair he stayed bottled up with the a-c on. He couldn't afford to let the breeze blow his toupe around. It had been especially stubborn about blending in with his natural hair this morning and he didn't have any more time to fuss with it. And this was his good piece. His back-up had been stolen during a robbery of his house last week, an occurrence that still baffled the hell out of him. He wished he didn't have to worry about wearing a rug. He had heard about a new experimental lotion that was supposed to start hair growing again. If that ever panned out, he'd be first on line to—

His right hand started tingling. He removed it from the wheel and fluttered it in the air. Still it tingled. The sleeve of his sports coat slipped back and he saw a faint indentation running around his forearm, just above the wrist. For a few heartbeats he studied it in horrid fascination.

What's happening to me?

Then he glanced up and saw the looming rear of a truck rushing toward his windshield. He slammed on the brakes and slewed to a screeching stop inches from the tailgate. Gasping and sweating, Milo slumped in the seat and tried to get a grip. Bad enough he was developing mysterious little constricting bands on his legs and now his arm, he had almost wrecked the new Mercedes. This sucker cost more than his first house back in the seventies.

When traffic started up again, he drove cautiously, keeping his eyes on the road and working the fingers of his right hand. He had some weirdshit disease, he just knew it, but he couldn't let anything get between him and this breakfast with Regenstein.

* * *

"Look, Milo," Howard Regenstein said through the smoke from his third cigarette in the last twenty minutes. "You know that if it was up to me the picture would be all yours. You know that, man."

Milo nodded, not knowing that at all. He had used that same line himself a million times—maybe *two* million times. *If it was up to me* . . . Yeah, right. The great cop-out: I'm a nice guy and I have all the faith in the world in you but those money guys, those faithless, faceless Philistines who hold the purse strings, won't let guys with vision like you and me get together and make a great film.

"Well, what's the problem, Howie? I mean, give it to me straight."

"All right," Howie said, showing his chiclet caps between his thin lips. He was deeply tanned, wore thick horn-rimmed glasses; his close-cropped curly hair was sandy-colored and lightly bleached. "Despite my strong—and, Milo, I do mean *strong*—recommendation, the money boys looked at the grosses for *The Hut* and got scared away."

Well. That explained a lot of things, especially this crummy table half hidden in an inside corner. The real power players, the ones who wanted everybody else in the place to see who they were doing breakfast with, were out in the middle or along the windows. Regenstein probably had three breakfasts scheduled for this morning. Milo was wondering what tables had been reserved for the others when a sharp pain stabbed his right leg. He winced and reached down.

"Something wrong?" Regenstein said.

"No. Just a muscle cramp." He lifted his trouser leg and saw that the indentation above his ankle was deeper. It was actually a cut now. Blood oozed slowly, seeping into his sock. He straightened up and forced a smile at Regenstein.

"*The Hut*, Howie? Is *that* all?" Milo said with a laugh. "Don't they know that project was a loser from the start? The book was a bad property, a piece of clichéd garbage. Don't they know that?"

Howie smiled, too. "Afraid not, Milo. You know their kind. They look at the bottom line and see that Universal's going to be twenty mill in the hole on *The Hut*, and in their world that means something. And maybe they remember those P.R. pieces you did a month or so before it opened. You never even mentioned that the film was based on a book. Had me convinced the story was all yours, whole cloth."

Milo clenched his teeth. That had been when he had thought the movie was going to be a smash.

"I had a *concept*, Howie, one that cut through the bounds and limitations of the novel. I wanted to raise the level of the material but the producers stymied me at every level."

Actually, he had been pretty much on his own down there in Haiti. He had changed the book a lot, made loads of cuts and condensations. He had made it "A Milo Gherl Film" but somewhere along the way he had lost it. Unanimously hostile one-star reviews with leads like, "Shut 'The Hut'" and "New Gherl Pix the Pits" hadn't helped. Twentieth had been pushing an offer in its television division and he had been holding them off—who wanted to do tv when you could do theatricals? But as the bad reviews piled up and the daily grosses plummeted, he grabbed the tv offer. It was good money, had plenty of prestige, but it was still television.

Milo wanted to do films, and very badly wanted in on the new package Regenstein was putting together for TriStar. Howie had Jack Nicholson, Bobby De Niro, and Kathy Turner firm, and was looking for a director. More than anything else in his career, Milo wanted to be that director. But he wasn't going to be. He knew that now.

Well, at least he could use the tv job to pay the bills and keep his name before the public until *The Hut* was forgotten. That wouldn't be long. A year or two at most and he'd be back directing another theatrical. Not a package like Regenstein's, but something with a decent budget where he could do the screenplay and direct. That was the way he liked it—full control on paper and on film.

He shrugged at Regenstein and put on his best good-natured smile. "What can I say, Howie? The world wasn't ready for *The Hut*. Someday, they'll appreciate it."

Yeah, right, he thought as Regenstein nodded noncommittally. At least Howie was letting him down easy, letting him keep his dignity here. That was important. All he had to do now was—

Milo screamed as pain tore into his left eye like a bolt of lightning. He lurched to his feet, upsetting the table as he clamped his hands over his eye in a vain attempt to stop the agony. *Pain!* Oh, Christ, pain as he had never known it was shooting from his eye straight into his brain. This had to be a stroke! What else could hurt like this?

Through his good eye he had a whirling glimpse of everybody in the dining room standing and staring at him as he staggered around. He pulled one hand away from his eye and reached out to steady himself. He saw a smear of blood on his fingers. He took the other hand away. His left eye was blind, but with his right he saw the dripping red on his palm. A woman screamed.

"My God, Milo!" Regenstein said, his chalky face swimming into view. "Your eye! What did you do to your *eye*?" He turned to a gaping waiter. "Get a doctor! Get a fucking ambulance!"

Milo was groggy from the Demerol they had given him. In the blur of hours since breakfast he'd been wheeled in and out of the emergency room so many times, poked with so many needles, examined by so many doctors, X-rayed so many times, his head was spinning.

At least the pain had eased off.

"I'm admitting you onto the vascular surgery service, Mr. Gherl," said the bearded doctor as he pushed back one of the white curtains that shielded Milo's gurney from the rest of the emergency room. His badge said, *Edward Jansen, M.D.*, and he looked tired and irritable.

Milo struggled up the Demerol downgrade. "Vascular surgery? But my eye—!"

"As Dr. Burch told you, Mr. Gherl, your eye can't be saved. It's ruined beyond repair. But maybe we can save your feet and your hand if it's not too late already."

"*Save* them?"

"If we're lucky. I don't know what kind of games you've been into, but getting yourself tied up with piano wire is about the dumbest thing I've ever heard of."

Milo was growing more alert by the second now. Over Dr. Jansen's shoulder he saw the bustle of the emergency room personnel, saw an old black mopping the floor in slow, rhythmic strokes. But he was only seeing it with his right eye. He reached up to the bandage over his left. *Ruined?* He wanted to cry, but Dr. Jansen's piano wire remark suddenly filtered through to his consciousness.

"Piano wire? What are you talking about?"

"Don't play dumb. Look at your feet." Dr. Edwards pulled the sheet free from the far end of the gurney.

Milo looked. The nail beds were white and the skin below the indentations was a dusky blue. And the indentations had all become clean, straight, bloody cuts right through the skin and into the meat below. His right hand was the same.

"See that color?" Jansen was saying. "That means the tissues below the wire cuts aren't getting enough blood. You're going to have gangrene for sure if we don't restore circulation soon."

Gangrene! Milo levered up on the gurney and felt his toes with his good hand. *Cold!* "No! That's impossible!"

"I'd almost agree with you," Dr. Jansen said, his voice

softening for a moment as he seemed to be talking to himself. Behind him, Milo noticed the old black moving closer with his mop. "When we did X rays, I thought we'd see the wire embedded in the flesh there, but there was nothing. Tried Xero soft-tissue technique in case you had used fishing line or something, but that came up negative, too. Even probed the cuts myself but there's nothing in there. Yet the arteriograms clearly show that the arteries in your lower legs and right forearm are compressed to the point where very little blood is getting through. The tissues are starving. The vascular boys may have to do bypasses."

"I'm getting out of here!" Milo said. "I'll see my own doctor!"

"I'm afraid I can't allow that."

"You can't stop me! I can walk out of here anytime I want!"

"I can keep you seventy-two hours for purposes of emergency psychiatric intervention."

"Psychiatric!"

"Yeah. Self-mutilation. Your mind worries me almost as much as your arteries, Mr. Gherl. I'd like to make sure you don't poke out your other eye before you get treatment."

"But I didn't—!"

"Please, Mr. Gherl. There were witnesses. Your breakfast companion said he had just finished giving you some disappointing news when you screamed and rammed something into your eye."

Milo touched the bandage over his eye again. How could they think he had done this to himself?

"My God, I swear I didn't do this!"

"That kind of trauma doesn't happen spontaneously, Mr. Gherl, and according to your companion, no one was within reach of you. So one way or the other, you're staying. Make it easy on both of us and do it voluntarily."

Milo didn't see that he had a choice. "I'll stay," he said. "Just answer me one thing: You ever seen anything like this before?"

Jansen shook his head. "Never. Never *heard* of anything like it either." He took a sudden deep breath and smiled through his beard with what Milo guessed was supposed to be doctorly reassurance. "But, hey. I'm only an ER doc. The vascular boys will know what to do."

With that, he turned and left, leaving Milo staring into the wide-eyed black face of the janitor.

"What are you staring at?" Milo said.

"A man in *big* trouble," the janitor said in a deep, faintly accented voice. He was pudgy with a round face, watery eyes, and two days' worth of silvery growth on his jowls. With a front tooth missing on the top, he looked like Leon Spinks gone to seed for thirty years. "These doctors can't be helpin' what you got. You got a *Bocor* mad at you and only a *Houngon* can fix you."

"Get lost!" Milo said.

He lay back on the gurney and closed his good eye to shut out the old man and the emergency room. He hunted for sleep as an escape from the pain and the gut-roiling terror, praying he'd wake up and learn that this was all just a horrible dream. But those words wouldn't go away. *Bocor* and *Houngon* . . . he knew them somehow. Where?

And then it hit him like a blow—*The Hut!* They were voodoo terms from the novel *The Hut!* He hadn't used them in the film—he'd scoured all mention of voodoo from his screenplay—but the author had used them in the book. If Milo remembered correctly, a *Bocor* was an evil voodoo priest and a *Houngon* was a good one. Or was it the other way around? Didn't matter. They were all part of Bill Franklin's bullshit novel.

Franklin! Wouldn't he like to see me now! Milo thought. Their last meeting had been anything but pleasant. Unforgettable, yes. His mind did a slow dissolve to his new office at Twentieth two weeks ago . . .

* * *

"Some conference!"

The angry voice startled Milo and he spilled hot coffee down the front of his shirt. He leaped up from behind his desk and bent forward, pulling the steaming fabric away from his chest. "Jesus H.—"

But then he looked up and saw Bill Franklin standing there and his anger cooled like fresh blood in an arctic breeze. Maggie's anxious face peered over Franklin's narrow shoulder.

"I tried to stop him, Mr. Gherl, honest I did, but he wouldn't listen!"

"You've been ducking me for a month, Gherl!" Franklin said in his nasal voice. "No more tricks!"

Maggie said, "Shall I call security?"

"I don't think that will be necessary, Maggs," he said quickly, grabbing a Kleenex from the oak tissue holder on his desk and blotting at his stained shirt front. Milo had moved into this office only a few weeks ago, and the last thing he needed today was an ugly scene with an irate writer. He could tell from Franklin's expression that he was ready to cause a doozy. Better to bite the bullet and get this over with. "I'll talk to Mr. Franklin. You can leave him here." She hesitated and he waved her toward the door. "Go ahead. It's all right."

When she had closed the door behind her, he picked up the insulated brass coffee urn and looked at Franklin. "Coffee, Billy-boy?"

"I don't want coffee, Gherl! I want to know why you've been ducking me!"

"But I haven't been ducking you, Billy!" he said, refreshing his own cup. He would have to change this shirt before he did lunch later. "I'm not with Universal anymore. I'm with Twentieth now, so naturally my offices are here." He swept an arm around him. "Not bad, ay?"

Milo sat down and tried his best to look confident, at ease. Inside, he was anything but. Right now he was a little afraid of the writer stalking back and forth before the desk like a caged tiger. Nothing about Franklin's physical appearance was the least bit intimidating. He was fair-haired and tall with big hands and feet attached to a slight, gangly frame. He had a big nose, a small chin, and a big adam's apple—Milo had noticed on their first meeting two years ago that he could slant a perfectly straight line along the tips of those three protuberances. A moderate overbite did not help the picture. Milo's impression of Franklin had always been that of a patient, retiring, rational man who never raised his voice.

But today he was barging about with a wild look in his eyes, shouting, gesticulating, accusing. Milo remembered an old saying his father used to quote to him when he was a boy: *Beware the wrath of a patient man.*

Franklin had paused and was looking around the spacious room with its indirect lighting, its silver-gray floor-to-ceiling louvered blinds and matching carpet, the chrome and onyx wet bar, the free-form couches, the abstract sculptures on the Lucite coffee table and on Milo's oversized desk.

"How did you ever rate this after perpetrating a turkey like *The Hut?*"

"Twentieth recognizes talent when it sees it, Billy."

"My question stands," Franklin said.

Milo ignored the remark. "Sit down, Billy-boy. What's got you so upset?"

Franklin didn't sit. He resumed his stalking. "You know damn well what! My book!"

"You've got a new one?" Milo said, perfectly aware of which book he meant.

"No! I mean the only book I've ever written—*The Hut!*—and the mess you made out of it!"

Milo had heard quite enough nasty criticism of that particular film to last him a lifetime. He felt his anger flare but suppressed it. Why get into a shouting match?

"I'm sorry you feel that way, Billy, but let's face facts." He spread his hands in a consoling gesture. "It's a dead issue.

There's nothing more to be done. The film has been shot, edited, released, and—"

"—and withdrawn!" Franklin shouted. "Two weeks in general release and the theatre owners sent it back! It's not just a flop, it's a catastrophe!"

"The critics killed it."

"Bullshit! The critics blasted it, just like they blasted other 'flops' like *Flashdance* and *Top Gun* and *Ernest Goes to Camp*. What killed it, Gherl, was word of mouth. Now I know why you wouldn't screen it until a week before it opened: You knew you'd botched it!"

"I had trouble with the final cut. I couldn't—"

"You couldn't get it to make sense! As I walked out of that screening I kept telling myself that my negative feelings were due to all the things you'd cut out of my book, that maybe I was too close to it all and that the public would somehow find my story in your mass of pretentions. Then I heard a guy in his early twenties say, 'What the hell was *that* all about?' and his girlfriend say, 'What a boring waste of time!' and I knew it wasn't just me." Franklin's long bony finger stabbed through the air. "It was you! You raped my book!"

Milo had had just about enough of this. "You novelists are all alike!" he said with genuine disdain. "You do fine on the printed page so you think you're experts at writing for the screen. But you're not. You don't know the first goddamn thing about visual writing!"

"You cut the heart out of my story! *The Hut*'s was about the nature of evil and how it can seduce even the strongest among us. The plot was like a house of cards, Gherl, built with my sweat. Your windbag script blew it all down! And after I saw the first draft of the script, you were suddenly unavailable for conference!"

Milo recalled Franklin's endless stream of nit-picking letters, his deluge of time-wasting phone calls. "I was busy, dammit! I was writer-director! The whole thing was on my shoulders!"

"I warned you that the house of cards was falling due to the cuts you made. I mean, why did you remove all mention of voodoo and zombiism from the script? They were the two red herrings that held the plot together."

"Voodoo! Zombies! That's old hat! Nobody would pay to see a voodoo movie!"

"Then why set the movie in Haiti, f'Christsake? Might as well have been in Pasadena! And that monster you threw in at the end. Where in hell did you come up with that? It looked like the Incredible Hulk in drag! I spent years in research. I slaved to fill that book with terror and dread—all you brought to the screen were cheap shocks!"

"If that's your true opinion—and I disagree with it absolutely—you should be glad the film was a flop. No one will see it!"

Franklin nodded slowly. "That gave me comfort for a while, until I realized that the movie isn't dead. When it reaches the video stores and the cable services, tens of millions of people will see it—not because it's good, but simply because it's there and it's something they've never heard of before and certainly have never seen. And they'll be directing their rapt attention at your corruption of my story, and they'll see 'Based on the Novel by William Franklin' and think that the pretentious, incomprehensible mishmash they're watching represents my work. And that makes me *mad*, Gherl! Fucking-A crazy *mad!*"

The ferocity that flashed across Franklin's face was truly frightening. Milo rushed to calm him. "Billy, look: Despite our artistic differences and despite the fact that *The Hut* will never turn a profit, you were paid well into six figures for the screen rights. What's you're beef?"

Franklin seemed to shrink a little. His shoulders slumped and his voice softened. "I didn't write it for money. I live off a trust fund that provides me with more than I can spend. *The Hut* was my first novel—maybe my only novel ever. I gave it everything. I don't think I have any more in me."

"Of course you do!" Milo said, rising and moving around the desk toward the subdued writer. Here was his chance to ease Franklin out of here. "It's just that you've never had to suffer for your art! You've had it too soft, too cushy for too long. Things came too easy on that first book. First time at bat you got a major studio film offer that actually made it to the screen. That hardly ever happens. Now you've got to prove it wasn't just a fluke. You've got to get out there and slog away on that new book! Deprive yourself a little! *Suffer!*"

"Suffer?" Franklin said, a weird light starting to glow in his eyes. "I should suffer?"

"Yes!" Milo said, guiding him toward the office door. "All great artists suffer."

"You ever suffer, Milo Gherl?"

"Of course." *Especially this morning, listening to you!*

"Look at this office. You don't look like you're suffering for what you did to *The Hut*."

"I did my suffering years ago. The anger you feel about *The Hut* is small change compared to the dues I've had to pay." He finally had Franklin across the threshold. "I'm through suffering," he said as he slammed the door and locked it.

From the other side of the thick oak door he thought he heard Franklin say, "No, you're not."

"Missing any personal items lately, mister?" said a voice.

Milo opened his good eye and saw the big black guy standing over him, leaning on his mop handle. What was *wrong* with this old fart? What was his angle?

"If you don't leave me alone I'm gonna call—" He paused. "What do you mean, 'personal items'?"

"You know—clothing, nail clippings, a brush or comb that might hold some of your hair. That kinda stuff."

A chill swept over Milo's skin like an icy breeze in July. *The robbery!* Such a bizarre thing—a pried-open window, a few cheap rings gone, his drawers and closets ransacked, an old pair of pajamas missing. And his toupe, the second-string hairpiece . . . gone. Who could figure it? But he had been shaken up enough to go out and buy a .38 for his night table.

Milo laughed. This was so ludicrous. "You're talking about a voodoo doll, aren't you?"

The old guy nodded. "It got other names, but that'll do."

"Who the hell *are* you?"

"Name's André but folks call me Andy. I got connections you gonna need."

"*You* need your head examined!"

"Maybe. But that doctor said he was lookin' for the wires that was cuttin' into your legs and your arm but he couldn't find them. That's because the wires are somewheres else. They around the legs and arm of a doll somebody made on you."

Milo tried to laugh again but found he couldn't. He managed a weak "Bullshit."

"You'll believe me soon enough. And when you do, I'll take you to a *Houngon* who can help you out."

"Yeah," Milo said. "Like you really care about me."

The old black showed his gap-tooth smile. "Oh, I won't be doin' you a favor, and neither will the *Houngon*. He'll be wantin' money for pullin' you' fat out the fire."

"And you'll get a finder's fee."

The smile broadened. "Tha's right."

That made a little more sense to Milo, but still he wasn't buying. "Forget it!"

"I be around till three. I'll keep checkin' up on you case you change you' mind. I can get you out here when you want to go."

"Don't hold your breath."

Milo rolled on his side and closed his eyes. The old fart had some nerve trying to run that corny scam on him, and in a hospital yet! He'd report him, have him fired. This was no joke.

He'd lost his eye already. He could be losing his feet, his hand! He needed top medical-center care, not some voodoo mumbo-jumbo . . .

. . . but no one seemed to know what was going on, and everyone seemed to think he'd put his own eye out. God, who could do something like that to himself? And his hand and his feet—the doc had said they were going to start rotting off if blood didn't get flowing back into them. What on earth was happening to him?

And what about that weird robbery last week? Only personal articles had been stolen. All the high-ticket stereo and video stuff had been left untouched.

God, it couldn't be voodoo, could it? Who'd even—

Shit! Bill Franklin! He was an expert on it after all those years of research for *The Hut*. But he wouldn't . . . he couldn't . . .

Franklin's faintly heard words echoed in Milo's brain: *No, you're not.*

Agony suddenly lanced through Milo's groin, doubling him over on the gurney. Gasping with the pain, he tore at the clumsy stupid nightshirt they'd dressed him in and pulled it up to his waist. He held back the scream that rose in his throat when he saw the thin red line running around the base of his penis. Instead, he called out a name.

"Andy! *Andy!*"

Milo coughed and peered through the dim little room. It smelled of dust and sweat and charcoal smoke and something else—something rancid. He wondered what the hell he was doing here. He knew if he had any sense he'd get out now, but he didn't know where to go from here. He wasn't even sure he could find his way home from here.

The setting sun had been a bloody blob in Milo's rearview mirror as he'd hunched over the steering wheel of his Mercedes and followed Andy's rusty red pick-up into one of L.A.'s seamier districts. Andy had been true to his word: He'd spirited Milo out of the hospital, back to the house for some cash and some real clothes, then down to the garage near the Polo where his car was parked. After that it was on to Andy's *Houngon* and maybe end this agony.

It *had* to end soon. Milo's feet were so swollen he was wearing old slippers. He had barely been able to turn the ignition key with his right hand. And his dick—God, his dick felt like it was going to explode!

After what seemed like a ten-mile succession of left and right turns during which he saw not a single white face, they had pulled to a stop before a dilapidated storefront office. On the cracked glass was painted:

M. Trieste
Houngon

Andy had stayed outside with the car while Milo went in. "Mr. Gherl?"

Milo started at the sound and turned toward the voice. A balding, wizened old black, six-two at least, stood next to him. His face was a mass of wrinkles. He was dressed in a black suit, white shirt, and thin black tie.

Milo heard his own voice quaver: "Yes. That's me."

"You are the victim of the *Bocor?*" His voice was cultured, and accented in some strange way.

Milo pushed back the sleeve of his shirt to expose his right wrist. "I don't know what I'm the victim of, but Andy says you can help me. You've *got* to help me!"

He stared at the patch over Milo's eye. "May I see?"

Milo leaned away from him. "Don't touch that!" It had finally stopped hurting. He held his arm higher.

M. Trieste examined Milo's hand, tracing a cool dry finger around the clotted circumferential cut at the wrist. "This is all?"

Milo showed him his legs, then, reluctantly, opened his fly.

"You have a powerful enemy in this *Bocor*," M. Trieste said finally. "But I can reverse the effects of his doll. It will cost you five hundred dollars. Do you have it with you?"

Milo hesitated. "Let's not be too hasty here. I want to see some results before I fork over any money." He was hurting, but he wasn't going to be a sucker for this clown.

M. Trieste smiled. He had all his teeth. "I have no wish to steal from you, Mr. Gherl. I shall accept no money from you unless I can effect a cure. However, I do not wish to be cheated either. Do you have the money with you?"

Milo nodded. "Yes."

"Very well." M. Trieste struck a match and lit a candle on a table Milo hadn't realized was there. "Please be seated," he said and disappeared into the darkness.

Milo complied and looked around. The wan candlelight picked up an odd assortment of objects around the room: African ceremonial masks hung side by side with crucifixes on the wall; a long conga drum sat in a corner to the right, and a statue of the Virgin Mary, her small plaster foot treading a writhing snake, occupied the one on his left. He wondered when the drums would start and the dancers appear. When would they begin chanting and daubing him with paint and splattering him with chicken blood? God, he must have been crazy to come here. Maybe the pain was affecting his mind. If he had any smarts he'd—

"Hold out your wrist," M. Trieste said, suddenly appearing in the candlelight opposite him. He held what looked like a plaster coffee mug in his hand. He was stirring its contents with a wooden stick.

Milo held back. "What are you going to do?"

"Help you, Mr. Gherl. You are the victim of a very traditional and particularly nasty form of voodoo. You have greatly angered a *Bocor* and he is using a powerful *loa*, via a doll, to lop off your hands and your feet and your manhood."

"My left hand's okay," Milo said, gratefully working the fingers in the air.

"So I have noticed," M. Trieste said with a frown. "It is odd for one extremity to be spared, but perhaps there is a certain symbolism at work here that we do not understand. No matter. The remedy is the same. Hold your arm out on the table."

Milo did as he was told. His swollen hand looked black in the candlelight. "Is . . . is this going to hurt?"

"When the pressure is released, there will be considerable pain as the fresh blood rushes into the starved tissues."

That kind of pain Milo could handle. "Do it."

M. Trieste stirred the contents of the cup and lifted the wooden handle. Instead of the spoon he had expected, Milo saw that the man was holding a brush. It gleamed redly.

Here comes the blood, he thought. But he didn't care what was in the cup as long as it worked.

"André told me about your problem before he brought you here. I made this up in advance. I will paint it on the constrictions and it will nullify the influence of the *loa* of the doll. After that, it will be up to you to make peace with this *Bocor* before he visits other afflictions on you."

"Sure, sure," Milo said, thrusting his wrist toward M. Trieste. "Let's just get on with it!"

M. Trieste daubed the bloody solution onto the incision line. It beaded up like water on a freshly waxed car and slid off onto the table. Milo glanced up and saw a look of consternation flit across the wrinkled black face towering above him. He watched as the red stuff was applied again, only to run off as before.

"Most unusual," M. Trieste muttered as he tried a third time with no better luck. "I've never . . ." He put the cup down and began painting his own right hand with the solution. "This will do it. Hold up your hand."

As Milo raised his arm, M. Trieste encircled the wrist with his long dripping fingers and squeezed. There was an instant of heat, and then M. Trieste cried out. He released Milo's wrist and dropped to his knees cradling his right hand against his breast.

"The poisons!" he cried. "Oh, the poisons!"

Milo trembled as he looked at his dusky hand. The bloody solution had run off as before. "What poisons?"

"Between you and this *Bocor!* Get out of here!"

"But the doll! You said you could—!"

"There is no doll!" M. Trieste said. He turned away and retched. "There *is* no doll!"

With his heart clattering against his chest wall, Milo pushed himself away from the table and staggered to the door. Andy was leaning on his truck at the curb.

"Wassamatter?" he said, straightening off the fender as he saw Milo. "Didn't he—?"

"He's a phony, just like you!" Milo screamed, letting his rage and fear focus on the old Black. "Just another goddamn phony!"

As Andy hurried into the store, Milo started up his Mercedes and roared down the street. He'd drive until he found a sign for one of the freeways. From there he could get home.

And from home, he knew where he wanted to go . . . where he *had* to go.

"Franklin! Where are you, Franklin?"

Milo had finally found Bill Franklin's home in the Hollywood Hills. Even though he knew the neighborhood fairly well, Milo had never been on this particular street, and so it had taken him a while to track it down. The lights had been on inside and the door had been unlocked. No one had answered his knocking, so he'd let himself in.

"*Franklin*, goddammit!" he called, standing in the middle of the cathedral-ceilinged living room. His voice echoed off the stucco walls and hardwood floor. "Where are you?"

In the ensuing silence, he heard a faint voice say, "Milo? Is that you?"

Milo tensed. Where had that come from? "Yeah, it's me! Where are you?"

Again, ever so faintly: "Down here . . . in the basement!"

Milo searched for the cellar door, found it, saw the lights ablaze from below, and began his descent. His slippered feet were completely numb now and he had to watch where he put them. It was as if his feet had been removed and replaced with giant sponges.

"That you, Milo?" said a voice from somewhere around the corner from the stairwell. It was Franklin's voice, but it sounded slurred, strained.

"Yeah, it's me."

As he neared the last step, he pulled the .38 from his pocket. He had picked it up at the house along with a pair of wire cutters. He had never fired it, and he didn't expect to have to tonight. But it was good to know it was loaded and ready if he needed it. He tried to transfer it to his right hand but his numb, swollen fingers couldn't keep hold of the grip. He kept it in his left and stepped onto the cellar floor—

—and felt his foot start to roll away from him. Only by throwing himself against the wall and hugging it did he save himself from falling. He looked around the unfinished cellar. Bright, reflective objects were scattered all along the naked concrete floor. He sucked in a breath as he saw the hundreds of sharp curved angles of green glass poking up at the exposed ceiling beams. They looked like shattered wine bottles—big, green, four-liter wine bottles smashed all over the place. And in among the shards were scattered thousands of marbles.

"Be careful," said Franklin's voice. "The basement's mined." The voice was there, but Franklin was nowhere in sight.

"Where the hell are you, Franklin?"

"Back here in the bathroom. I thought you'd never get here."

Milo began to move toward the rear of the cellar where brighter light poured from an open door. He slid his slippered feet slowly along the floor, pushing the green glass spears ahead of him, rolling the marbles out of the way.

"I've come for the doll, Franklin."

Milo heard a hollow laugh. "Doll? What doll, Milo? There's just me and you, ol' buddy."

Milo shuffled around the corner into view of the bathroom. And froze. The gun dropped from his fingers and further shattered some of the glass at his feet. "Oh, my God, Franklin! Oh, my *God!*"

William Franklin sat on the toilet wearing Milo's rings, his old slippers, his stolen pajamas, and his other hairpiece. His left eye was patched and his feet and his right hand were as black and swollen as Milo's. There was a maniacal look in his remaining eye as he grinned drunkenly and sipped from a four-liter green-glass bottle of white wine. The cuts in his flesh were identical to Milo's except that a short length of twisted copper wire protruded from each. A screwdriver and a pair of pliers lay in his lap.

M. Trieste's parting words screamed through his brain: *There is no doll!*

"See?" Franklin said in a slurred voice. "You said I had to suffer."

Milo wanted to be sick. "Christ! What have you done?"

"I decided to suffer. But I didn't think I should suffer alone. So I brought you along for company. Sure took you long enough to figure it out."

Milo bent and picked up the pistol. His left hand wavered and trembled as he pointed it at Franklin. "You . . . you . . ." He couldn't think of anything to say.

Franklin casually tossed the wine bottle out onto the floor where it shattered and added to the spikes of glass. Then he pulled open the pajama top. "Right here, Milo, old buddy!" he said, pointing to his heart. "Do you really think you want to put a slug into me?"

Milo thought about that. It might be like putting a bullet into his own heart. He felt his arm drop. "Why . . . how . . . I don't deserve . . ."

Franklin closed his eye and grimaced. He looked as if he were about to cry. "I know," he said. "It's gone too far. Maybe you really don't deserve all this. I've always known I was a little bit crazy, but maybe I'm a lot crazier than I ever thought I was."

"Then for God's sake, man, loosen the wires!"

"*No!*" Franklin's eye snapped open. The madness was still there. "I entrusted my work to you. That's a sacred trust. You were responsible for *The Hut*'s integrity when you took on the job of adapting it to the screen."

"But *I'm* an artist, too!" Why was he arguing with this nut? He slipped the pistol into his front pocket and reached around back for the wire cutters.

"All the more reason to respect another man's work! You didn't own it—it was only on loan to you!"

"The contract—"

"*Means nothing!* You had a moral obligation to protect my work, one artist to another."

"You're overreacting!"

"Am I? Imagine yourself a parent who has sent his only child to a reputable nursery school only to learn that the child has been raped by the faculty—then you will understand *some* of what I feel! I've come to see it as my sacred duty to see to it that you don't molest anyone else's work!"

Enough of this bullshit! If Franklin wouldn't loosen the wires, Milo would cut them off! He pulled the wire cutters from his rear pocket and began to shuffle toward Franklin, sweeping the marbles and daggers of glass ahead of him.

"Stay back!" Franklin cried. He grabbed the pliers and

pushed them down toward his lap, grinning maliciously. "Didn't know I was left-handed, did you?" He twisted something.

Searing pain knifed into Milo's groin. He doubled over but kept moving toward Franklin. Less than a dozen feet to go. If he could just—

He saw Franklin drop the pliers and pick up the screwdriver, saw him raise it toward his right eye, the good eye. Milo screamed,

"No!"

And then agony exploded in his eye, in his head, robbing him of the light, sending him reeling back in sudden impenetrable blackness. As he felt his feet roll across the marbles, he reached out wildly. His legs slid from under him and despite the most desperate flailings and contortions, there was nothing to grasp on the way down but empty air.